Ninety Six

A Ryan Conner Detective Novel

By

Robert Messenger

Author's Note

This is a fictional story, any similarities between any person living or dead is purely coincidental. This fictional story is based on real events and personal experiences from my time in the British Army and the Police Service. It is a story I have wanted to tell for a very long time. I have changed a few locations and all of the names to protect people's privacy. I created the Royal Mounted Rifles Regiment as I did not want to single out and condemn one regiment in particular. The vast majority of soldiers are brave and professional. I am very proud to be a fourth-generation soldier myself. However, within any large organisation there will always be a number of *bad apples*. I have just chosen to place them all in the same barrel. I have not changed the name of the Metropolitan Police because as an organisation it is so huge and complex it would be difficult to identify a specific individual or team. Furthermore, some of the most professional, dedicated and courageous police officers I have ever worked with were from The Met. They are all too often lumped in with their own bad apples, but they can take it. The Metropolitan Police and its officers can take anything.

I would like to thank my mentor, editor and friend Matthew Dunn for his assistance in this book and a big thank to the multi talented Kathleen for getting me out of a hole with the proof reading. I could not have written this book alone.

Robert Messenger
July 2023

Chapter 1

London, 2223 hours, 3rd May 1996.

Mimi stood on the Albert Embankment, looking through the swirling mist and rain at two men walking into the alleyway opposite her. She could not have known that, within minutes, one man would come out barely alive and the other would be starting on a journey to becoming a serial killer.

Two years ago, Mimi had escaped Rwanda to France and made her way to Paris by selling sex to truck drivers and the occasional taxi driver. She was nineteen years old, pretty, slim, and currently an illegal immigrant. Whilst in Paris, she had found out the hard way that French men do not like facial scars on women despite her beautiful smooth skin. The scar was a present from the Hutu militia, given to her when she was seventeen years old at the end of a brutal gang rape. A friendly Nigerian girl, working the red-light district on the Boulevard de Clichy, had told her that English men were less fussy, and so she had found herself in the fringe areas of South London's red-light district to ply her trade.

Pulling up the collar on her black denim jacket, she shielded herself from the wind and rain, and started to feel the pull of another crack high. She lit her last Gauloises cigarette and placed the lighter back into her small purse amongst the carefully folded twenty-pound notes, loose cheap condoms and an unopened ten pack of Marlboro Lights. The shitty weather and weak cigarettes were what she hated most about London. Leaning against the Embankment wall with her back to the river she looked over to an area known locally as the *Dark Walk*. This was mainly a pickup place for London's gay community, but Mimi often found men here with a mixture of tastes. It was just after 10 pm and deathly quiet, but she decided she would give it another twenty minutes before returning to the couch she slept on in the back of a newsagent next to Brixton Tube station. She decided she would score a rock of crack from outside the tube.

Across the Thames Path pavement and behind the streetlights she could see the metal shuttered shop fronts, decorated with graffiti and a thousand piss stains. The shops ran along a short alleyway leading to Black Prince Road and there was a collection of bin bags and old sodden cardboard boxes on the corner. Mimi could see that the two men had stopped just inside the alleyway, the other side of a pile of rubbish. She could see the figure of a tall man standing with his back against the wall. She was used to assigning labels to men in her profession and so *Tall Man* seemed to fit. He was partly illuminated by a security light and the second figure was knelt in front of him. The kneeling man was dressed in a suit and raincoat. This figure became *Raincoat*. He looked short, fat and appeared to be perched uncomfortably on his knees, struggling to undo the waist belt and trouser fly of the Tall Man. She was used to seeing such acts, so inhaled on her cigarette and decided to watch the show. The Tall Man's trousers were now gaping open at the fly, and this seemed to be a cue for him to take a small bottle from out of his left-hand trouser pocket, unscrew the lid and take a deep inhale of whatever was inside. Probably Amyl Nitrite, thought Mimi, the legal high often referred to as *poppers*, which gives a chemical boost to sexual pleasure and was used by gay and straight alike.

But what she saw next, she would never forget.

The Tall Man dripped two small droplets onto Raincoat man's head, indistinguishable amongst the light rain, and placed the small bottle back into his pocket with his left hand. With his right hand he reached behind his back and pulled out a short silver pole, glinting in the dim alley. He then extended his right arm out to the side, still at

5

waist level height. Mimi's eyes bulged as she could now see it was a long-bladed knife. Raincoat was still kneeling, his eyes closed, fully concentrating on the job in hand, unaware of the danger he was in. With a lightning quick movement, the Tall Man struck the kneeling man in the left-hand side of the neck with the glinting blade. Mimi saw a thick black liquid spurt out of the man's neck. Raincoat tried to scream but the tall figure had already put his left hand over his mouth and pushed him back onto the floor. The Tall Man sat astride his writhing victim and struck him again and again, into Raincoat's stomach, chest and neck. He then swivelled around and plunged the glistening blade over and over into the dying man's loins.

Mimi collapsed to her knees and was sick against the Embankment wall. The sight of the violence had brought back to her the horrors she had suffered at the hands of the Hutu's soldiers. She spat out the last of the bittersweet vomit from her mouth and knew she had to get away. Standing up, she steadied herself on the Embankment wall, took off her high heels and ran barefoot towards Vauxhall Bridge. After a hundred metres, she turned to see if the Tall Man was following her. She could see that he was at the side of the Embankment where she had stood and witnessed the attack. The tall dark figure had the body of his victim slumped over his left shoulder, legs sticking forward, arms dangling down behind him but still twitching. The Tall Man perched the dying body on the ledge of the Embankment wall. Mimi saw him push the fat round body of his victim backwards into the wet darkness of the river Thames below. She watched, frozen in terror, as the Tall Man stood staring silently into the cold black void of the river. The rain was now beating down on him, washing away any obvious traces of the violent attack. The Tall Man smoothed his dark hair back and adjusted his clothing, He then turned and walked towards her. She spun around and ran as fast as she could, her bare feet splashing in the pools of rain on the pavement and didn't look back until she was under the covers on her threadbare couch.

****

No one really noticed when Bernard West – a forty-four-year-old, single senior IT manager -failed to turn up for his work at The Bank of Indonesia in City Road. Not even after a week. After two weeks, Bernard's line manager tried to ring and email him, but there was still no reply. At the end of April, Bernard's senior manager, Kathy Seymour, walked into Bishopsgate Police Station in The City of London and filed a report of a missing person. She explained to the Front Enquiry Officer, as politely as she could, that Bernard was short, rotund, and bald. He was very quiet and lived alone. He had no known family. He had never been in trouble with the police, as far as she was aware. He took long holidays to Indonesia, a perk of the job, she said with a self-satisfied smile, but had not mentioned to anyone he was planning to go. The Front Enquiry Officer took the report as best he could from the lady in an expensive business suit. He noticed she was constantly looking at her watch and mobile phone. The details taken, the lady was given a City of London Police Missing Persons reference number, and she left as quickly as she could. Her next stop was at a temporary job agency to request an IT Manager. Mr West's details were recorded on the Police National Computer as reported as missing, but then went into a cabinet drawer with a hundred others.

****

The Essex Police Marine Unit at Crayford Ness patrols one of the largest coastlines in the country, including the east end of the Thames estuary. With only two boats on duty on an early turn shift, even in mid-April, things can get remarkably busy. So, a call to a body part found churned up in a fishing boat's propeller at East Tilbury Docks would have to wait with everything else. Four hours after the initial call was received, Alpha Echo Zero Four, a small patrol boat with two Marine police officers on board, attended the scene to find three pissed off fisherman waiting by the dock, complaining that they had lost a day's fishing. With an air of disgruntlement, they showed the officers a white and green fleshy lump which they had placed in a transparent plastic bag. The lump was clearly a human back with an arm and the top of a leg. The male genitals were there, but they had been mutilated.

One of the fishermen observed that the body could have been floating around for weeks, being chopped up by every propeller in the Thames. The police officers looked at the bloated cold mass of fat and muscle and then looked at each other. The white and green lump was partly covered in an open shirt and suit jacket. The older officer of the two looked at his slightly younger partner and nodded at the bag. With a sigh of resignation, the younger cop took off his hat, placing it on the deck, put on a pair of blue medical gloves, opened the plastic bag and started to search the body part and clothing remains. There were no identifying marks on the body but there were lots of wounds, most likely caused by propeller strikes. There were no documents in the jacket pockets and the suit was a typical *St. Michaels* make and design. Gently standing up on his aching knees, the officer put his cap back on, thanked the fishermen for their time and said he would take the remains and book them in. With that, the officers got back onto the patrol boat and went to a report of ten illegal immigrants found in a trawler at Shoeburyness. At the end of a long shift, the body parts were photographed, a DNA sample was taken and submitted to a lab for an identification that would never come. Four weeks later, what was left of forty-four-year-old Bernard West was then destroyed along with the evidence of a murder.

Chapter 2

Central London, 0905 hours, 3rd June 1996.

Ryan Conner accepted that police undercover work was dangerous, but what he was struggling to accept was the rough, bitter aftertaste of super strength *Special Brew* lager at just after 9 am on a Monday morning. He was standing on the corner of Piccadilly Circus, sipping from his can and trying not to wince at the taste. He took a drag on a rolled-up cigarette he had made from discarded tab ends to help disguise the bitter alcohol swirling around his mouth. It was hot. A bright summer's morning. The traffic was bumper to bumper, struggling to get across the traffic light system from Regent Street onto Shaftesbury Avenue and the Haymarket. Conner looked out across the hot smog towards the statue of Eros and into the Lillywhites sports shop. The shop window was festooned with the flags and football strips of all the nations taking part in the Euro 96 Football Championships being held in England in a week's time.

"It's coming home, it's coming home, football's coming home!" was the national mantra and despite some negative press there was a feeling in the country that this was England's time. This air of expectancy, coupled with the *Britpop* bands currently ruling the airwaves, had led to a feel-good factor in the air that had not been seen in London since the swinging sixties.

However, the air that Conner was currently surrounded by did not feel good at all. This air did not care about football, music, the country or anything else for that matter. This was the air of London's underclass. Drug addicts, rent boys and the homeless. And they only cared about one thing. Their next score of crack and heroin. But what made matters worse was that their dealer was late.

Ryan Conner, Police Constable 347 EK, Metropolitan Police, was a Level Two Undercover Test Purchaser Operative, known throughout the Police Service as a *TPO*. A TPO's job is to purchase drugs, guns, caravans, stolen goods or anything really, and *test* to see if a crime has or would have been committed. For example, are the drugs really drugs or just brick dust and chewing gum? Is a firearm really a lethal barrelled weapon or a cheap toy? The evidence collected by the TPO would then form part of the prosecution case file and ultimately be tested in court.

It was a tough, dangerous, and demanding role, requiring the operative to have one part of his brain function in a very real-time scary world, whilst the other half constantly worked out the legal implications of his actions, and those of everyone around him. His specialism was as an open drugs market street buyer, and he was extremely good at it. Although still technically on the books at Kentish Town Police Station as a *General Duties Officer*, he had been seconded to the Met's Elite SO10 Undercover Unit for the last six months and as far as he knew he was staying there until his SO10 Inspector told him otherwise.

At 7 am that morning he had arrived at a safe house, a disused office building in Covent Garden, and had received his test purchase instructions. These were known as the *1 and 10s*, and they had been read to him by the Operation Atlantic Senior Investigative Officer, or *SIO*. A young University of Sussex educated Detective Inspector called Henry York. DI York liked to be called *Sir* rather than the tradition *Guv* and this annoyed mostly everyone. But this was DI York's operation, and he was keen to do well.

Conner had also been given his intended targets for the day and issued with his drug buy money and some expenses money known as *exes*. He was given some technical equipment, which he put on, and was taken to a dusty office room on the first floor of the disused office block. As he entered the room, he saw that lines of battered old desks and chairs had been pushed to one side and dumped underneath a large window with a crack across it. The damage had been covered over with several old copies of The Sun newspaper. A semi - transparent picture of a Page Three model with ginger hair and a big smile was centre stage. He suspected this was no accident. The rich Dublin brogue of his *Granda's* voice came into his head: "All tits, teeth and ginger hair, that'll be trouble son."

The office had been converted to a police briefing room, with radio battery chargers, pictures of his targets on the walls and, most importantly of all, a makeshift brew kit. All the targets for Operation Atlantic were Jamaicans, with an equal number of men and women staring blankly back at him. Conner was ushered into a chair by the SIO and introduced to his Foot Protection Team as *Mark,* a pseudonym. They took a good look at this scruffy *scroat* so they could recognise him when he was wandering about on the ground amongst the other scroats. Conner looked at his Protection Team, who were sitting slumped on chairs, either looking at mobile phones or attempting to write obscenities on each other's arms and foreheads. He suspected they were from One Area (Central) Tactical Support Group. Despite the joviality and childishness, he knew he was in good hands. The *TSG* dealt with the worst violence, the worst protests and could even give the Millwall *firms* a run for their money. Looking at them he saw the familiar group of large built blokes and athletic-looking women all wearing plain clothes. Their clothing was basically the same for all cops who were plain clothed, rather than *covert* like Conner, and was a uniform all its own. It generally consisted of blue jeans, a hoodie or Berghaus jacket and a baseball cap. The team of six officers were now staring back at him with amusement tinged with admiration on their faces. Everyone knew you had to be a bit crazy to be a TPO.

Conner said "hi" to each of them in turn, looking them straight in the eye so they could see there was another cop under his stinking, ripped and dirty clothes. He knew his life may depend on them remembering that.

Day fifteen briefing over, the Foot Protection Team officers adjusted their earpieces and re-checked their personal protection equipment worn in a harness under their clothing.

Conner slipped quietly out of the room. He gave himself a last look in the mirror and could just about make out his twenty-four-year-old boyish good looks under the filth his face was covered in. He had thick black unkept hair and blue eyes. He was slim but muscular. His baggy *druggie* clothing covered up his athletic frame and it had the effect of making him look like he was on the heroin or *H plan* diet. After taking a few deep breaths he checked his mobile phones, his buying money and his technical assets and left the safe house via a fire exit. He made a mental note of his deployment time. It was 8.20 am.

The bright sunlight hit his eyes immediately after the dingy office block. He blinked a few times before making his way to his now regular off-licence corner shop. Stepping over a sleeping drunk as he entered, he picked up two cans of Special Brew lager, a sausage roll, and a copy of the Daily Sport before paying a young Asian girl behind the counter. He turned left and sat down on the pavement in a doorway near to the off-licence. He got out a mobile phone, a simple Nokia which had been issued to him at the start of the operation and which was solely used for the purposes of buying drugs. Going into the electronic phone book he found the name *Jam* and pressed the dial button. The number rang for what seemed like an age and was suddenly answered.

"Yeah man?" said a heavy Jamaican accent that sounded like it had just been woken up.

"Are you working, bruv? It's Mark," said Conner, reverting to his natural Midlands accent rather than the Thames estuary one that the Army and the Met had given him. He could also do a passable Dublin or Belfast accent, thanks to his family roots.

"Yeah," said the voice on the phone, accompanied by the sound of scratching.

"Can you do me one white and one brown."

"Twenty each yeah, Boots Piccadilly at nine."

"Sound," Conner said. "Cheers, man."

"Ok, ok," said the voice, as it went back to sleep.

He hung up and put his drug phone back into his front pocket and then slipped out a slimmer Ericsson phone which was concealed in a pouch sewn into the waistband of his jeans. He sent a text to the SIO in the safe house.

"JAM 9 PICCADILLY BOOTS"

His Ericsson phone vibrated with the reply: "OK".

One white and one brown were street terms for a rock of crack and a small bag of heroin. This was known on the street as a *Molotov Cocktail* and was a classic upper and downer. The conversation on the phone had gone well and he was often surprised at how many Jamaican drug dealers, with their cool, easy manner, he liked. That was conditional on not pissing them off of course, as they also had a well-earned reputation for extreme violence.

He now had half an hour to get to the corner of the Boots store at Piccadilly Circus which was about half a mile away. He opened a can of lager and took a long drink. The lager helped him look the part of *a down and out*, the smell of alcohol on a person's breath before 10 am can tell you a lot about them. Then he tucked into his sausage roll. It was breakfast time. The tourists and commuters walked past him without a second look.

****

Conner paced up and down the pavement underneath the arches of the old County Fire Office opposite the large Boots the Chemist at Piccadilly Circus. He looked as impatient as the other *crackheads* who were smoking furiously and kicking at pieces of trash. The Boots at Piccadilly is set back from the pavement and has the world-famous electronic billboards above it. The arches opposite provide a perfect place to keep out of the way while waiting for your dealer.

He adjusted his open sleeping bag, which was cradled over his left arm like a comfort blanket and took a drag on his roll up. He had found the sleeping bag in a bin whilst on a deployment to Brixton earlier in the year. It was blue on the outside and the lining, which was supposed to be white, was now a sort of yellowy grey. Grey was good, as bright colours in this game were best avoided. The sleeping bag's main asset was that it stunk. It smelt of piss, fags, and the sort of damp you get in soiled mattresses. He once had to spend three hours in it in a shop doorway in West Hampstead while waiting for a dealer who was messing him around. He'd been sick twice in it, which ironically, had just added to the bag's credibility. He was dressed in his usual drug buying attire. He had on his oversized green hoodie and blue jeans, which were in a similar style and condition to his sleeping bag, and underneath his hoodie he wore a filthy white Umbro t-shirt with a rip under the armpit. On his head he wore a battered old blue baseball cap, and on his feet he had a pair of black Adidas Samba trainers which had seen better days. He had also done his normal routine before the start of an operation, by not shaving his face or washing his hair for two weeks. He had freshly dirtied his face and hands up with dust and mud that morning. He knew of some TPOs that would go to the extremes of not showering for a month, or even cutting themselves to give the impression they had been fighting. They didn't stay deployable for too long.

He had given himself a single ear stud and the overall effect seemed to work for him. He suspected that his accent was a major help. He was from Coventry and to your average drug dealer, whether they be from Clapham Junction or Jamaica, that meant *The North*. The look, the drinking, the chat was all about one thing. Credibility. Convincing the drug dealers and the other drug users that you belonged. The basic premise was that if it looked like a duck and quacked, chances were it was a duck.

The last piece of attire was his backpack. It was black, old and battered, and it looked heavier than it should. He had already placed his sleeping bag, a blanket and a can of lager into it. However, the bag's real purpose lay underneath the blanket. For it concealed a large *Nagra* video and audio tape recorder which was linked by wires to a camera and microphone sewn into the front of the bag's straps. The camera and microphone were very small, but the recorder wasn't. It was about the size and shape of an average car battery and almost as heavy. Basically, if you were to get searched, you were fucked. This was the kit the TPOs were issued, and it certainly wasn't James Bond standard. All the fancy gadgets, sports cars and trips abroad were saved for the *Level Ones*. The TPOs were the poor bloody infantry of the undercover world.

It was now 9.45 am and Conner took the very last extended drag from his roll-up cigarette and flicked it away. The thing about drug dealers was they didn't go a whole lot on customer service. Jam's *Unique Selling Point* was that he sometimes got out of bed before midday. He rubbed his stubbly chin and had a sly look around at the collection of characters waiting impatiently with him. The loudest was a short, slim woman, who may have been in her thirties but looked closer to fifty, with her sharp drawn features, brown teeth and dyed blonde hair pulled back in a tight ponytail. She was dressed in a scruffy blue leather jacket and black leggings and was smoking furiously whilst having an argument with a black male who was at least twice as old as her, skinny, drunk, and clearly living rough. He mentally tagged the female as *Blue Leather Jacket.*

"I'm not giving you fucking half, Tommy," said Blue Leather Jacket. "You're giving me a tenner so you get what you get, or you can fuck off elsewhere and find some other mug!"

Conner recognised Tommy as a local drunk who frequented the West End. Tommy mumbled something in a quiet sing-song tone and threw his hand up in exasperation as if appealing to the world at large at the scale of his injustice.

Stood at the front of the Arches, smoking and checking her phone, was a slim black girl in a black demin jacket. She was pretty, despite the long scar on her right cheek, but she looked like she had not slept for a month and the heroin was taking its toll. Clearly a *Tom* he thought, the local slang for a prostitute. Over to his left and leaning against the wall was a male and female couple in their thirties. They were relatively clean and well dressed and were clearly shitting themselves. Probably moved up on bail from some shit hole in Kent or Essex, Conner observed. God knows what they had done, but it probably involved kids to have been placed in the anonymity of central London. The only clue they were using was the blackened teeth caused by the crack smoke. He knew the same effect could be mimicked by TPOs using Cola and toothpaste.

In the corner of the alcove was a tight knot of young scruffy males who looked like they had been sleeping rough for months. They were sharing cans of Special Brew and anxiously looking at the one pay-as-you-go mobile phone they had between them. He had seen a couple of them before on previous buys and nodded to one male, saying, "What's he fucking doing, man!" The male shrugged and went back to looking at the phone.

Although Conner was only twenty-four years old, he knew that life was about suffering. Illegal drugs brought nothing but suffering - to the individual, their families and the wider community in the form of crime. The money from drugs went to arms sales, funded child sexual abuse, human trafficking, its effects went on and on. But this collection of individuals were the masters of suffering. The premier fucking league of suffering.

In his police probation, Conner had taken a trip to the Old Bailey Central Criminal Court. He had stared at a stone inscription that was above the main doors.

It read "DEFEND THE CHILDREN OF THE POOR AND PUNISH THE WRONGDOER". He felt he was doing both as a TPO.

"Jam's definitely up," said a young male voice from behind him. "My friend has just text me to say he's seen him at Leicester Square tube."

Conner turned around and saw a young, slim white male he had not seen before sat in the corner of the alcove. The male looked no older than eighteen and was dressed in a scruffy blue Kappa shell suit, battered white Ellesse trainers and a rigid-peaked black baseball cap with the word "BOY" sewn on to it in gold-coloured thread.

He mentally tagged him as *Boy Cap* in case he became of value to the operation in the future.

"When was that, mate?" Conner asked.

Boy Cap took a drag on a cigarette, which he held between the ends of his right index and middle finger.

"About 10 minutes ago, he'll be here," he said with a theatrical wink, whilst breathing out a smoke ring.

Conner was aware of Boy Cap's femininity and strongly suspected that he was one of the local rent boys who plied his trade around Soho's *meat racks*. Not that all the rent boys were so effeminate. Since he had been on Operation Atlantic, he had met some rent boys who would be loud, tough, shouting at the football and built like the proverbial outhouse. But through fair means or foul they had found their way to survive by selling sex to men. If it was their choice and they weren't robbing their clients, then he didn't have a problem with it. Boy Cap, however, was not in the butch category.

"I fucking hope so," Conner replied, then waited a breath before asking, "have you got a spare smoke, mate?"

Boy Cap gave a small laugh and made an exaggerated sigh before saying, "Oh, go on then." He took out a packet of Marlboro Lights and handed a cigarette to him.

"Cheers, mate," Conner said, placing the cigarette behind his ear with a grin.

Just then the knot of young homeless men started to get agitated. "Shut up, man! It's Jam!" said one of them with a Geordie accent. Conner could hear their pay-as-you-go phone ringing.

"Yo!" said *Geordie* as he answered the call. He was listening intently, nodding, and looking up at his fellow druggies.

"You're not fucking us about are you, man?"

Some mumbled expletives came out of the phone.

"Ok, ok, ten minutes, aye."

Geordie put the phone in his pocket.

"Jam's going to be next to the Burly Arms in ten minutes," he said to the group as a whole. Ten minutes, Conner thought to himself, that's a bit tight, and he knew what it meant. There was going to be a *Junkie Yomp*.

A junkie yomp occurs when a group of junkies need to get a specific area before their dealer sells all the drugs. Drug addicts are generally not the most dynamic of people, except when they are on a Junkie Yomp. The head down, arms swinging approach, which never breaks into a run, can get up to some tremendous speeds and they won't stop for pedestrians or traffic or World War Three for that matter. The group suddenly set off with Blue Leather Jacket taking Tommy's money and getting an early lead. Conner gathered up his sleeping bag and set off at pace with everyone else.

The group, who had remarkably stayed together, arrived at Old Burlington Road like starships coming out of hyperspace. A small group of other users were gathered around a doorway next to The Burlington Arms. A loose line of junkies was going into the doorway one at a time and coming out slipping small cling film wrapped packages into their mouths, pockets, or socks. Conner's group formed a sort of gaggle and he made sure he was in the middle, so he did not stand out. He had bought from Jam before, but this being the third buy it needed to be on camera. The recording device had been switched on since he had breakfast, but now he readjusted the straps, so the camera and microphone were at a good height. He took some breaths. Despite having scored from Jam before, drug dealers were very unpredictable. They could decide to serve you up or search you or rob you. You could have looked at them funny last time you bought, and they would give you a punch or a kick just to make a point. He remembered a time when he was meeting a dealer, a large Jamaican wearing a bulletproof vest. The dealer had made the universal symbol for a pistol with the two fingers and thumb of his right hand and put it to the head of another dealer and then used the exact same gesture to beckon him forward. He had suspected he may be shot but went forward anyway. He was served up and, on that occasion at least, wasn't shot.

At The Burly pub, he knew that his foot protection would be somewhere about trying to keep him safe, but they generally stopped you from dying rather than stopping the blows that could cause it.

The gang of homeless men dived in and out of the doorway one at time and then it was his turn. He got out his buying money. *Always let them see the green* he had been taught. Jam was leaning back and had just taken a fresh batch of little white and brown packages out from his mouth and backside respectively. He was tall and slim with short dreads and wore a puffer jacket, with a yellow string vest underneath. His jeans were slung low, showing his *Miami Penitentiary* underwear, which was worn like a badge of honour. This likely meant Jam had been caught dealing by the British Police, served twelve months in a UK prison. Then he had been deported to the US, where he was wanted for similar offences, and locked up for a further eighteen months in a Miami prison. But as soon as he was out, he was flown straight back to London by his *Yardie* gang, where it would all start again. Leaving a trail of misery and death along the way. Not for the first time, Conner marvelled at the lunacy of the British justice system, as he handed over the two twenty-pound notes he had been issued.

"One and one," Conner said. Jam passed over one small brown and one small white cellophaned package into his hand. This was all going a bit quick, and he wanted to be sure he got a good picture of Jam's face.

"Is it good gear, bruv?" Conner said, looking at his drug wraps.

Jam looked at him, and annoyed, spat out, "Yeah man, shiittt."

Conner turned around and, not wanting to push his luck, moved away quickly. Got you, you bastard, he thought as he walked away with the two small packets of drugs held tightly in his right hand.

And then everything changed.

He heard a commotion from behind him in the doorway. He continued walking, but could not help looking back. He could see that Jam had Boy Cap by the throat and was smacking him in the side of the head with an open hand whilst Boy Cap tried in vain to kick Jam between the legs.

"You fucking little bitch!" the tall Jamaican shouted as he slapped Boy Cap around the head. "Fucking batty boi!"

Jam took Boy Cap's legs from under him with one sweep, making the frail-looking white man fall to the ground, his hat flying off into the gutter.

Conner stood watching, quickly assessing the situation. During his undercover course at Hendon, it had been stressed to him he was to be the grey man. That was his role. He was not to get involved in anything unless it was life-threatening. If a pedestrian gets run over and a good-natured member of the public goes to help, great, walk off. If there is no one else around and the pedestrian may die, then help. If you're with a load of junkies, then pinch the pedestrian's phone or wallet to maintain your cover and book it into police property later. The same applied to assaults. Ask yourself, is it life threatening? He looked on and saw that Jam was now kicking Boy Cap in the head with a brand new pair of Air Jordans. Ok, not good, but survivable. Drug addicts are notoriously difficult to kill in a fight. It was known. Then came a stamp to Boy Cap's head and the thin young white man stopped making noises. Then another one. Stamp. Then another. Stamp.

"Shit," Conner said to himself, as he stuffed the drugs he had bought into the small front pocket of his jeans and tightened his pack straps. Test Purchasers don't carry any Personal Protective Equipment when they are deployed. And this is where the copy of the Daily Sport comes in. Rather than read about what bullshit was being said about Paul Gascoigne today, Conner had folded it in half and then long ways, several times. He had then placed it in a side pouch in his backpack. He reached for the folded newspaper and then bent it in half again. This produced quite a small but handy club. It also had a couple of sharp points that at a pinch, through a puffer jacket for example, can feel like the point of a knife blade. Taking a deep breath, he ran towards Jam with his newspaper club.

A few seconds later, he impacted Jam at speed just below the drug dealer's right eye, sending them both flying into a metal food bin at the back of the doorway. Both men were now in a tussle in a dark, stinking, confined hole. Conner felt his head hit the brick work, but he was sure he had got a knee into Jam's face. He continued to lash out with his paper club. A foot came up and caught Conner under the chin and he kicked out at what he suspected was a rib cage. It became a whirlwind of arms and legs. Suddenly, from the daylight, two hands grabbed Conner and pulled him out of the doorway. He looked up and expected to see another angry Jamaican face staring back at him. What he actually saw was a friendly Jamaican face wearing a baseball cap and a large smile, shouting, "Leave that nice gentleman alone!"

Conner recognised the man as a member of the Foot Protection Team and allowed himself to be dragged along the street and thrown into the road. His head was spinning and started to throb with pain as the adrenaline started to wear off. Somehow, he got himself to his feet.

He could see that Boy Cap was sitting up crying and holding his head, blood pouring from his nose. Back in the doorway, he saw the Jamaican Foot Protection officer and another female officer were pretending to be concerned members of the public. They had knelt next to the drug dealer and were consoling Jam, who was sitting down holding his right side. Conner could not help but notice that the female Foot Protection officer had taken off her cap to reveal long ginger hair. She was slim, pretty, and was

making a good job of filling the front of a blue baggy
hoodie. Clever, he thought, Jam is not going to want to
leave the attention she was giving him any time soon. He
then recalled the Page Three picture in the briefing room
and now it made sense.

Conner staggered over to Boy Cap and helped him
to his feet.

"C'mon, let's get the fuck out of here."

Boy Cap was swearing softly to himself, but
nodded and bent down to pick up his black hat. Conner
held up the bleeding and dazed man by the shoulders and
they started to hobble and then break into a run as they
could hear Jam shouting at them.

"You're dead, motherfuckers, both of ya, fucking
dead, ya hear me!!"

****

Ten minutes later, Conner and Boy Cap were sitting in
bushes with their backs against the railings of Berkeley
Square. It was almost 10.30 am and it was still hot. The
bushes smelt of rat urine and human excrement. There were
flies everywhere. Bags of discarded glue were alongside
used needles and rusty spoons that had been used to prepare
heroin. He had checked that his drugs and his technical
equipment were intact, switched off his recording
equipment and texted "I AM OK" to the SIO, whilst Boy
Cap was distracted by trying to stop his nose from
bleeding. Boy Cap had been lucky, but the partial Air
Jordan tread mark on his forehead was evidence that he had
received a right kicking. He threw a packet of Marlboro
Light cigarettes at Conner, who opened the pack to see a
disposable lighter, a small piece of cannabis resin and
around six cigarettes. Conner lit a smoke and gave the pack
back to him, then lit one for himself.

"What's your name, mate?" asked Conner, taking a draw on his cigarette.

"Peter," Boy Cap replied, dabbing at his nose with his sock.

"Mark," Conner said, wiping the sweat from his forehead and pointing at himself. "Peter, what the fuck was all that about?"

"Christ knows. He's not my usual dealer but he served me up a couple of weeks ago. I was a fiver short, so I offered him a blowy and he fucking freaked out. Queer bashing black bastard."

"You need to go to A&E at St Thomas's mate. Your nose is a mess."

"Nah, it'll be fine. I've just got to get myself cleaned up." He sniffed. "I can't let *my adoring public* see me like this," Peter said, as he investigated the blood-filled sock.

Conner could now see that Peter had fine features, piercing green eyes and mousy hair over his ringed ears. He looked older than Conner had first thought with his short, slim stature covering the fact he was probably in his early twenties.

Peter stubbed out his cigarette. "Thanks, Mark, I owe you." He used the railings to heave himself up to his feet. "I would offer you a *real* reward, but I suspect you wouldn't be interested."

Conner gave a small laugh and looked down. "No, not for me, mate. I'm firmly on the other team."

"Your loss," Peter said, still dripping blood from his now bulbous nose. He bent down and picked up his hat. He then took out four cigarettes and threw them at Conner's feet.

"Cheers, man," he said, picking up the smokes and putting them into his bag. "See you around."

Peter smiled. "Be lucky, Mark. Lots of crazy people in this city now." He disappeared into the bushes towards the centre of the park.

Conner gave himself five minutes to tidy up a cut to his chin, then followed on. He needed to get back to the office block. The SIO would be going berserk.

Chapter 3

Undisclosed Location, Covent Garden, 1045 hours, 3rd May 1996.

Half an hour later, PC Conner walked into the safe house in Covent Garden. As he approached the fire exit it was opened as if by magic and he was met by the friendly face of Nigel *Nash* Collins, his welfare and technical officer. Nash had been with SO10 forever, a gentle giant of a man. Conner trusted him completely. It was to be the last friendly face he was going to see for a few hours. Nash held out two property bags, rolling his eyes as the SIO burst out of a door trying to contain himself and standing behind them watching proceedings.

Conner put his wraps of drugs into separate property bags, whilst saying to Nash, "1047 hours, exhibit Mark 23, property bag number P2356786 and exhibit Mark 24, property bag number P2356787." Conner then pulled the self-sealing strip off the bags and handed them to Nash as he silently mouthed the word "Shit" to Nash's amused face.

"Received at 1048 hours," Nash said. "I'll take the tech now, so I can get it downloaded."

Nash took the recording equipment from under the stinking sleeping bag and blanket in Conner's backpack.

"I want to go straight to the debrief," DI York said looking flustered.

"Yes, Guv... sorry - yes, Sir," he replied, and left Nash to it.

Conner sat at the front of the briefing room, facing everyone else like a naughty school boy. He looked around the room as the final stragglers from the Foot Protection Team came in and sat on chairs or perched on windowsills. He noticed that a giant cock and balls had been drawn where the Page Three model's head had been. DI York and his Deputy SIO, a crusty old Detective Sergeant called Dave Holland, came into the room. The DI wore a tight smile and looked like he was about to enjoy being *Billy Big Potatoes* in front of the staff. On his lap was his blue day book. The detective's blue book was a badge of honour carried by all worthy detectives and collected within its pages was all the misery, harm and death that could be dealt out by an uncaring universe.

"Right, *Mark*," said York, crossing his arms. "You had better tell us all what led up to this mess."

Conner took a deep breath. He had been here before. He would take his time and provide his rationale step by step. He talked through the phone call with Jam. The characters he had seen at Piccadilly and then tagging *Boy Cap* as a person of interest. He would be known by that name rather than Peter for the purposes of the operation. He would also be subject to some intelligence checks and his picture would appear on the operational intelligence board. He had got up to the point when he saw Boy Cap was taking a kicking, when the SIO interrupted him.

"Ok, Mark, thanks for that. We shall come on to what happened next in a minute. Foot Protection Team Leader, anything from you at this stage?"

A sturdy-looking male in a blue Nike hoodie sat up straight in his chair and took out his log. As he cleared his throat, it was clear that he was an officer with a loose aspiration to be a Sergeant, so had been given the job of Team Leader for the day.

"No, nothing from us at this stage, Sir. We had Mark all the way to the buy, but of course lost him after the, er...altercation." He smirked and looked about the room for approval, which was muted.

"The altercation!" bellowed York. "Good description. Go on then, Mark, what the bloody hell happened there!" The Deputy SIO took his glasses off and wiped his eyes in a vain attempt to distract himself from the embarrassment.

Conner again counted to five in his head and composed himself. He spoke in his best court voice.

"I had completed my tasking when I heard a fight behind me. I looked round and saw that Boy Cap was being beaten to a pulp. I risk assessed the situation and I believed that it was life-threatening so I... intervened."

"Well, your *intervention* could have burnt the operation, damaged the technical equipment or gotten yourself injured - or even worse, a member of the public," said York, now sitting forwards in his seat.

"Why not leave it to the Foot Protection, Mark, why get involved that early? I thought it was reckless," the Foot Protection Team leader sniped in.

Conner looked at the Team Leader with what an ex-girlfriend had called his *Paddington Bear* hard stare. The TL shuffled nervously in his seat and then looked back at his log.

"Well, I was about five feet away and I believed that one more stamp to the head could have killed him. The Foot Team were nearby, but they would have stood out more by getting involved and I would have been burnt. This way we have lost a dealer, but we may have saved a life while gaining a new contact and we've also come away with the drugs."

He shifted his attention directly to DI York.

"Sir, I believed that with your experience you would understand that the operation is going well and what would have taken the shine off it would have been a dead druggie, surrounded by plain-clothes cops, in the middle of Old Burlington Road at 10 o'clock in the morning."

There was a silence in the room as what Conner had said slowly sunk in. Then a female voice from the back of the room said, "I agree."

Conner looked to see the red-haired female perched on a desk with her arms crossed, looking towards the SIO.

"Me and Roger were the first there, but it still took two minutes and Jam was really going for it. He could have snapped Boy Cap's neck on the pavement at any time."

DI York looked at the female and then at Conner, before saying, "What about the loss of line of sight when you ran off?"

Nash had slipped into the room. "I can help with that, Guv. The Council CCTV had Mark all the way into Berkeley Square. And the technical equipment has worked a treat. Good image of Jam. I've field tested the purchases and it's gear alright. That's three buys, with one on video, so he can be nicked at any time."

Not for the first time, Nash had taken a noose from around Conner's neck.

The SIO sat back in his chair and thought for a bit. The Deputy SIO piped up. "Becky, where are we with the targets?"

A young studious-looking female Detective Constable in a smart business suit and sensible shoes stood up and went to the board. "That's all eight of the SE24 gang accounted for, three buys on each. Once we get the lab result for the drugs and Mark's statement for Jam today, the prosecution files are ready to go."

York nodded and bit the end of his pen whilst thinking aloud. "Ok, well if we nick them this week, that means Jam is out of the way for Mark when he goes back on the ground."

There was an exaggerated round of positive comments from the group, sensing this could now all blow over very quickly. "Good idea, Sir."

Looking pleased with himself, DI York, the Operation Atlantic SIO, sat back in his chair.

"Ok, Dave, can you get those arrests in motion?" he said looking at his Deputy, who nodded in return.

"Mark, have you got any leave owed?" York asked, glancing up from his blue book now with a smile on his round face.

"Yes, Sir, I'm sure I have some cancelled rest days on my card somewhere."

"Right then, take them. It'll give us some time for things to cool off."

The SIO then walked out of the room, no doubt eager to tell the Divisional Superintendent how well it was all going. As an afterthought he shouted back "Well done, everyone!" DS Holland walked off after him, vigorously rubbing his temples with both hands.

The crowd in the room broke up, as they started to pack up their kit and wipe white board ink from their faces. Conner looked at Nash, who smiled back at him, making a letter T with his hands. He nodded, and as he was putting his chair back against the wall, he noticed the red-haired officer was standing near to him, unplugging her radio piece from her ear, and packing up her personal protection equipment. He looked at her and smiled.

"Thanks for backing me up. I really did appreciate it...sorry, what's your name again?"

The redhead woman glanced up at him but did not stop packing her bag. "Amber," she said, with a hint of sarcasm, pointing at her hair which had been tied back into a ponytail. "And it was the right thing to do, crazy, but the right thing. I was a TPO for two years at Clubs and Vice."

In the TPO world, the Clubs and Vice Unit was the closest you got to glamour. The unit was made up of attractive female officers who frequented London's most exclusive and trendy nightclubs whilst undercover. Their job was to buy cocaine and amphetamines from Essex wide boys and pop stars' entourages.

Conner scratched the cut on his chin. "Now, would you let me buy you a drink to show how grateful I am? I need to write my statement and have a shower, but I could be done in an hour with some encouragement."

Amber thought for a second whilst still packing up her bag. She smiled a thin-lipped smile. "No, thank you, I don't drink." She put her cap on, slung her backpack over her shoulder and walked to the door.

"A Haagen Dazs ice cream?" he said, more in hope than expectation.

Amber stopped and stood in the doorway. Without turning, she thought for a second then walked out laughing and said, "It's going to take you hours to clean yourself up. Maybe another time when you're less smelly."

He smiled to himself at the retort and then got a whiff of himself. He realised he had a lot to do if he wanted to catch a train to Coventry anytime soon.

Chapter 4

North London, 0530 hours, 8th June 1996.

King's Cross Police Station was built in 1867 and it showed. Once used to stable horses for the Met's Mounted Branch, it was now no longer accessible to the public. Instead, housed on its dilapidated six floors, were various *Jeans and T-Shirt* units such as the Confidential Source Unit, Local Crime Squad and Vice Squad – all of which struggle to work amongst leaking roofs and mice infestations. It being so bad at times, that officers had to resort to working from The Carpenter's Arms pub directly across the road, or at least that's what they tell the Detective Chief Inspector when they are found there during the day. But *The Cross*, as the nick is known, does have a decent briefing room and a nearby café that opens at 5 am, freshly supplied with sausages, bacon and black pudding from the nearby Smithfield meat market.

That was why, just under one week on from her Foot Protection Team duties with Operation Atlantic, PC 113 CX Amber Mills was sitting in the King's Cross briefing room dressed in full Level 1 riot clothing, with her blue NATO standard Police Riot helmet rolling around between her feet.

Whilst she was waiting for everyone else in the packed room to settle down, she found herself wondering if she had done the right thing by adding an extra egg to her sausage sandwich. Wiping the last bit of yolk from the corner of her mouth, she decided she had, but would have to do a few extra miles on the treadmill before her shift finished. Amber was twenty-five years old and had been with the Metropolitan Police for four years after leaving a comfortable job in an upmarket health club and gym in Colchester. Although she had enjoyed the atmosphere and free gym sessions, she had felt that she was destined for more. After kicking the idea around for a few months, she had joined the Met in June 1992 to see where it would take her. Initially, it took her to West End Central, dealing with drunks, tourists and drunken tourists, before she was recruited by The Met's elite Clubs and Vice Unit. She was excited by the thrill of buying drugs in London's top night clubs, but she soon became disheartened by the revolving door of drugs policing. Looking for a new challenge she had joined One Area Territorial Support Group, or TSG, and found what she had been looking for. Excitement, hard work and the ability to exercise on *Job* time. Once she had proved herself in the pub fights, the shield wall and the long, long hours, she had found colleagues who would die for you no matter your background, race or sex. The feeling was mutual.

The only light in the King's Cross briefing room was provided by an overhead projector that was waiting eagerly for a PowerPoint presentation to start and give its existence any meaning. Amber heard the clinking of metal and the clumsy shuffling of feet, as six heavily armed men tried in vain to sneak into a cramped room. This signalled that the Firearms Teams from SO19 had arrived, and the briefing would begin.

A presentation appeared on the screen five metres in front of Amber and she looked at the pictures of the solemn faces of today's targets. The aim of today's operation was the successful execution of seven Misuse of Drugs warrants as part of Op. Atlantic, the overhead projector cheerfully informed her. DS Dave Holland, whom Amber recognised from the operation's safe house, had come to the front of the room and was reading the next slide, entitled *Intention and Information,* whilst stroking his grey beard. Another collection of images of men and women appeared on the screen. Some were from custody photos, others were grainy and from odd angles, which meant they had been taken from the covert cameras used by the undercover officers. Looking at the board, Amber recognised one of the males as *Jam* from the tussle between him and Mark on the last buy. She smiled to herself, remembering the astonishment she had felt when she saw Mark hurtle into Jam. Not what she was expecting, but the right call in the circumstances. She smiled again, remembering when Mark, looking like a bag of shit, had asked her out. She had declined, not wanting to make it too easy, but it took some nerve, looking and smelling the way he did.

Whether through luck or judgement, and probably the former, she thought, her serial had been allocated to another target on the Caledonian Road Estate and Jam, by virtue of his firearms markers, would get a visit from SO19. Serves him right, she thought to herself.

The briefing finished, she collected her helmet off the floor, picked up her day sack and woke up Roger with a gentle slap to the head, which made him open his eyes immediately, but otherwise remain in the same position. PC 82 CX Roger Kelly was a 6-foot 3-inch ex Jamaican Policeman who had moved from Kingston, Jamaica, to London five years ago with his wife and three children. Back in Kingston, he would often have a gun fight with local Yardies just to get into work. Big, tough and unflappable, he was always destined for the TSG. Amber and Roger had become inseparable whilst at work.

"Come on, sleeping beauty, we're off to the Caley," Amber said whilst looking down at the big Jamaican stirring in his chair. Roger sat up, rubbed his eyes and lifted his huge frame from his seat, and they both negotiated the six flights of stairs down to the Police Mercedes *Sprinter* Van parked outside the Station.

Twenty minutes later, they were standing outside a ten-storey block of flats and looking up.

"Why is it always the top floor?" Roger observed, as he, Amber and the rest of their TSG serial entered the grey concrete stairwell that would take them to 1023 Samwell House on the Caledonian Estate.

This flat was the sometime address of a William Johnston, or *Green beanie* to give him his Operation Atlantic name. William was a twenty-two-year-old Jamaican national and was already on bail for several drug offences. He had not yet graduated to firearms but was known to carry knives and the occasional machete.

The serial naturally fell into a single file formation with the lead officer carrying the Method of Entry Kit. Despite its grand name it comprised of little more than a red battering ram and crowbar. The rest of the serial had paired off and been assigned specific rooms, which for a one-bedroom flat wasn't many. Amber and Roger had been assigned the bedroom - standard practice on the serial as Amber was the only female – given that many rack dens had girls for *entertainment.* Some of the time these girls, some as young as twelve, wanted to be there but many didn't really get a choice.

As the serial approached the target flat, they became stealthier in their approach. A second serial, who had been in the lead, branched off to the left on the same floor and their Team Leader, or *TL*, had given Amber's TL a double-handed flash to signify ten seconds until they hit both addresses simultaneously.

Her serial gathered pace as they reached the top floor and turned right. Five doors in they stopped and formed up in a stack. She dropped her visor and took out her pepper spray. Roger removed his Met baton, a 2-foot piece of hollow metal with a foam handle and placed it over his right shoulder. The flat and the front door was a standard Islington Council fitting. The kitchen was at the front of the flat and on the left-hand side of the front door as Amber faced it. There was a light on in the kitchen, but the front windows, some smashed, had been covered with newspaper and old cardboard. The TL whispered into his radio whilst giving a small nod to the Method of Entry officer.

"Charlie Uniform Five entering target address."

The MOE officer lifted the *big red key*, took a deep breath and slammed it against the lock of the door. The whole door shook, but held. A second slam followed shortly after, and the door flew back on its hinges.

"Police with a warrant! Stay where you are!" shouted the TL through the now open door as the serial ran in to secure their assigned rooms.

Amber and Roger ran to the bedroom and hurled the door open. Through the early morning light that was spilling in through a dirty white blanket over the window, she saw a stained, brown-patterned duvet on a filthy white mattress. It was surrounded by beer cans, which were spilling over with ash and cigarette butts, next to piles of pizza boxes, McDonald's bags and old Steven Segal video tapes. The room stunk of the sickly-sweet smell of cannabis and there were numerous knives and broken bottles laying around. Amber could now see that under the duvet was a young black female looking back at her in terror. The face was pretty and had a long scar on the right-hand side of it. Amber could hear "Room clear!" being shouted by the other police officers in the flat.

Suddenly, Amber noticed that a pair of black skinny legs were hanging into the bedroom while the rest of the body was trying to scramble out of the window. Roger, who had seen what had caught her attention, had dropped his baton and ran over to the window ledge, dragging the now kicking legs, writhing body and a screaming head back into the bedroom. A foot came up towards Roger's face, which he casually avoided before returning the favour with a single kick between the legs of the now prone male. The male stopped kicking and screaming and instead curled up into the foetal position and started crying softly to himself. Roger calmly returned his baton to its ring holster on his belt and, almost as an afterthought, said in his deep Jamaican accent to the crying male, "Stay down."

With both occupants of the bedroom placed in *quick cuffs*, a double handcuff held together with a solid piece of plastic in the middle, Amber and Roger led out their prisoners.

Roger took out Johnston, who had been arrested for Supplying Controlled Drugs, and who was now on the block landing wearing only a pair of Orlando Magic basketball shorts.

Amber had tried to get some details from the young black female, but she had refused to speak, so she had been nicked on suspicion of being an illegal immigrant. She was allowed to put on underwear and a white Snoopy nightie. Amber held the plastic bar of the quick cuffs that had been placed on the female's wrists and led her out onto the concrete landing. She could hear that the other serial were having issues getting into their allocated address. The sounds of banging on the door reached her, along with shouts of "Open the fucking door, dickhead!!" As Amber turned to lead the female down the stairs, she could see an aluminium ladder go through the resisting target's address front window and two officers climb up and start to kick out the rest of the glass before jumping into the flat, batons flying. The Met would always win in the end.

Amber sat opposite the pretty young black female in the police van. The prisoner cage at the back of the vehicle was already full. Two angry young men, still in cuffs, were alternating between trying to kick the van door and arguing between themselves. Amber knew that the female would never speak at length to a police officer with them watching, but tried to build trust by taking her cuffs off and smiling gently at her. The black female rubbed her wrists but still looked down at the floor. Amber could see there were other scars on the female's shaved head and bruising on her arms and knees.

"What's your name?" Amber asked with a light smile.

"Fuck you, bitch!" came a shout from the prisoner cage. Amber gave a look in that direction, which said, if I have to stand up and come over there, you'll be getting a smack for my trouble. The prisoners went back to arguing amongst themselves.

"Do you speak English?" Amber asked the female and received a small curt nod in return.

"C'mon then, what's your name?" she asked again.

The female looked out of the tinted window next to her and after a few seconds said, "Mimi."

"Where you from, Mimi?"

"France."

"Ok, good." Amber nodded.

Just then the van's side door slid open and a man's face, wearing a blue NATO Police helmet with the three yellow Sergeant's stripes stuck above the visor, looked in.

"What's happening with her?" the Sergeant asked, nodding at Mimi. The radio on his shoulder was trying to get his attention.

"She's been nicked as an illegal, Sarge," said Amber.

The sergeant sighed. "Ok, take her to Islington Custody, serve her an IM3 immigration notice and leave her for the Immigration Service." And with that, he slid the van door shut.

Mimi looked at Amber. Amber turned away. There was nothing more to be said at this stage.

In the back yard of Islington Police Station in Tolpuddle Street, TSG Police Mercedes vans were dropping off officers and prisoners before both parties went on very separate journeys. Amber's van pulled up. She helped Mimi out of it and kept hold of her elbow, having left the cuffs off.

"I must piss," Mimi said, as they walked in through the door to the custody suite. Amber could see a queue of prisoners sitting on the bench waiting to be booked in and knew she was looking at an hour wait at least.

"Alright," Amber said, "this way." And she led her prisoner off into the female staff toilets near to custody.

As they walked into the toilets, Mimi turned to Amber and said, with desperation in her voice, "You must help me. I'll help you if you'll help me."

"How can you help me?" Amber asked, intrigued.

"I saw something, a murder. I can make you famous, you can solve big murder, be a big star."

Amber gave a small laugh.

"Well, it doesn't always work like that. What did you see, Mimi?"

"Please, please. I can't go back to my country." Mimi grabbed Amber's hands and pleaded.

"France?"

"Rwanda." The pretty round face had terror in her eyes.

"Ah, right," said Amber, releasing Mimi's grip. "I can't promise anything, but you'll be treated fairly. I'll make sure of that. What did you see?"

Mimi slumped to the floor on her knees and Amber knelt beside her. Amber could smell the white spirit cleaning fluid on the grubby tiles and looked at Mimi in increasing shock as she told her about what she had seen a *Tall Man* do on the Albert Embankment.

After Amber had booked Mimi in with the custody sergeant, she completed the IMMIGRATION 3 form, adding *"Suitable for Bail"* in big red letters at the top. Amber knew that the Immigration Service would probably take a few details and release her, pending an assessment on her asylum claim, but her endorsement should help secure that outcome. Amber made her way out of the custody suite through twisting corridors and into the refreshing sunlight of the police station yard. The sergeant from earlier was in the smoking area, his helmet at his feet, listening intently to the police radio via his earpiece, whilst dragging on a Benson and Hedges cigarette. He responded that he had received the message, then looked wearily at Amber as she approached.

"Sarge, you know the illegal I brought in? I did an intelligence interview with her and... well, she says she witnessed a murder about a month ago. On Albert Embankment."

"Right?" the sergeant said, rolling his eyes.

"I believe her, she seems genuinely upset."

"What checks have you done?" the sergeant asked, taking another drag.

"She's no trace on police systems, but if she's an illegal that would explain it. She says she saw a *Tall Man* carry out some sort of ritual stabbing on another man and then drop him in the river. I don't have much of a description of the victim, I've tried Missing Persons reports, but there is nothing on our database that matches him in the last three months."

"Ok," said the sergeant, taking a last draw on his cigarette. "Albert Embankment is Lambeth Division, so put an Intel log in for them before you finish duty. Then leave it."

"But I think it's genuine, what if..."

"I said, leave it, Amber. It's probably a load of shit to stop her being deported. Now get back to your van and put your Level One kit back on, there's a protest at the American embassy so we're going back to Central."

With that, he threw his cigarette to the ground, picked up his helmet and walked back to his van, speaking into his radio.

"Probably a load of *shit*," she said to herself as he walked off. But Amber was far from convinced.

Chapter 5

Villiers Street, London, 1000 hours, Monday 8th June 1996.

The Griffin Pub is situated opposite Charing Cross railway station and is a five-minute walk from the Embankment tube. The pub looks modern from the outside but has an old world feel inside and is popular with the city types from the nearby big six accountancy firms as well as commuters and tourists. It's also handy to watch the football on a Sunday afternoon, before heading back to your hotel or a semi-detached in Surrey. Ryan Conner could see all the evidence of this, as he was currently sitting amongst a pile of discarded England flags and plastic glasses that had been dragged out into the street by The Griffin's disgruntled clientele. The England football team had started their opening Euro 96 game against Switzerland in good form, with a goal by Blackburn Rover's star striker Alan Shearer, but had then reverted to type and attempted to soak up Swiss pressure that inevitably led to an equalising goal. It was that, he suspected, that had led to The Griffin having a barstool-shaped hole in one of its windows.

Conner took his stinking sleeping bag off his shoulders and laid it behind him to lean back against. He adjusted the blue baseball cap that was laying upturned between his crossed legs and contained fifty-seven pence that he had put in. He did not expect that amount to increase anytime soon. The spot he occupied was generally a good place to beg. It was also a prime area for the *Real Issue* homeless magazine sellers who, as in most towns and cities around the country, were the oracles of where drugs could be bought and sold. He had hoped to bump into one or two and see what the word on the street was since he'd been away. But today was slow, real slow. The football had provided an excuse for people not to turn up for work. It was hot, overcast and muggy, and thanks to the enforcement arm of Operation Atlantic, there were currently no drug dealers about. Drug dealers are of course like weeds. You pull a load out and within a relatively short time some more sprout back up again. It was important for him to be there when they did. He would then look an *old face* on the druggie scene, rather than suddenly appearing just when the new dealers did.

He took a sip from his super strength lager and laid back against the wall of Charing Cross train station, closing his eyes. He was in the shadow of a stall selling London-themed tat, such as t-shirts, mugs and oversized Union Jack hats. The stall holder had given up as well and was sitting on his chair reading a copy of The Sun and smoking a roll-up. He had already asked the stall holder for a cigarette and had been told to "Piss off" without him even looking up from Page Three.

With his eyes closed, he remembered that he had watched the England game with his *Granda* Pat in the small front room of his Ma's terraced house in Coventry. The street she lived in had the familiar accoutrements of old mattresses propped up in alleyways and smashed glass from car quarter lights glistening on the tarmac. He had spent the week sleeping on an overstuffed sofa in the front room. The room had been dark, damp and smelt of his Granda's pipe tobacco. It was all strangely comforting. Conner had of course shouted for England, despite his strong ties to Ireland. His mother, who didn't care much about football, would bring in cups of tea and cakes from the small kitchen that was directly adjacent to the front living room, shouting, "C'mon! Fecking beat England!" and then busy herself in the kitchen again. His Granda Pat, ever the diplomat, would remain neutral and just appreciate the game.

Pat Hayes had grown up in Dublin and had enjoyed some football success as a tough no-nonsense centre back with Waterford Town in the seventies. Pat had married Angela, a typist at the club, and they had been blessed with a baby daughter, Lucy, Conner's Mum. But he had lost his wife to cancer a few years later and his footballing career ended soon after that. Lucy had moved to the UK as soon as she was old enough with a man from the *North*. Pat had followed her to Coventry eight years later, after the man, Conner's waster of a father, had cleared off with the car, the rented TV and the meagre family savings. Lucy was found by police, unconscious at the bottom of the stairs with cuts and bruises, the day after his father went. Pat had stumbled back into a father's role, despite his advancing age, not only for his daughter's sake, but for Conner's.

Sitting on the sofa, watching the slow pace of the game, Conner had found his mind wandering, not unlike England's midfield, he observed. He had left Coventry in a hurry in 1988, having upset a local crime family, the Coopers. He had unwittingly prevented a robbery in the white goods warehouse where he had worked since leaving school at sixteen. He had been working late unloading fridges, when he saw two men in balaclavas attacking the warehouse security guard by the front gate. He had boxed from the age of eight and so had fought one felon off and managed to knock the other to the ground while the guard called the police. The security guard was an old boy in his seventies and subsequently died of a heart attack two months later. It became a big local story and the public were outraged.

Conner had thought he would be treated as a hero by the warehouse owners, the Cooper family. But he was badly mistaken. The Coopers were behind the crime as an insurance scam. Lots of money had been lost. Charlie Cooper, Billy Cooper's only son, had been linked by the detained man and both went to prison. Even worse, the Coopers had lost respect amongst their criminal rivals for the death of the security guard and the family were never a crime underworld power again. But the Coopers' money was as good as anyone else's, and a price had been put on Conner's seventeen-year-old head. He now risked a severe beating, the loss of his kneecaps or worse, if found out and about. Although comfortable with himself that he had done the right thing, and this strong sense of right and wrong would define his life, he had joined the British Army within the fortnight to escape the heat and distance himself from his family. Disgraced crime families have long memories, so he had only been back to Coventry for short spells, preferring to meet his family in Oxford or Leicester when he had the chance. His Granda's reputation and connections had been enough to keep any trouble away from his mother, but one day he knew he would need to sort it all out with the Cooper family.

Just not yet.

Conner had watched his Granda sitting in his usual chair, stroking the end of the chair arm in a soothing circular fashion. He loved his Granda and enjoyed the old man's passion for the beautiful game. Behind the old man's chair was a mantelpiece packed with photographs in varying styles of frames. The first one he could make out was of him as a baby in a white gown being baptised into the Church of England. The only contribution his father had made to his life. Then there was a picture of him in school uniform, aged around eight, with a bowl haircut, big patterned collars and an even bigger grin. Another photo showed him in a Sidney Stringer secondary modern school football kit, aged fifteen, kneeling next to two large silver cups, his captain's armband proudly displayed on his right arm. Conner's natural leadership skills and emotional intelligence had been recognised by a PE teacher who was ex-Army and would fascinate the class with stories of

Germany, Malaya and Canada. The PE teacher had made him school football team captain after their first training session. Conner recalled that it was a rough school back then. English, Irish, Asian and Jamaican kids all thrust together. Poverty and single parent families were the only thing they all had in common. There were gang disputes and fights, but when they got onto a football pitch, they had a great first eleven, feared across Coventry.

Then there was a picture of him in his British Army khaki number two dress, standing to attention, chin up, eyes obscured by the black, shiny, slashed peak on his red and green parade cap. A bright silver cap badge, portraying two crossed rifles propping up a crown with a running horse across the middle, gleamed in the sun, along with a boxing trophy at his feet. The photo had been taken by his Granda outside his accommodation block in Catterick Garrison on the day of his pass off. His mother hadn't come. Despite this, he remembered feeling proud and excited of what the future might hold. If only he knew then what he knew now, his smile would have been a bit more reserved. There were no photos of him in Northern Ireland or police uniform. His Ma had not allowed it. In the house his job wasn't discussed and he was happy with that. When the game had finished, he had eaten a tea of sausage, mash and gravy, shared a tin of Stout with his Granda, kissed his Ma goodbye and went by taxi to the nearby train station. It had been dark when he left Coventry and dark when he had arrived at his police section house accommodation in Hounslow.

Back on Charing Cross Place, Conner opened his eyes and decided he would visit his old employer. He took out his operational phone from his waist band and typed in "WHITEHALL" to the SIO and gathered up his stuff. He told the stallholder that perhaps he would make more money if he smiled occasionally and got a two-finger salute in return.

Setting off along The Strand, the vehicle traffic trundling along at walking pace, he turned left towards Trafalgar Square, or *T Square* as it was known in the Met, then crossed over into Whitehall. Just past The Silver Cross pub on the corner of Whitehall Place, there was a begging spot where every self-respecting homeless person knew there was money to made from gullible tourists and civil servants full of liberal guilt and self-loathing. From here he could see the front of Horse Guards Parade, despite the throngs of tourists surrounding it. The road traffic had already been closed off by armed police, a precaution put in place after an IRA mortar attack on Whitehall in 1991. The iron barred gate at the front of Horse Guards was traditionally the official entrance to St James's Palace, but the building was now used as offices for British Army's London District HQ. Either side of the black metal gate were two large black wooden sentry boxes and each box contained a large black cavalry horse and a Mounted Dutyman soldier sitting on top. Each soldier carried a large Wilkinson's steel cavalry sword sloped over their right shoulder. Today the *Dutymen* were wearing the blue jacket, silver breast plate and the red plumed silver helmet of The Blues and Royals. But it was their reliefs Conner had come to see. He knew that they would be along any minute, because what he was watching was his first legitimate job. He had once been one of these elite soldiers and it was nearly time for the 11 am changing of the Queen's Life Guard. He was pretty confident of that fact. After all, it had happened at this time every day since 1689.

Settling down on his sleeping bag, he saw the two Blues and Royals Mounted Dutymen dig their heels into the horses' flanks and move them forward out of the sentry boxes. They were immediately replaced by two identical looking horses, the sound of their metal horseshoes clanking on the cobbles, but the new Mounted Dutymen looked different and carried a small highly polished wooden rifle instead of a sword. They wore midnight green jackets with red facings, a highly polished brown leather bandolier lay across their chests and both wore a black riding busby hat with a black plume. This was a special regiment with a special reputation. Conner had served six years as one of them and knew their history well. The midnight green jacket represented their infantry roots, as one of the first regiments to use what would now be termed guerrilla tactics. The black plume had been given to the regiment in disgrace after they had looted and then burnt down the village of Vellaloor in India in 1767, killing five hundred civilians. The red facings recognised their overzealous treatment of the enemy at the Battle of Roliça in Spain in 1808. All this history seeped out from the two Mounted Dutymen and even the tourists could sense the increased menace these new soldiers radiated. A gaggle of tourists, who had mistakenly got too close, all took one step back as the horses shook their heads, rattled their steel mouth bits and loudly blew out hot air through their flaring nostrils. This regiment was officially titled The Royal Mounted Rifles, but they were more commonly known, and feared, throughout the British Army as *the Green Mafia*.

The Royal Mounted Rifles were the third regiment in the Household Cavalry along with The Life Guards and The Blues and Royals. Unlike their sister regiments, who were armoured troops when operational, the *RMR* were mechanised infantry and were often used as decisive shock troops. They were generally seen as a particularly ugly and ill-mannered sister by the other two more refined regiments and although they did carry out Queen's Life Guard duties, they were not trusted with state occasions.

Originally formed from the remains of the Horse Grenadier Guards, which had been disbanded after refusing to take part in the brutal quashing of the Anti-Catholic Gordon Riots that threatened to bring revolution to London in 1780, the regiment had survived as *The Mounted Rifles*. It had revelled in its reputation of being above the law ever since. This was often encouraged as *esprit de corps* by its officers and the private soldiers did not want to let their officers down. However, it was in the Boer War that they really came to prominence. The regiment played the Boer Commandos at their own game with mounted hit-and-run tactics, terrorising homesteads, carrying out ambushes and attacking heavily-defended supply columns. Due to their exploits, they became a personal favourite of Queen Victoria, who bestowed on them the title of The *Royal* Mounted Rifles and instructed that they should be part of her own Household Cavalry. This was not universally popular amongst her generals. The regiment had gone on to fight with distinction in the First and Second World Wars, if you don't count art theft and forgery as war crimes.

More recently the *RMR*'s reputation had spawned a more sinister element. Since the turn of the 20th century, a large part of Central London's prostitution, protection rackets, unlawful weapons supply, stolen goods and, increasingly, its open drugs markets had all been under the command and control of *the Green Mafia*. This Organised Crime Group, or *OCG*, was perfectly placed. The civilian police were often kept out of the loop of what was happening on military premises and the Royal Military Police were not equipped to deal with high levels of organised crime. The *Top Floor* were the brains behind their criminal activities. This group of soldier-criminals consisted of a relatively small number of middle-ranking non-commissioned officers who ran their crime empire from the top floor of Sloane Square Barracks in Cadogan Place, hence the name. Being posted to Sloane Square Barracks was known within the regiment as *Going Downtown*. The Green Mafia identified potential criminal members from the soldiers who came from all the hellhole estates of the United Kingdom as they passed through Downtown. Each private was required to complete a two-year tour of ceremonial duties before moving on to the mechanised infantry units. If they proved themselves as an asset to the criminal group, they remained Downtown enjoying all the monetary and criminal benefits that went with the Green Mafia's activities. Perhaps they would even be invited to become part of the Top Floor itself. In 1989, an eighteen-year-old Ryan Conner had found himself dropped into this cauldron of crime, fear and violence and it would define him for the rest of his life.

However, times were changing, and Queen Victoria's disgruntled generals may yet have the last laugh. An upcoming Strategic Defence Review had earmarked several regiments for *suspended animation* or disbandment in non-governmental speak. And all the rumours were saying The Royal Mounted Rifles were at the top of the list.

With the inspections completed by the duty officer and the foot soldiers posted to their positions, the changing of the Queen's Life Guard had been done for another day. The tourists had started to move on to the next item on their itinerary whilst looking at guidebooks and gathering in excited children who were running rings around them. Conner gathered up his belongings and accepted he had to get back to the grimy world that is the Central London open drugs markets. He realised he would need to raise his game if he was going to get served up today. He would need to engineer an accidently-on-purpose meeting known as a *bump*, with a contact who could introduce him to a new dealer. He would need to bump into Peter.

****

Curzon Square, London, 11 am, Monday 8th June 1996.

The Tall Man had carefully placed his knife and fork at the 5 o'clock position on the fine white China plate. He had enjoyed his lightly poached eggs. His long thin legs were casually crossed and his arms were lightly folded across his muscular chest. He had a sharp, intelligent face with dark collar-length hair, still wet from his morning shower. Looking out of the large bay window across Park Lane and into Hyde Park, he watched its young couples laying together on the grass enjoying the hot sun, whilst avoiding footballs kicked in their direction from groups of male tourists shouting apologies in Italian and Turkish.

He felt uncomfortably warm inside the one-bedroom flat. He considered opening a small window but as it would be just something else to clean, he decided against it. Picking up the plate, he went to the kitchen area and placed the dinnerware and cutlery into a washing-up bowl that already contained a pan, a coffee mug, a wine glass, a set of house keys, the TV remote and a large blood-stained cooking knife. Looking under the sink he found a bottle of bleach and a cardboard cylinder of Vim cleaning powder. There was a pack of fresh cloths and kitchen scrubbers neatly arranged on a shelf. He reflected that one of the *few* things he admired in gay men was their organisational skills. *They* could always be relied upon to have sufficient cleaning products at hand.

He filled the washing-up bowl with hot water, added a splash of bleach, and thoroughly washed the items before putting them away where he had found them. Then he soaked a fresh cloth in bleach and sprinkled Vim powder on top and carefully went around and cleaned all the places he had touched since arriving in the flat late last night. This included a glass topped coffee table which took most of his efforts. Whilst working away the Tall Man thought about how easy the pick-up of his target had been. His prey had been a fifty-three-year-old fund manager called Clarence Bale. The Tall Man had followed him for a week before they had met. He had gone to a pub at Earl's Court where Bale was known to drink. A simple coloured handkerchief in his suit pocket, and Bale's lust for meaningless sex, was enough to entice him in. The Tall Man had not even needed to go into the pub to meet Bale. Their conversation and drinks had all taken place in a beer garden and went on late into the night. Apparently there had been a football game during the day but neither man cared, preferring to discuss horse racing and literature. Eventually he had been invited back to Bale's flat. It had been dark by then. There was no concierge, no CCTV, no one around. Perfect.

Having finished the washing up in the morning sunlight, the Tall Man walked into the bedroom at the end of a short corridor and pushed the door open using the cloth. The large naked dead body of Clarence Bale was on its back on the bed, a fat distended white stomach protruding into the air. This was in part gluttony on Bale's behalf and in part the accumulating of bodily gases. The body was in a state of *rigor mortis* and the blue marbling of lividity was forming on Bale's skin. The legs of the deceased man were dangling off the end of the bed and his right arm draped to the floor. The left arm was still held fast by a handcuff to the bedpost.

The Tall Man recalled how he had taken part in a disgusting charade as the fat monster had defecated on top of the glass table whilst he laid underneath, closing his eyes in revulsion. But he knew that he would have Bale's full trust once the obscene act had been completed. It had worked. Bale had allowed himself to be handcuffed to the bed and the Tall Man had agreed to return the obscene favour on to Bale's fat bare chest. He smiled as remembered the look on Bale's face when the fat pervert saw the knife the Tall Man was holding and it became clear he had other ideas. The Tall Man had started his questioning and dropped the *special* liquid onto Bale's body whilst the pig was in a state of fear-induced sexual arousal. The Tall Man had then known immediately this was not his ultimate target. He had shoved the man's shit from the coffee table into the fat monster's mouth when questioning had gone badly. The smell of the liquid, the disgusting visage, the very repulsiveness of the man himself had then taken over the Tall Man's mind and the knife in his hand did the rest.

Now looking down on Bale's deceased body the Tall Man was reminded of *Porky Pig*, a cartoon character he had enjoyed as child. He gave a small laugh at the dark cartoon-like scene and admired the contrast of the red-brown dried blood stains on the slowly blueing body against the white sheets. It reminded him of dirt tracks across a snowy hill. The blood had streamed out in a flow from the neck and then had pooled at the bottom of Clarence Bale's dismembered head. There was a look of horror and amazement on the fleshy face, its eyes now glazed over staring into never-ending nothingness.

The Tall Man sat on the edge of the bed, looking at his night's work. Bale would be discovered of course, and he would be labelled a sex killer. Just like those other crazies. But those fiends were mere amateurs. Only targeting gay men because of the easy way in which they could be put at the killer's mercy. He knew he was not like them. They were sloppy and only motivated by common thievery and lust.

The Tall Man's purpose was righteous. Had not his mission been inspired by the very centre of justice in this country? The Old Bailey itself. There above the Central Criminal Court entrance, carved in stone, was his purpose: "DEFEND THE CHILDREN OF THE POOR AND PUNISH THE WRONGDOER". No one would suffer like him again.

He stood up and walked from the bedroom, cleaning as he went. At the front door he wiped the inside and outside handles with the bleached cloth, which he then carefully folded up and put into his pocket. Finally, he quietly and carefully closed the door to the flat. He then left the near-deserted building thinking of his next target, who was out there, somewhere. Waiting for the Tall Man's justice.

Chapter 6

Leicester Square, London, 1425 hours, Monday 8th June 1996.

The city had stubbornly refused to cool down. American tourists in their beige shorts, loud shirts and jaunty baseball caps were even feeling the heat, paying out top dollar for ice creams and cans of fizzy drinks. Conner watched the transactions from a bench in the small park in the centre of Leicester Square. Large men and thin women handing over English pound notes from *fanny packs* and receiving a small Mr Whippy and few pence change in return. His *Nagra* recording equipment was safely in his backpack, so he had taken his t-shirt off and draped it around his shoulders. His hat was perched peak down on the back of his sweaty head, protecting his neck from the blistering sun. He sat hunched forward, staring at an open can of lager on the floor in front of him. Around an hour ago he had spoken to the Operation Atlantic detective sergeant on the phone and asked if the Foot Protection Team could keep an eye out for the operational target known as *Boy Cap*. Conner had noticed that the team had included Amber. This had cheered up his day. He had received a text back within thirty minutes: "BOY CAP MOON UNDER THE WATER NOW".

Conner had taken up a position in a small park to watch the front of the famous tourist pub in the bottom corner of Leicester Square. He had immediately seen the young rent boy sitting at an outside table smoking and still wearing the same clothes from two weeks earlier. Boy Cap had been identified by the Operational Intelligence Cell as Peter David Collins, born 12/03/74 in Northampton. He had fifteen previous convictions, including shoplifting and possession of Class A drugs. He was of *No Fixed Abode* but was rarely seen sleeping rough, so probably sofa surfed. He was also known to the sex worker team at Charing Cross nick. Despite an intelligence log stating that he carried a knife in his sock, he wasn't known to be any trouble to the punters and seemed to be a professional with his activities.

From his position, he could see that Peter was trying to meet the gaze of single young men that walked into the outside seating area. He'd had no luck for the last 30 minutes, but he knew Peter would be desperate to score so would stick in. Suddenly he saw Peter get up from his seat and go over to where a tall, slim, blonde male, wearing a pastel-yellow jumper casually draped over his shoulders, was taking an overly long time to look at the menu on a stand near to the pub entrance. There was a brief conversation between the two men, a couple of exaggerated false laughs, and then they both went into the pub.

Twenty minutes later, Conner saw the blonde man, his yellow jumper now around his waist, leaving the Moon Under the Water pub, followed by Peter a few moments later. Given the speed that the rent boy was now walking, Conner knew he was off to score drugs and followed at a safe distance. Peter turned left onto Charing Cross Road and stopped outside Bar 79, placing forty pounds into his left sock. He then continued over Shaftesbury Avenue and Conner suspected he would go along Moor Street to Old Compton Street. Conner now had a small window of opportunity, so he turned left onto Shaftesbury and started to run up Greek Street, trusting that his foot security would keep up. If he timed it right, he would intercept Peter near the Mackintosh Theatre. Sprinting up the street, his heavy backpack slapping into his back, he reached the junction and spun around, wiping his sweaty face with his t-shirt. He jumped slightly when he heard Peter's voice behind him.

"Fucking hell, are you alright Mark? Why are you running, bruv?" the rent boy asked.

He turned to see Peter's still bruised face looking straight at him.

"Cops mate," Conner said breathlessly. "Fucking Cops."

"C'mon, I know just the place those pigs won't look. You scored yet?"

"Nah man, there's fuck all about." He placed his hands on his hips trying to get his breath back.

"Right, let's kill two birds with one stone." Peter took hold of Conner's arm and led him off into the Soho heat.

Walking along arm-in-arm with Peter, Conner realised this was not an area that he knew particularly well. He recognised the main entertainment venues on Old Compton Street. G-A-Y was a famous nightclub and had hosted big names such as The Pet Shop Boys, Gloria Gaynor and Kylie Minogue. A few doors down, a queue was already forming outside Ronnie Scott's jazz club, despite it being lunchtime. They continued along the street and past the open façade and electric blue internal lighting of The Admiral Duncan Pub. Groups of young and older men stood outside, soaking up the hot sun with a beer. Conner had no issue with the gay community. As far as he could see they were just another tribe. The Army was a tribe. The Police were a tribe. Criminals were a tribe. Football supporters were a tribe. City traders were a tribe. Drug dealers and drug users were a tribe. The list went on. Each had its own rules and conventions. Its dos and don'ts. Its heroes and villains. The tribes mixed along as best they could day-to-day, but when it came down to it, you would fight and die for your own tribe. That's how you survived. It had been ever thus.

As the tourist part of Soho gave way to more run-down shopfronts selling sex toys and leather clothing, Conner started to see scraps of paper with the rather optimistic word "MODEL" scribbled in felt pen attached to grim-looking doorways. The local populace had become different. Gleaming white muscle shirts and high-top trainers had given way to stooped men in overcoats rifling through bins. Chinese people from the nearby Chinatown ferried produce around on carts and argued on street corners. The Chinese never bothered the Police and the Police never bothered them.

Conner had gently released Peter's grip from his arm and was now following him along Wardour Street, when they suddenly turned right on to Duck Lane. Situated at the end of a short road was a pub Conner had heard of but never thought he would ever get to go into. This was a no-go zone for the local cops, and you would need a good proportion of the *Commissioner's Strategic Reserve* just to get in the front door. The building was late Georgian and imposing. The very top floor had plywood covering smashed windows. Old beer and milk bottles could be seen on some of the windowsills. The second floor had all its windows painted black with just the white window frames clearly visible. The windows on the ground floor where especially unwelcoming. The bottom half was frosted glass with heavy net curtains covering the rest. As Conner approached the front door, he could see it was shut tight. Unlike most of the other pubs in the area, who were trying to entice tourists and their wallets in, this door was saying a big fat *piss off*. It reminded him more of a social club in Coventry than a West End pub. In fact, the whole place projected the vibe, *if you don't like what you see, good, go away, we don't want you.* Above the door was an ageing picture sign with the name of the pub in faded black writing. This was The Rutting Stag, and it was legendary.

Conner had heard the stories like everyone else. The Rutting Stag pub first came to police notice during the war as a bar that would be frequented by criminals running black market scams and selling stolen fuel vouchers. As homosexuality was also a crime back then it became a safe pickup point for likeminded men not on military service or on leave. It was a strange mix of clientele. After the war it was, outwardly at least, more respectable, but was also known as haunt of local criminal gangs who would offer protection to the homosexual community for their activities in return for cash. The old stars of the theatre mixed with the new stars of the big screen. Private parties were held where boys, girls and amphetamines were all on the menu. The parties continued for decades and changed with people's tastes. Cannabis and free love for the sixties. Cocaine and sado-masochism for the seventies and early eighties. There were police raids, of course, but these became so problematic for the police that any excuse was made not to go in. The pub, a veritable gold mine, often changed hands as part of violent turf wars between rival gangs, but the upstairs parties always remained the same. Absolute privacy and security for whoever was in attendance.

Today, The Rutting Stag was a shadow of its former self. There was no need to hide as much in the *Anything Goes nineties*. But it still held onto its reputation as a haunt of tough criminals and even tougher queens and that was a combination you didn't want to mess with.

Outside the pub, two heavily built skinheads sat opposite each other at a rotting old picnic table chained to a drainpipe. As Peter and Conner approached the entrance, the skinheads turned and looked Peter up and down.

"Who's this?" asked one of the skinheads, wearing a black sleeveless Judas Priest top and nodding towards Conner.

"This is Mark," said Peter. "He's cool, man. He's trying to get away from the filth."

Judas Priest, as Conner had mentally tagged him, slowly got up from the table using his powerful tattooed arms and walked over to him. Conner dabbed the sweat from his face with his t-shirt and knew he would be in a world of pain if the Nagra recording device was found. He drew in some breaths without it being too obvious and prepared to front it out.

"What's your name, *sweetheart?*" Judas Priest said in an East London accent.

"Mark Doyle."

"Why are the filth after you, *Mark Doyle?*"

"It's bullshit, mate, a fucking poxy warrant."

"We don't want any extra heat. You understand me, sweetheart."

"Nah man, it's bollocks, shoplifting or some shit. I'll be straight back out if I'm nicked. Waste of fucking time but I want to score before I go in, know what I mean."

"What's in the bag?" Judas Priest asked, looking him up and down.

"Fuck all mate, my sleeping bag, blanket..." He said, as he started to pull everything out.

"Ok, for fuck's sake don't get all your stinking shit out." Judas Priest turned up his nose. "Go in and no fucking about."

Peter and Conner thanked the two men profusely and went into the pub.

"Bloody hell," thought Conner. "I'm in!"

****

One mile away in an old office block converted into a police operational control room, a nervously sweating DI York was listening in to the Operation Atlantic back-to-back radio channel. Slamming the radio on the desk, he shouted angrily at his DS.

"For fuck's sake! He's only gone in!"

DS Holland, who was making a brew in the kitchen, took his glasses off and started to vigorously rub his temples.

****

As Conner walked into The Rutting Stag the first thing that hit him was the smell of stale beer and the sweet sickly smell of cannabis. No longer the low-level recreational drug of the sixties and seventies, it had been perfected into a strong psychoactive substance, grown on an industrial scale in warehouses by Organised Crime Groups. The pub décor was overwhelmingly brown. Stained beige wallpaper sat uncomfortably above scratched, dark wood veneer panelling. The heavy wooden bar took up the whole of the back wall with pumps and optics jostling for space. Pinned to the walls behind the bar were packets of peanuts partly revealing a smiling, and potentially topless, blonde-haired girl. The barmaid, a large white lady with jet black hair wearing an oversized Madonna t-shirt, eyed him suspiciously as she made a show of cleaning a glass. Behind her, an open doorway led into a back room with empty beer crates stacked up around beer kegs. The drinkers in the pub were sitting together in clumps around circular tables with a mixture of styles of chairs. A few drinkers were sitting on stools at the bar and turned to look at Peter and Conner as they entered, but soon went back to their drinks. In the bottom right-hand corner of the room were the toilets and next to them a heavy mahogany brown door had a small sign on it that discreetly but firmly said "PRIVATE".

Underneath the front windows were cushioned bench seats with long rectangular tables and this is where Peter headed. In the corner there was a group of young men sitting around a table, smoking and nursing bottles of Pilsner lager. They looked at Peter and one or two nodded a friendly welcome. A young muscular Chinese boy smiled widely as Peter sat down next to him and gently took the boy's hand.

"Alright, you bunch of old queens," Peter breathed out.

There was some laughter and a general chorus of "Fuck you, darling!"

"Sit down, Mark, they won't bite. But they might give you a nasty suck," he added with a wink. "This is Mark everyone. He's the one who stopped me getting my brains bashed in by a fucking yardie the other week."

"What the fuck did you do that for! He probably deserved it," said a laughing voice. Peter showed one middle finger to the person responsible.

Conner sat on a chair at the end of the table and placed his backpack underneath his seat and hooked his ankle into a shoulder strap. He crossed his arms and lent on the table, his dirty white t-shirt still over his shoulders, his grimy face a patchwork cleaned by his sweat.

"Hi mate, I'm Ken," the Chinese man said in perfect English, leaning over to shake Conner's hand.

"Ken, good to meet you, mate".

"Lager?" Ken asked.

"Yeah, cheers, man. I'm gasping after running around all morning."

"No point asking you," Ken said, looking at Peter ,who said, "Yes, please" and smiled back at him.

Conner could not help but notice a strong connection, a love, between the two men.

"So, what's happening?" Peter asked the group.

"We're celebrating," said a slim black male. "That fat bully Bernard West has gone. Not been seen for over a month. I normally have a meet with him in Smithfield toilets every Thursday, but he didn't show again. He pays well but he was too violent, scarily so. I was dreading it, but he's disappeared off the face of the fucking earth! Good riddance." The black male extinguished a cigarette in an ashtray with real feeling. "He beat you bad once, didn't he, Peter?"

Peter brushed his mousey hair back from his face. "I went to his flat and he tried to put a plastic bag on my head when I was high. He said it was for a laugh but then turned nasty and broke a few of my ribs. Fat bastard. I hope he's fucking dead."

Ken came back with the drinks and sat down. "So, where you from Mark?" he asked Conner.

"Coventry." Conner took a long drink from the bottle of cold lager. It tasted like an angel crying on his tongue. "I came down for work four months ago, and to get away from some heat up north, but it's gone to rat's shit, no work, nowhere to stay, no gear. Pigs still on my back."

He raised his bottle then took another long drink. "Fuck it," he added.

"Anyone getting served up?" Peter asked, taking a cigarette from someone else's pack and lighting up.

"Daz's got a new number," the slim black male answered, nodding at a fair-haired male sat at the opposite end of the table from Conner.

Daz looked startled now being the centre of attention and checked his pay-as-you-go Samsung mobile phone.

"I got a number from a regular punter from here. Dealer's called *White Boy*. I've sent a text an hour ago to see if he's working but got nothing back."

Mark carried on with the general banter. Topics included the current HIV threats, who was best avoided, where to get free condoms and general piss-taking. It was like any other work conversation, a mixture of moaning and mirth. Meanwhile PC Ryan Conner, the police officer, had kicked his legal brain into gear. He'd never heard of this new dealer and if indeed he was a *White Boy,* then that would be unusual as most of the white London gangs had got out of drug dealing when the Jamaicans and Asians moved into it. Cocaine came from South America and heroin came from Pakistan. It didn't take an economic genius to work out who was better connected. The new gangs were also more desperate, which made them more violent. At the end of the day, they were simply better at it. The white criminal firms had kept shoplifting, imported cigarettes, burglary, armed robberies, brothels and protection rackets, but everything else was moving online. Fraud, child pornography, counterfeit goods. That was the new frontier. However, a few East End gangs had refused to throw in the drug dealing towel, so he was eager to see who would turn up.

Daz's phone suddenly vibrated on the table, killing the conversation dead. He picked it up.

"It's White boy," he said, then read out the text message.

"WHAT DO YOU WANT WHERE R U". Daz looked expectantly around the table. "Who's in?" he said, excitedly.

Conner knew he would have to be very careful. The Misuse of Drugs Act 1971 was very clear on the issue. He could buy drugs but if he passed the drugs to anyone else, even as part of a chain, he'd go to prison. If he split the drugs with anyone else, he'd go to prison. If he took anyone else's money? Yep, he'd go to prison.

The group shouted up their orders of *whites* and *browns*. Ken kept silent and started to rip the label off his lager bottle.

"I'll have one white and one brown, but if no one knows this geezer how you know you're not getting *skanked*. How do we know its real gear?" Conner asked calmly.

"It's cool man, the punter who gave me the number is straight up. If we get skanked, I'll bite his balls off next time they are in my mouth," Daz said, as he texted the order.

A few seconds later the phone vibrated again and Daz read the text. "It's thirty quid per wrap," he said after a few seconds.

This was meet with a chorus of swearing. "Look there's fuck all about, what choice have we got?" Daz pleaded.

Peter turned to Conner. "Wanna split a rock?"

"Can't mate, I'm already splitting it with a bird *Up West*. She'll be doing her nut as it is."

Ken put a ten-pound note on the table in front of Peter and then sat quietly. Peter picked it up and kissed him theatrically on the cheek.

Doing foolish things for the people we love is universal, Conner observed.

"Do it, Daz," said Peter excitedly and the text went off.

Thirty minutes later, he was waiting with all the other boys from the pub, except notably Ken, on the second floor of Brewer's Street car park. An old, rundown, concrete edifice from the Sixties, it stunk of urine in the stairwells and had litter on the breeze in every corner. There were needles and bent rusty spoons everywhere and no CCTV that worked. He also observed that unsurprisingly there weren't many cars either.

White Boy had texted Daz "10 MINS" thirty minutes ago and the motley bunch had stood around waiting and sharing cigarettes since. Abruptly, the screeching of tyres could be heard coming up the ramp and a blue BMW four door 3 series car, with blacked out windows, swung into the parking area and came to a stop, reverse parked against the rear wall. Daz took a deep breath and walked over to the passenger side door only to be redirected to the driver's side. There was a brief conversation and an exchange and Daz walked off towards the stairwell exit, giving a thumbs up as he went. Peter went next. Conner jumped ahead of the queue, not wanting to stand out as being last. As he approached the driver's car window, he noticed that the vehicle's registration plate had been taken off. The driver was a thin white male aged around twenty-four with fine black hair severely gelled back. He was wearing wraparound shades and a black Ralph Lauren polo shirt. He had a large gold earring in his left ear. He looked like *Bono* from U2, so that's what Conner tagged him as.

"One and one," Conner said to *Bono,* handing him his drugs money with the recorded serial numbers so they could be traced later. The driver took the money without saying a word.

Bono then took out one small white wrap and one small brown wrap from the car's central console and handed him the drug wraps without looking at him. Conner had not activated his video recorder, with it being a new dealer and the dangers of being searched being higher, but he could do with a better look at the new target so he stalled.

"Can I have your number, bruv?" he asked Bono, leaning into the motor through the window. Suddenly a hand came over the headrest from the back of the vehicle and grabbed him by his chin.

"Fuck off and ask your queer mate, prick!" said an angry male voice.

Conner pulled back instinctively. "Sorry bruv. Sorry mate. No problem," he said acting submissively and backing away. Do not be a threat. Give them their power trip. He will have the last laugh when they are all doing time. He then saw the hand that had grabbed him and his brain glitched. He could feel himself going pale. On the wrist of the hand was a watch. But it was not just any watch. It was a Swiss-made, Cabot Watch Company watch, a G10 V5 Pilot model, to be precise. Conner knew only two things about this watch. One – it was prohibitively expensive, and two – it was issued exclusively to British Army Special Forces.

****

Oxford Street, London, 1735 hours, Monday 8th June 1996

The Police Mercedes *Sprinter* van was ironically moving at snail's pace along Oxford Street. PC Amber Mills was sitting in the rear offside door seat looking out through the tinted windows at the bustling shoppers busying themselves with the delights of capitalism. Amber was thinking back to the Test Purchase Officer *Mark's* debrief she had just sat through in the repurposed office block in Covent Garden. She knew from her own time as a TPO that this wasn't his real name, but it would do for now. He had given a good account again, but he had also given his foot security a heart attack. First by sprinting off and then second when he walked, as bold as brass, into The Rutting Stag Pub. The foot security had found an observation point and got a few cars to cover all the exits, but they were blind until he came out and moved to the car park. He had been given space for the deal and it turned out well. DI York was less impressed of course. The last thing he wanted to do was explain to his Superintendent why there was a riot at The Rutting Stag. Amber thought that DI York was going to burn Mark on the spot. Sack him off and return him back to the joys of missing children and domestics on General Duties policing. But Mark was a good TPO. He had the look and the patter. He could think on his feet and knew the law. He was also brave and a bit crazy which helped in that line of work. And he hooked into another dealer on his own initiative. Not easy to do.

Amber had felt that Mark was holding something back about the deal. But he could not or would not add anything else when she'd asked him about it. He hadn't asked her out again, but had given her his best *boy next door* smile when he first saw her. She had smiled back. Amber had steered away from having relationships with cops. She had tried it once. With her first *street duties* tutor. It had started off full of excitement just like the *Job* itself. But then came the shifts, the stress, the tension. The lying on both sides. The violence on his. She had left him shortly after.

But Mark seemed different. There was a burning light in his eyes to do the right thing every time. No matter the fallout. Amber admired that. If she was honest with herself, she liked it. Liked him. Maybe she would go for that ice cream after all, she thought to herself.

The van trundled its way to Hyde Park corner and turned left. The Team Leader had accepted a shout to assist some local cops to get into an address in Mayfair. The serial had *spoofed*, a game of chance where you had to guess the total number of coins in everyone's hand, and Roger had lost. Amber had volunteered to go with him of course. Around five minutes later they were outside a rather upmarket block of flats on Curzon Square. Amber and Roger had taken the big red key out of the rear of the van and had placed their stab proof jackets over their civilian jackets. They shoved on their blue police baseball caps with the distinctive black and white checks and set off towards a block of expensive looking flats. They could see a Met Police Astra vehicle parked up outside the block. Once on the top floor, Amber saw two male uniformed police officers standing with their arms crossed, leaning against a corridor wall, opposite a flat's front door. The older one of the pair looked up at the ceiling as he saw them and swore quietly to himself. The younger one just looked exited to be there. A tutor and his street duties probationer, Amber thought to herself.

"What took so long, been to the gym?" the older cop said with half a smile.

"Traffic," Amber said putting the red lump of metal down on the floor. "What have we got?"

"Neighbour rang in, saying there was some sort of commotion in the flat last night, and no one's seen or heard from the occupant since. It's probably an overdose or a heart attack. We can't kick the door in and neither of us are MOE trained so we called *the big dogs*," the older cop added, with a hint of sarcasm.

"Ok, well we're here now."

Roger squeezed his huge frame past the young probationer, who backed up against the wall and stared open-mouthed as the huge Jamaican lifted the red battering ram in one hand. Giving the door a quick look to see were the hinges where situated, Roger took as step back, and two large thumps later the door was smashed open.

"Hello, Police! Anyone there?" Amber shouted into the flat, then looked at the older cop who made himself busy writing in his pocket notebook. Amber sighed and went in. Around two minutes later she came back to the front door and spoke to the tutor constable.

"You'd better get on to your control room. We have a murder scene."

"How could you possibly know that?" said the Tutor scornfully, still scribbling in his pocket notebook.

"Well, there's a naked man lying on his back and his head has been cut off," Amber said, smiling *sweetly*. "Oh, and his head is covered in excrement."

The older officer went white as sheet and the younger one threw up.

Amber resigned herself to being late off again. She knew how this would play out. The Metropolitan Police is an extremely busy organisation. Of course, everyone these days is busy at work. But then there is being busy and then there being Metropolitan Police busy. The two are light-years apart. It's extremely busy on a normal day, but it can sometimes reach astronomical levels.

One Area, of which West End Central, Charing Cross and Mayfair are part, could deal with up to ten thousand incidents a day. This did not include prisoners, bed watches, court cases and everything else that goes with policing a city of around twelve million people. Each police station within One Area would perhaps parade twenty cops, of which only half would be available for calls. London averaged around a murder a day which accounted for half of the yearly national total. This did not include suspicious deaths, sudden unexpected deaths and traffic-related deaths. So, Amber knew that this meant, even if a man had been found beheaded in his own bed, there would not be long lines of police cars with their blue lights swirling, parked up outside Curzon Square with twenty smart police officers wearing hats and carrying clipboards. That was for TV.

Amber understood that what would happen was more sedate and routine. It would be, however, extremely thorough. She had seen it a hundred times before. There was a suspect on the loose, sure, but they were long gone. And in the *Five Building Blocks of Investigation* the block entitled *Identifying the Suspect* came last for a reason. There was work to be done.

What would happen was this. Following the call of a suspected murder by the officers at the scene to the control room, the Duty Uniformed Inspector would be notified. In this case, he turned up with a uniformed sergeant and two police officers. The sergeant had found the unwitting constables in the canteen planning to have a brew after spending all shift dealing with prisoners. Trying to hide in the canteen was of course a fundamental error as that is the first place a sergeant will go when looking for more *troops*.

Once all available officers were at the scene, which amounted to about six, the cordons that were put in place by the two initial officers were quickly extended to make the controlled area bigger. A *crime scene log* would be commenced detailing everyone going in and out of the scene. The two thirsty constables and two more from Amber's serial (who had been waiting in the van) were despatched to carry out local enquiries with neighbours and recover any CCTV. This was a lot of work for four tired PCs, but they would do it to the best of their ability, despite knowing that some detectives would come down and do it all again later, because most people would be out at work and the CCTV would be unavailable today.

The uniformed Inspector would then have a very quick look at the scene in the flat using an *uncommon approach path*, that is, a path to the deceased that the suspect would have been unlikely to take and therefore there would be less chance of destroying any evidence. This quick look was to establish if the death was suspicious or not. In this case it took the uniformed Inspector approximately two seconds to decide that it was and to breathe a sigh of relief as he rang the Duty Detective Inspector and ruined his day. The Duty DI would in turn ruin the day of his Detective Sergeant by dispatching him down to the scene with a few detectives to start the crime scene management. The Duty DI would also speak to a *Scenes of Crime Officer*, known as SOCO, who would grab a colleague and attend in the white suits beloved of the media. No one else would go into the scene until SOCO had finished.

Finishing the call to SOCO, the Duty DI would then have the most important call of the day with the *On Call* Duty Detective Superintendent, who would decide if the investigation was to remain on One Area, and suck up all its limited resources for months, or go to the *Area Major Investigation Team*, known as AMIT. Once again within five seconds of the Detective Superintendent being told the circumstances of the beheaded man, the Duty DI was told to inform AMIT. Another sigh of relief was made by the Duty DI, before he called the AMIT Detective Chief Inspector who listened to the tale of woe and agreed it should be theirs.

And that's how DCI Colin Hammond became the Senior Investigative Officer for the murder of Clarence Bale. His day, and his plans to go for dinner with his wife, were also ruined, for the second time this week.

Chapter 7

Sloane Square Barracks, London, 2305 hours, Monday 8th June 1996.

The Royal Mounted Rifles' Sloane Square Barracks at Cadogan Place was an imposing series of Sixties-style concrete edifices and were in direct contrast to the grandeur of the Kensington and Chelsea Borough that surrounded it. The barracks consisted of a block of stables attached to an indoor riding school, *Other Ranks* accommodation, split into four-men rooms, and the NCOs' and Officers' Mess rooms. Army Mess rooms are like private drinking clubs for soldiers and they host their meals, parties and events. All Messes throughout the British Army have their own strange practices and archaic rules.

At the front of the barracks, a large wooden gate was permanently guarded by armed troops to control access and egress of pedestrians and vehicles. It was watched over carefully by the *Regimental Provost,* who were housed in a large purpose-built annex which also contained *jail* cells. Once through the main gate you were greeted by a large central drill square which also doubled as the main parade ground. A constant smell of hay, horse muck, leather and sweat wafted across the square and pervaded every corner of the complex. Looming over the whole site was a large tower block where the married quarters and the officers' apartments were situated. The top floor of the block, some twenty storeys high, was a flat like any other with a kitchen and bedrooms, but as the air conditioning units were just above the flat nobody wanted to live there, so it had been left empty, even if it did offer some amazing views of London, especially at night.

Contrary to fire regulations, the flat only had one way in and one way out, via a single elevator which also made it almost impregnable. This fact had not been lost on the Green Mafia forefathers who took it over shortly after it was abandoned and it fitted out as an *unofficial* Mess room with a bar, pumps and optics. In the living room, a large, ornate, varnished dining table took centre stage and for over thirty years the people who had sat around the table were known as the Green Mafia's *Top Floor* and they had been responsible for a large proportion of the serious crime committed in central London ever since.

At this moment Sergeant Tom *Ginger* Bailey was sitting directly opposite an empty, but still imposing, highly decorated, wooden leather-backed chair. It was situated at the head of the table, behind which were regimental paintings of famous battles and important-looking men sitting in this distinctive chair, staring down on proceedings. Around the wooden table there was space for thirteen seats. They were currently all occupied by the Green Mafia's Top Floor members. There were a few glasses of beer and whiskey in front of those seated and the smoke from their cigarettes had wafted up to form a cloudy smog around a central light. Those in attendance were dressed either in clean stable dress of green lightweight trousers and light brown shirt or in smart civilian clothes, just as it stated in the Top Floor Mess rules.

Ginger Bailey was chairing the meeting as the second-in-command of the Top Table. A short, stocky, bright ginger-haired man with a quick temper, he was reading from the Apologies in a thick Glaswegian accent, but managing an agenda was not his forte. He prayed the *boss* would appear soon, as he stumbled over the minutes from the last meeting. His prayers were suddenly answered when he heard the lift that led directly into the Mess open and in stepped Staff Sergeant Vivian Mason, the Green Mafia's current elected *Master*.

Ginger watched as Mason, immaculately dressed as always in stable uniform and highly polished black boots, walked over to his *Master's* Chair. Mason stood well over six foot and had the gait of a fighter but moved with natural athleticism, despite being in his mid-forties. He took his seat at the top of the table. Although not being the most senior Army rank present, everybody went quiet and stood up, waiting for Mason to sit down.

"Thank you, Gentlemen," said Mason, pulling his chair up behind him. He stroked his dark moustache and smoothed down his neat black hair.

"Please sit down and accept my apologies. I had a disciplinary matter to attend to," he said in the ubiquitous Thames estuary army accent, with just a hint of his Bethnal Green roots. He put a cigarette to his mouth, and someone lit it for him.

"We had just finished the agenda, Viv." Ginger sounded relieved.

"Ok, well I'll carry on from here, thank you, Ginger. Now, can I have your weekly reports please, gentlemen?"

Ginger sat back in his chair, while the tension increased around the rest of the table as the attendees moved drinks, shuffled papers and cleared their throats.

"The burglaries at the NAAFI shops at Knightsbridge, Wellington and Pirbright Barracks all went off no problem," said a short, thin corporal with a Mancunian accent. "We got lots of electricals, aftershave, beer and fags, as well as a total of three grand cash."

Mason nodded in appreciation.

"The goods have gone to our normal handlers for the usual fee and the cash went straight into Mess funds," the corporal continued, now sounding pleased with himself.

"Good. Next?" Mason asked, looking around expectantly for another report.

"A new customer has been found for our *protective services*." said a large-built black sergeant wearing a gleaming white Yves Saint Laurent collared shirt. "He owns several brothels around the West End. It took some *persuading*, but after a few visits at peak times he came round. He eventually agreed to the normal monthly fee of five hundred pounds."

Mason nodded, drew on his cigarette and thought for second before commenting. "Give him a reminder not to mess us about. Burn down one of the knocking shops and put the price up to seven hundred."

"Yes Viv," said the sergeant unquestioningly, as he adjusted the cuffs on his immaculate shirt.

The business of the meeting continued with a list of new customers, regimental recruitment, scores that had been settled, bribery money and the revenue brought into Mess funds, which currently stood at fifteen million pounds, all held in an off-shore British Virgin Islands bank account. As the meeting ended, Ginger Bailey looked around nervously at the other attendees and received a few nods of support. He then cleared his throat before speaking.

"Viv, we think we should talk about the move into the open drugs markets and The Rutted Stag."

"Oh." Mason raised half an eyebrow and lit another cigarette "What's troubling you, Ginger?"

"I, er…we think the link with White Boy is a good one. We all know we have struggled with drug dealing in the past, but with *Scarecrow* and his Provost sorting out the Southend problem we now have complete control of the White Boy line."

In every British Army regiment there was a Provost platoon. They were a cross between local law enforcement and base security. They manned the security gate and dealt with drunkenness and ill-discipline. But this being the Royal Mounted Rifles, they also happened to be trained in covert and countersurveillance techniques, breaking and entering, advanced driving, hostage tactics, releasing and *taking*, to name just a few of the tricks in their repertoire. They also possessed a well-stocked and advanced armoury of weapons and ammunition completely off the Army's books. But their speciality was a high level of intimidation and the permanent disposal of anyone who Viv Mason believed was standing in the way of the Green Mafia's objectives. Assisting him in this was Provost Sergeant Darren *Scarecrow* Tully. A six-foot-two steroid-infused monster with light blonde hair and a pockmarked face, he had been recently returned to the regiment after being thrown out of the Parachutes Regiment's elite *Pathfinder* Platoon for insubordination. Mason had welcomed him back and placed him in charge of his most valuable resource. Scarecrow was sitting at a right angle to Mason at the top of the table and quietly picked his nails clean with the blade of a Fairburn Sykes Commando knife.

Ginger continued, looking for signs of condemnation on Mason's impassive face.

"The concern I have is The Rutting Stag. We haven't got a good history there, Viv. We all remember the near downfall of '87. I'm just not sure it's worth the risk to us sat around this table."

Mason put his cigarette out in a nearby ashtray and lent forward on crossed arms. The room went deadly silent as he spoke.

"Yes, we've all heard about the trouble we had with those queer parties back in the day. Our predecessors did what they felt was best for the Green Mafia and its members at the time. The company parties were a solid revenue stream. But they went wrong. It cost us and now of course the regiment is moved out of London during the late summer months. What's done is done. However, my understanding is that plans are afoot which will eliminate the few loose ends that remain from them days and reduce the risk of our exposure in our future ventures."

Mason paused for effect, then continued.

"The Rutting Stag is strategically important because of its location, its difficulty for *CivPol* to control and its influential customer base. Let me be clear. The

Rutting Stag and its customers are to continue to be serviced by the White Boy line. It is through this drug line we will eventually gain full control of the Stag again."

Viv looked around the table and received affirmative nods. Finally, he looked straight at Ginger, who felt the white heat of the stare and nodded back in submission. Ginger felt he need a large drink.

"Good, the business concluded. Social Secretary, what do you have for us?" Mason asked, turning to a chubby-faced Warrant Officer in designer horn-rimmed glasses. The mood started to lift.

"Of course, Viv. Gentlemen, please enjoy the fruits of our collective labours with this light distraction."

Just then the lift opened and five young ladies, who had first been squeezed into tightly fitting dresses and then tightly squeezed into the lift, burst out in fits of drunken giggles. The Green Mafia members smiled, finished their drinks and started to form queues. Ginger made sure he had first pick.

Mason stood smoking on the balcony of the flat looking north towards Harrods and Hyde Park. He could see the lights from the tower block at Knightsbridge Barracks and the airplane warning lights of the BT Tower blinking red in the distance. The glass patio door behind him slid open and for a few seconds he could hear a baseline mixed with singing and laughing before it slid shut again.

"Viv, I know you don't normally partake, but there's a black girl in there with the arse of a ten-year-old boy." It was a drunken Ginger Bailey. He was sweating profusely. His straight ginger hair had been sleeked back and his beige stable shirt was open at the chest.

Mason smirked as he flicked the butt of his cigarette into the night and spoke. "I have to go to a *Supreme Lodge* meeting this month."

Ginger appeared to sober up by at least fifty percent on the spot, Mason noticed with some satisfaction. The Supreme Lodge – or The Grand Supreme Lodge of the Near East Temple as it was more formally known – was part secret society, part executive committee, but mainly a wide-ranging criminal enterprise. Within their ranks there were senior armed forces officers, senior police officers, doctors, bank executives and politicians, amongst other professions. The Supreme Lodge consisted of males and females, straight and gay, black and white. After all, the desire for money and power does not discriminate. Formed at the turn of the twentieth century from a remnant group who had split off from Aleister Crowley's *New Dawn* organisation, its aim was ensuring that the right people held the wealth and decision-making of the civilised world. They were global and had connections at every top level of society. They were also known to be ruthless and demanded absolute loyalty on the pain of death. The rewards for cooperation were also equally as great. When both organisations were newly formed, the Supreme Lodge elders had recruited the Green Mafia as their attack dogs. The relationship was mutually beneficial and had worked exceptionally well for nearly a hundred years.

"The Lodge, why? Have we fucked up?" Ginger asked, steading himself on the balcony rail.

"No, but they have a special operation running and, apparently, I need to have sight of it. My eyes only. But just in case, the boys need to be on top of their game over the next few weeks. And make sure Scarecrow and his Provost are ready to go if needed."

"Yes Viv, of course," Ginger said, fastening up a few buttons on his shirt.

"Oh, and Ginger, the request for the takeover of The Rutting Stag has come from the Supreme Lodge. The Council members believe that enough water has run under the bridge and the time has come to get back into the high-end prostitution game."

Mason turned and looked Ginger Bailey dead in the eye. "Don't question this again, understood?"

"Yes, Master." Ginger stood as close to attention as he could in his half drunken state.

Mason took a last look at the view and walked past Ginger, patting him on his shoulder as he did so. Ginger let out a deep breath and decided he need a drink and half an hour with a certain African hooker to calm him down.

Chapter 8

Trafalgar Square, London, 2100 hours, Tuesday 11th June 1996.

A thin blue line of round Police NATO helmets from the Metropolitan Police's Tactical Support Group pushed its way through the centre of *T Square* towards The National Gallery where a large screen was showing the Euro 96 Group D game, Turkey v Croatia. It was the seventy-fifth minute and tensions between rival fans and the police had been rising all day. Red flares were being set off from both groups of supporters, whilst bottles and cans rained down on the police lines, who were frantically trying to keep the two groups apart. The stewards had long since retreated and One and Five Area Tactical Support Groups had been called in to restore order. The local police were forming an outer cordon to stop the situation getting worse, as pockets of England hooligans decided that they wanted some of the action. The game itself was being played in Nottingham, but fans from both countries had descended on London to watch the game in the pubs and take advantage of the large screen provided by Westminster Council. It had been a disaster in the making. Ten thousand fans had packed into *T square*. Turkey had never qualified for a European Cup since their formation in 1923. This had led to Turkish football fans from clubs such as Galatasaray, Besiktas and Fenerbahce putting their deep-seated hatred of each other to one side and joining with first and second generation Turks living in North London. When combined, this became one of the loudest, passionate and fearsome footballing firms on the planet. In fact, the only other national team supporters that could match them, other than England, were Croatia.

The red and white checked shirt of Croatia was packed full of nationalist pride whether it was worn by a player or a supporter. The modern country was formed in 1990 after splitting away from the Former Yugoslavia. A bitter civil war between Croatia, Bosnia and Serbia had followed. Ethnic cleansing had reared its ugly three-mouthed head and thousands of people were killed on all sides. In 1995 the Croatian Army launched Operation Storm which brought an end to the fighting and the three countries went their own ways. Croatia had taken this as a victory and every victory by the Croatian national football team was an echo of it. Croatian supporters were known as *Il Furioso Incendio* by their Italian rivals, *The Blazing Fire,* and they had a terrifying reputation amongst the world's football hooligans. Some of its members would have taken part in Operation Storm when they would have been armed with guns, grenades and bayonets. Now around five thousand of them were taking out their frustrations with bottles, cans and metal fences on the Turks and the Met Police. As the game inched towards an unsatisfactory nil-nil draw, the violence was increasing. Admiral Nelson looked down disapprovingly.

One mile away, in a disused office building, Undercover Test Purchase Operative Ryan Conner was busy writing his deployment statement under his pseudonym of *Mark*. Nash, his friend and welfare officer, had made him a brew. Conner took sips of sweet tea between writing sentences. A police radio was squawking away on a window ledge behind him. Today's second buy from White Boy had gone as planned. He'd been served up one white and two brown for fifty pounds. The drugs lay in property bags in front of him so he could note the serial numbers before they went off to the lab. Amber's TSG serial were on the football duty, but he had been given the Brixton Crime Squad as foot security which he was more than happy with. They were tough, blended in and most of them smelt worse than him. He had gone along with the locals from The Rutting Stag to the Brewer's Street Car

Park. The same car, which was untraceable on police systems, had turned up with White Boy sitting motionless in the driver's seat. Although he was sure that there was a presence in the back of the car, he couldn't tell if it was the same man as before. Conner had kept the military angle to himself as he didn't want to put the balloon up before he was absolutely sure there was some Army involvement.

The debrief had gone as well as could be expected. DI York had been frosty with him ever since he had gone into The Rutting Stag, but his Detective Superintendent, Alan Jones, knew Conner from a previous operation and rated him very highly. Detective Superintendent Jones had authorised White Boy as a target. So, DI York was stuck with *Mark* the TPO for the foreseeable, but he knew he couldn't push his luck.

The police radio behind him sprang into life and a voice from the T Square control room made a formal sounding announcement. "A Goal for Croatia. Eighty-sixth minute, Vlaovic. Current score, Turkey 0 Croatia 1." There was a heartbeat of silence and then all hell broke loose on the air. Static voices started to scream over the radio as the background noise became deafening.

"Urgent assistance, urgent assistance. Northwest Corner T Square. Croatian fans have broken through cordon and are now fighting with England fans," said a male voice.

"Units to Northwest Corner please," instructed a calm female voice in the control room.

"Turkish fans are now ripping up the metal fences and attacking Croatia fans. There are families trying to get out. Can I have an ambulance to South Africa House. Male unconscious and bleeding," came a breathless male voice over the air.

"Ambulance required," said a female voice. "Can I..." She was suddenly cut off as an emergency button was activated.

"Code zero," said a female voice with a Scottish accent. Then silence. The radio came back on, but the voice was clearly shouting at some else. "... Get back! Get back!" Sounds of a struggle. "Code zero!"

"Location please," said the voice in the control room. Silence. "Location please."

"The screen, the..." The radio went dead.

"Units to the screen, please, for a code zero."

The chaos went on.

Conner had stopped writing and was sipping his tea, listening to the radio calls, when the door was opened by a young black male with an afro comb sticking out the side of his hair and a pen behind his ear. It was Dale Alderton, the Brixton Crime Squad Team Leader.

"We've got to go, mate. The want us in unmarked vehicle patrols around T Square. Just wanted to say a pleasure working with you again."

He looked at the young man, who was dressed in a Chicago Bulls basketball shirt and cut-off jeans. They had worked as TPOs on a number of jobs and he had nothing but admiration and respect for the young lad from Croydon, wiser than his years.

"No problem, Dale. Thanks for the help. You're always welcome on my jobs, mate, when you want a break from bandit country."

Alderton laughed.

"You've got it, and I still owe you a night out," he said, now putting his police radio to his ear. "Take care, *Mark,*" he said with a smile and closed the door.

Conner finished his statement just as Nash came into the office to see how he was getting on.

"You done that yet or are you kicking the arse out of the overtime again?" Nash asked with a smile.

"You can't put a price on a good job," he smiled, as he took an overlong sip of tea.

"Oh, fuck it!" Nash said, suddenly noticing the two property bags on the desk. "They need to go to the lab tonight or the *Governor* will do his nut."

"So?" Conner said, reading his statement. "Get a local unit to do it."

"They're all *tucked up* with T square kicking off. There is only me and you left in here. And you may remember I can't drive police vehicles, after the *Brighton* incident."

Conner remembered it well. Two months ago, he had guested as a TPO for Sussex Police on a job in Brighton. He had been bundled in a car for questioning by a local drug dealer and his muscle. They had been satisfied with the lies he'd given them, but they had dumped him in the Sussex countryside just for badness. The counties were very different in their approach to safety of Met TPOs and the DS in charge had told him to make his own way home, as he could not afford the overtime to come and pick him up. In desperation he had phoned Nash back at the safe house. Nash had taken an unmarked Sussex police car in order to *rescue* him, and the powers that be couldn't decide if had constituted a *Taking Without the Owner's Consent* offence or not. It was a shitstorm in a teacup. But it being the police, they had taken Nash's police driving authority while someone in the Crown Prosecution Service worked it all out. That was *The Job* all over. They have to be seen to be whiter than whiter, even if it meant screwing your own people.

"I'll do it," Conner said. "It will be fine. It's only Lambeth. I'll clean up a bit, take one of the pool cars and a radio. Twenty-minute job."

"No. I'll just get the bus down." Nash sighed.

"Don't be daft. Go home to Anne and the kids." Nash didn't argue too much. He'd been pushing sixteen-hour days since the operation began and he had promised to put the girls to bed at least once this week.

"Ok. Thanks, *Mark,*" Nash said, with a wink.

"You can thank Mark, but you can buy Ryan a beer."

Nash laughed as he raised himself up from his seat and overly ruffled Conner's hair before wiping his hand on Conner's shirt.

Conner took a shower then changed into some clean clothes. He put the police radio and drug evidence bags on the seat of a battered old Vauxhall Corsa police pool car, before driving off towards the Strand. The trip to the Forensic Science Services laboratory at Lambeth Bridge would only take around twenty minutes even with a detour to avoid Trafalgar Square. The traffic was light, with most people staying out of the way of Central London as it was fast becoming a war zone. He had put the police radio on the local West End Central talk group and was listening to all the calls. The fighting between rival fans had spread outside the square with restaurants and pubs coming under attack. He drove on to Millbank as the radio chattered away.

"All units standby unless urgent," said a male voice in the control room over the radio.

"Units to 15 E Lord North Street. Report of a male stabbed. Life-threatening injuries. London Ambulance Service assigned, but stuck in traffic."

There was radio silence. Conner knew that the scene of the stabbing was behind the Virgin Active gym on Great Peter Street, which was now just in front of him.

Come on, someone answer, he thought to himself.

Silence.

The control room continued. "Reports from hysterical neighbour that a fifty-year-old male is bleeding badly, struggling to breath, any units, please?"

He could see the turn off that would lead to Lord North Street. He closed his eyes for a split second and resigned himself to his fate.

"Charlie-X Ray, this is 347 Echo Kilo. I will attend".

"You're not shown on duty, 347?"

"Do you want me to go or not?" He turned up Great Peter Street.

"Received... showing you assigned," the voice in the control room acknowledged.

Conner pulled up outside a large block of executive apartments on Lord North Street. He picked up the radio and stuck it in the back of his jeans pocket and went to the car boot. He looked for a green plastic first aid box, which was standard issue in all vehicles used by the police. He rifled through the large plastic bags, paper evidence bags and general trash until he found it at the back of the car boot. His heart then sank as he picked it up and it felt concerningly light. Opening it up, he found three small battles of eye wash and a small used bandage. Swearing, he threw it back into the car and slammed the boot shut. He ran to the front door of the block and pressed a random selection of buzzers, shouting, "Police, Police!" The door buzzed open and he ran up a set of stairs figuring 15 E would be near the top of the block. After three flights of stairs, he saw a young blonde woman crouched outside a flat, crying hysterically. Conner stopped running, took a few deep breaths, and kneeled down next to the woman.

"What's happened, where is he?" he asked as patiently as he could.

"He's in there, in the bathroom. I had a key. I just found him there," she said pointing to an open front door. She clasped to her hands to her face and continued to cry.

Conner walked into a finely decorated flat. There was no sign of disturbance in the main living room other than a wooden table that had been knocked over. Through an open internal door, he saw a large mirror and realised it was the bathroom. He pushed open the door, not knowing what horrors he would find. The small room was white tiled on the floor and walls, but it had been turned bright red with blood. The thick fluid had pooled on the floor and in the grouting. He was aware of a smell like an expensive cologne, but this wasn't unusual for what looked like a bachelor pad. The white bath was also covered in blood and laid back in it was a large white male face up with his eyes closed. The man was naked. Wheezing and holding his chest, he laid back almost motionless. Conner went to the bath and knelt in a puddle of blood that had gathered on the tiles. He could see that the man had around twenty stab wounds to his chest, stomach and groin. He was sure it was only the size of the male that was keeping him alive. There were puddles of thick red blood forming in the bath, winding their way to the plug hole. He could see three large white towels on a rack, and he pushed them against the male's stomach and chest. Pushing down as hard as he could to try to stop the bleeding.

"What's your name, buddy? Come on, what's your name?" Conner asked in desperation.

The blood-soaked male opened his eyes and let out a rasping noise.

Conner applied pressure to the largest wound on the man's stomach. Blood oozed out of the gaping holes in the man's flesh. Occasionally a spurt would arc out of an artery and onto the white tiled wall.

With a free hand he grabbed his radio and pressed the send button. "CX, 347, where's LAS? Where's the ambulance? Male has serious stab wounds!"

"I'll chase them up," came the reply from the radio.

"Come on, mate, try to breathe with me," Conner said, as he tried in vain to cover all the wounds with the now red-streaked towels.

The male fixed him with a look. His lips moved, trying to form a word. Conner leaned over and placed his ear next to the man's mouth.

"He…" the male said, with huge effort.

Conner put a towel behind his head. He knew the man was not going to survive, all he could do was make him comfortable. The man tried to speak again, grabbing Conner's head to pull him closer as he did so.

"He called me…"

Conner soothed the man's head, but sensed the stabbed male was slipping away. The terror of the unknown, the realisation of everlasting nothingness, dawning on the dying man.

With one last effort, the man said: "…a *crow*.". Conner checked; the injured man was no longer breathing. The man's chest was no longer going up or down. Any attempt at resuscitation would just push more blood out. The man had died. Murdered.

He laid the man carefully down against the bath and then he slumped himself on to the bloody floor. He had seen lots of dead people, but he had never looked into the eyes of a dying man before. The horrifying look of disbelief and terror would always stay with him. He looked down to see his hands and arms were covered in blood. He said aloud the words the dying man had whispered to him. "He called me a *crow*."

Then it hit him like a steam train. There was only one organisation that uses that term in a derogatory manner. He knew the slur only too well, as he had been called it many times before. The term was a military one. A slur for a recruit. Someone lower than low, a green horn, a maggot, a red arse. Every Army regiment had its own term, but "*crow*" was only used by one. The Royal Mounted Rifles.

The bathroom door was pushed further open, and two paramedics came in and fumbled with their medical bags. One medic went to the man in the bath and after some cursory checks proclaimed life extinct and gave a time of death. A female medic started to get out some bandages for Conner, staring at his arms.

"Don't bother," he said, "the blood's not mine."
He stood up and took hold of his police radio.

Just then he caught his own reflection in the
mirror. The figure looking back at him was almost
unrecognisable. His face, arms and hands were covered
with another man's blood.

He said into the radio, "CX, can you notify the
local Inspector, CID and AMIT that we have a murder
scene at Lord North Street." Conner then looked away from
his own horrific reflection. "The suspect may be nearby.
There is no direction or description other than he is likely
to be covered in blood."

****

The *Tall Man* hurried along Greycoat Place containing the
panic that most others in this situation would be riddled
with by now. He knew that to survive the chaos he had to
be focused. Analytical. More intelligent than the knuckle
draggers who were chasing him. The streetlights had come
on, giving patches of orange light which, he quickly flitted
cross. He could hear police sirens in every direction.
Thoughts whirled in his mind. They must be for him. How
could it have gone wrong so quickly? He was in control,
wasn't he? He quickly put such thoughts out of his mind.

He was at least thankful that when he came
out of the flats on to Great Peter Street the area had been
full of football fans. A few had taken their tops off, and so
he had done the same and joined in with them. He had then
discarded his shirt after wiping what blood he could from
his face and hands. He dropped the knife he used to stab his
target at Lord North Street down a storm drain. His trousers
were also bloodied, but only on close inspection would you
notice it. He was also not the only one, as this particular
group of England fans had been looking for trouble and

clearly found it. A casual observer would write him off as just another football thug.

He went over what had happened in his mind, the adrenalin still coursing around his body. The pickup had worked as planned. The target had gone to Bar 79 on Charing Cross Road, a well-known gay cruising bar. The conversation had gone well and he had been invited back to the Lord North Street Flat. The Tall Man had made the excuse that he needed cigarettes and left the bar separately from his target, meeting up again a short distance away. They had walked and talked as they took the tube back to the flat. Once inside, he now realised, he had started to lose control. The target was large and was no push over and had started to tell the Tall Man what to do. The target had wanted to defecate into his mouth. The Tall Man was prepared to do almost anything to get the job done, but this appalling suggestion, along with the target's dominating style had broken the killing fantasy. The Tall Man had panicked and hurried off into the bathroom to compose himself. This was not how it was supposed to go. The target had come into the bathroom naked and tried to kiss him, insisting that the revolting act was done.

"Don't be nervous," the target had said. "You'll enjoy it. And then you can do it to me."

The Tall Man had lost control. He was no longer that young recruit. He was no longer timid, nor could he be told what to do. This large brute was the fucking *crow* and he would show him who was in charge. The Tall Man had surprised the target and had pushed him back over the side of the bath. The heavily built male had tumbled with some force, hitting his head on the tiled wall. The Tall Man had grabbed a kitchen knife from a knife block and come back into the bathroom. He had showed the fat brute who was the *crow*, screaming the insult into his face as he plunged the knife into the fat bulbous mass of the man's stomach and chest. There was blood everywhere as both males thrashed about. But the knife thrusts were having an impact and the bleeding man started to slow down, and then just occasionally shudder.

The Tall Man stood back and looked at his victim wheezing. He felt disappointed with himself. He had not done his questioning. He had lost control. But all was not yet lost. He had taken out the small bottle of liquid from of his pocket and dropped a few splashes on the dying man's head. But then came a knock on the front door, a neighbour no doubt. The knocks had carried on. A female voice was asking if everything was ok. Inhaling the dying man's odour, he confirmed what deep down he already knew. This was not his ultimate target. The Tall Man went back into the living room and looked out of a large side window. The knocks at the door were getting louder. He saw that a fire escape ladder was one floor below him. Climbing out of the window he dropped the one floor, then took the ladder down to the street and ran off into the hot summer night, until he fell in with the football hooligans.

As he now walked along Artillery Row, his subconscious threw up challenges to him. He would have left his fingerprints and most likely his DNA in the flat. Was his target dead? Would they link the crimes? He acknowledged the thoughts then compartmentalised them for later analysis. Right now, he had to get away. He ducked into an alleyway beside a pub that had closed for the evening, sunk to his knees and started to breathe deeply.

Calm your mind, he repeated to himself, wiping the sweat from his eyes. I had committed two murders before tonight. I thought I had mastered the art. But clearly I still have some learning to do.

After a few minutes of anguish at his failures, his breathing started to return to normal. His cause was just, he told himself. He had been careful not to set patterns, he could not be linked. He was sure. This target could not have survived the frenzy of his attack. He had also ensured his vile manhood had been erased from existence. It was another name off the list. Another potential abuser dead. He stood up and composed himself. He needed to work smarter. He had started with a list of seven people. One of the names was the first person to abuse him. Rape him. Ruin his life. He just didn't know which one. But he had a foolproof mechanism for confirming who his first abuser was. He now had four names left. One of them was his ultimate target. Once that person was dead, his job would be done. The killing would stop. Others had died and more may still, but they would be no loss to society. He would look at the list of targets again. Study them in more detail. Plan in more detail. Yes, he had almost failed tonight. Yes, he had grown more deadly because of it.

There was a half drunk glass of lager in the alley way. He washed his arms and face in the stale smelling liquid. This would also add to the illusion of him being just another drunken football fan. The police were too busy dealing with the football disorder to care about just another drunken lout. The fates were smiling on him again. He set off back to his flat with a new energy.

Sixty-eight minutes later, the Tall Man was standing outside his flat in Kilburn. A fine rain washed over his face. It was a flat that was in the name of Simon Gee. That was one of the few things right now that was above board.

Because he was Simon Gee.

A real name with a real history. Real taunting at school for his abnormal height. His effeminate nature. Being a loner.

And here he was now. Simon Gee, the adult. A man. A man who had been twisted out of shape by the evil deeds of others. But he had remoulded himself. Flawed, yes, but infinitely stronger. More powerful. A good man turned bad. A bad man turned to doing good.

He would bring hellish revenge to his first abuser. The one who first took his innocence and sent him on this path to self-destruction. But self-destruction was long gone. He was going to destroy the lives of his targets.

Then when his job was done, he would have his day on the steps of the Central Criminal Court and tell the world.

Chapter 9

Paddington Green Police Station, Area Major Investigation Team (AMIT) briefing room, 0800 hours, Wednesday 12th June 1996.

Conner had finished late, following his attendance at the Lord North Street murder scene. He had written up his Incident Report Booklet, spoken to the Duty DI and had a short trauma debrief with the Fed Rep. In his *IRB* he had included the dying declaration from the victim and explained his understanding of the term *Crow*. He had then travelled back to his section house in Hounslow arriving at three in the morning to find a note under his door saying he was requested by the AMIT SIO to be at the murder briefing in Paddington Green Police Station at 0800 hours that morning. He got up four hours later after failing to get any sleep and travelled in. He sent a text to Nash explaining that wouldn't be on *plot* today and that he would explain later with a phone call.

Conner knew that there are several widely held *Golden Rules* within the Metropolitan Police. For example, there are no forks in police station communal kitchenettes, so take your own. The first time you park your brand-new car in a police station yard, when you return from your shift, it will be covered in police cordon tape and, the *biggy*, never, ever, sit at the front in a training event or briefing. He resigned himself to the fact he had broken a golden rule as he walked into the briefing room at two minutes to eight and did the walk of shame to the completely empty front row of seats. Thirty pairs of world-weary detective eyes stared at him as he sat down. He took out his notebook and pen from his day sack and shuffled uncomfortably. The chatter behind him eventually returned to normal levels. The room was large and modern with huge electric screen at the front. An impressive lectern with a Met Police crest was situated off to the left and he suspected the room was used for media briefings and witness appeals. He could hear the low hiss of the air conditioning and the fan in the projector. On the screen was the familiar blue Metropolitan Police PowerPoint slide with "Operation Pulse" and the date emblazoned on it. Beneath that there was a name, DCI Colin Hammond AMIT SIO.

From the back of the room, Conner could hear voices and some muted laughter as a group of senior detectives entered the room from a back office. All were white, middle-aged males. Detective sergeants, no doubt, he thought to himself. They sat to the side of the screen on reserved chairs. A minute later, a slightly older man and a slightly younger man in identical plain grey suits walked from the back of the room to the lectern and the atmosphere became more formal in an instant. The older of the two men placed a book on the lectern, whilst the younger one sat down. Other than the age difference they were almost carbon copies of each other. White, tall, slim and with sharp, intelligent features.

A microphone crackled into life.

"Good morning, everyone. For those joining us for the first time, I am Detective Chief Inspector Colin Hammond. I am the SIO for Operation Pulse. The *Silver* is Detective Chief Superintendent Alan Tomkins, and the *Gold* is Assistant Commissioner Callum McQueen. My recorded strategic aim is to investigate the suspected murder of Michael Granger at Flat 15 E, Lord North Street, Westminster, and bring the person or persons responsible to justice.

I will also be investigating if there are any grounds to consider the murder's connection to other offences. I am the principal decision-maker and I have sufficient resources at my disposal for this investigation. However, I will keep this under review. "

DCI Hammond closed the book in front of him and looked directly at the audience.

"Ladies and Gentlemen, most of you know how this works. We investigate the crime, not the criminal. We work towards the first day of the trial, with the first forty-eight hours of the investigation being the most important. We must remember it is both a burden and honour to give closure to a bereaved family. Thank you."

DCI Hammond turned around as the younger man stood up and they effortlessly swapped places.

"Good morning. I am Detective Inspector Tony Hanson and I will be the Deputy SIO for Operation Pulse." There was a comment made from the back of the room, which was met with a few giggles. DI Hanson seemed to share the joke as he fiddled with a remote control that advanced the briefing slides.

"Michael Granger was found with serious stab wounds, initially by a neighbour, who obviously is our first *significant witness*, and who subsequently called the police. The first officer on scene was PC Ryan Conner, who is here today, I believe?"

He put his hand halfway up.

"Where are you? Ah there. Good. At the front I see. Nice and keen. Good. Thanks for coming. I'm sure the investigation team will have some questions for you." DI Hanson looked back to the screen.

"Michael Granger, 13/4/46, born in Maidstone, Kent. He lived alone in the flat. Next of kin is a sister in

Melbourne who's on her way over. He was a successful TV executive working for an Australian production company. He played rugby and liked his field sports. He was also a discrete homosexual and had a conviction for Gross Indecency from 1986. There is nothing to suggest robbery was a motivating factor for the murder at this time. He was described as bullish and arrogant by most of the neighbours we talked to, but other than a few raised male voices over the years, there were no real concerns and nothing on the address on police systems. He did make a dying declaration, I have it here… 'He called me a *crow*.' PC Conner this came from you, I believe."

The room swivelled as everyone turned to look at him.

"Yes, sir," he said, sitting up and clearing his throat. "As I explained to the Duty DI last night, I believe it's a term used in the Army for a new recruit. A bit like *Proby* for a probationer constable, but not as affectionate, more derogatory. The thing is, it's only used by one regiment, the Royal Mounted Rifles. I know, because I served with them for six years."

He could feel the easing of the stares at his back. Being ex-military was often a free pass to credibility in the police – until you fucked up at any rate.

DI Hanson turned to DCI Hammond who give a curt nod.

"Yep, we picked up on that last night. It could mean anything, of course, but we've got an action for the Royal Mounted Rifles we would like you to do for us. So, as from now, you have been transferred to AMIT."

Conner went cold. "Right, but I have other duties. I..."

"It's all been sorted with your Superintendent at Charing Cross. We are going to share you with DI York."

"Ok Guv, if you say so."

Conner was inwardly shocked, but would not let it show. He was an undercover operative, not a blue book desk jockey in a cheap Asda suit and pointy shoes.

DI Hanson continued. "As the DCI said we are also trying to establish if there has been a series of offences. You've probably seen on the news the murder of Clarence Bale, who was beheaded in Cobalt Square. Well, that has now been incorporated into Op. Pulse. We will be taking it off AMIT 3's hands."

This was meet with groans from the back of the room. Nobody liked picking up other people's work.

"Now, I know Team 3 have had their issues, but I'm assured by Dave it's in good order."

Jeers from the back of the room.

"The other... well, an incident really, is the report of a male stabbed and pushed into the Thames in Lambeth. This came from an Intel log submitted by PC Amber Mills. Is she here?"

"Yes, sir."

Conner turned, to see the attractive redhead from Operation Atlantic standing up, dressed in a black business suit and white blouse. Amber looked at him with a *get back* stare.

"Welcome to the team. I think we have you for the week."

"Yes sir," Amber said and sat down.

"We're going to pair you with PC Conner and tie up the enquiries."

"Wonderful," Amber said, less than enthusiastically. It was an act for the room.

DI Hanson smiled to himself, but pretended not to hear.

"You and PC Conner will be working for DS Carl Parsons. I'm sure you can find him after the briefing. We are clearly keeping an open mind as to the military angle and the links between these two other offences. It could very easily turn into a media shitstorm just a few years after the Colin Ireland investigation. But the official line is that while we are investigating the other offences there is no *evidence* to suggest we have a serial killer targeting gay men at this time. Any press questions are to be directed to Clare in media liaison. Is that clear?"

A mumbled chorus of "Yes, Guv" trundled through the room.

"Good, ok, Fast Track Actions then..." DI Hanson then went through a list of actions, including revisiting the house to house enquiries, statementing the neighbour, and finding and viewing the CCTV which would show Granger's movements over the last 24 hours.

A Family Liaison Officer was assigned from within the room for the sister. Hanson finished off with the time of the second briefing which was to be 1800 hours that day. By then the post-mortem and the scene examination would have been completed. The briefing broke up and the detectives found their respective DSs to be given their actions. Conner looked up from his notebook to see Amber standing in front of him.

"You're a lucky boy," she said, with a slight smile.

"We shall see whether SO10 feel the same way," he replied, grabbing his backpack as they went to look for a DS Parsons. He scratched his nose to cover a big wide smile as they did so.

The murder investigation process was basically a paper-based system. Jobs to do or *Actions* were written out on numbered action sheets and underneath was a blank space for the result. Once the job was completed by a pair of detectives, the action sheet was given to a *Receiver*, normally a DS, who would check it had been done correctly and then identify further actions or mark it as closed. The sheet then went to an *Inputter*, a DC or a civilian, who would update the HOLMES murder investigation software. HOLMES had been introduced after the Yorkshire Ripper investigation where the South Yorkshire murder teams were drowning in paper actions and were unable to cross reference links and spot that a certain *Peter Sutcliffe* kept popping up in the investigation. History records the rest.

Conner managed to find DS Carl Parsons sat at his desk. He was in his mid-forties with the small, thin physique of a runner and looked devoid of any form of humour. He felt they may struggle to get on. Parsons was sitting at a table writing out action sheets and was handing them out by name to his detectives without looking up from the action sheet pad.

As Conner and Amber approached him, he held up a sheet.

"Derek!" he shouted.

A large built detective with a cigarette in his mouth snatched the piece of paper and winced as he muttered, "CCTV, bloody hell," and walked off.

Amber took the lead. "Morning Sarge. I'm PC Mills, this is PC Conner. Do you have our actions?"

DS Parsons looked Amber up and down, taking longer than was necessary, before giving Conner a fleeting glance.

"Ah yes, our two *attachments*. I have the actions here. They are periphery enquiries really. Nothing too taxing. Just fill out the results section and hand them back to me as soon as you can and we'll get you back to your home stations before you know it. Leave a mobile number on the sheet on the desk and take a car from the board. Be back by 5 pm."

"Yes, Sarge," said Amber, as she took two pieces of paper from the table. They both turned and walked off towards a large white board with car keys hooked on it. Conner selected a set for an L registration Corsa and wrote his collar number next to it. Turning to Amber, he said,

"I don't know about you, but I've got a bad case of mind fuck. Coffee?"

"Definitely," she replied.

Twenty minutes later, he and Amber sat in a sunlit canal barge that had been converted into a café in Little Venice. He had found it some months ago while researching a back story for a covert job. The heat from their coffees was depositing condensation on the windows and obscuring the view of the calm brown canal and overgrown bushes. It was quiet at this time of the day, and there was nobody around to listen in to their conversation. They both stared at the action sheets in front of them.

"You don't smell," Amber observed, taking a sip of coffee.

"I try," he replied, with a sarcastic smile.

"In fact, you scrub up reasonably well," Amber said. "I like chinos and a blue shirt. Very David Niven."

"Flatterer," Conner said, as he rubbed his eyes.

"So, first things first." Amber placed her cup down on the table. "I got a phone call from my Governor late last night to say AMIT were interested in my Intel Log. And because I was first at the scene at the Bale murder, I was to go to the briefing this morning. Now, as I understand it, you went to the Lord North Street scene and found Granger dead?"

"Dying."

"Dying, right. Despite you being a TPO working undercover. Which is, once again, interesting and reckless."

"That would appear to be the case," he said, taking the hands from his eyes.

"So, what are you going to do about Op. Atlantic?" she asked.

"Well, it won't hurt to be off plot for a while. Junkies disappear all the time. I'll keep my druggie phone on for texts. I've spoken with Nash. SO10 and DI York are not happy but are wearing it for the moment."

Amber picked up her action sheet.

"I'll go first then, shall I?"

Conner nodded.

She read aloud. *"Trace and interview a female known as Mimi who reportedly witnessed an unknown male being stabbed and pushed in the Thames on the 3 April 1996 on Lambeth Embankment."*

Taking a sip of her coffee, she said: "Ok, well, she was picked by Immigration Services, then immediately let go. So that's going to be a challenge."

He looked quizzical. Amber told him about the raid and the Rwandan working girl, Mimi, and how she had broken down and told Amber what she had seen.

"And you believe her?" he asked.

"Yeah, she was distraught, terrified. You can't fake that."

He thought for a bit and said "Ok, well, we'll start with Immigration Services and then look at the red-light areas in south London. I can make some calls based on description for Soho and King's Cross. What about the murder scene. Beheaded? Sounds grim."

"It was rough, but I had Roger with me. I suspected he'd seen things like this plenty of times before in the yards of Kingston. But… the thing that seemed really weird, aside from the headless corpse, was the smell on the body. It was a cologne or Eau de Toilet. I used to work on health and beauty stands sometimes, when I worked in a gym, and this was not a duty free special. It was expensive, designer. I just thought it was strange. A decapitated body, but wearing fresh cologne?"

He looked up from his coffee.

"When I went into the bathroom in Lord North Street. I could smell something like aftershave. I put it down to it being a bachelor pad. But there were no bottles out. From all accounts, Granger was not the expensive cologne type. More of a splash of Brute at Christmas."

"Coincidence?" said Amber.

He gave her an incredulous look.

"Yeah right," she said. "There is no such thing. I know. What about your action?"

Conner read aloud from the sheet in front of him. *"Investigate any connection between the victim, the unknown suspect and the Royal Mounted Rifles based on the victim's dying declaration.* Well, that's very wide-ranging… and the Army are not known for their openness to police."

He turned his head to stare out of the barge window at the locks and wildlife. What a beautiful place, he thought to himself. Peaceful, and a million miles away from the shitstorm going on around him.

He turned back to Amber, who, he pleasingly noticed, was looking straight at him with a gentle smile.

"A penny for your thoughts?" she said, cocking her head lazily to one side.

"Well, there is only one place to start. Ever heard of Sloane Square barracks?" Conner asked.

"Nope," came the frank reply.

"Come on then, finish up, and I'll explain on the way."

Conner knew they were going straight into the lion's den.

Chapter 10

Edgware Road, London, 0930 hours, Wednesday 12th June 1996.

Sloane Square Barracks was a twenty-minute drive from Little Venice, but at this time of the morning it might as well have been in Italy itself. The traffic was bumper to bumper. The day was heating up and Amber was driving with both front windows down. Conner was telling her about his time with the Royal Mounted Rifles. He was impressed that she was actually listening. She was concentrating on driving, of course, but she seemed genuinely interested in his story. In his experience this was rare. In fact, it was a first. Was she interested in him? He wondered, he hoped.

Conner explained how he had joined the Mounted Regiment of the Royal Mounted Rifles based in Sloane Square at the end of June 1989. He had arrived from basic training in Catterick with a reputation as a good sportsman, particularly in football, boxing and adventure sports. But he was a bit too *gobby* or opinionated for his own good. This willingness to state what he believed to be right, no matter the cost, had not gone down well with some of his instructors in basic training and word had reached Downtown that he was one to watch. After one weekend to sample the delights of London, he was thrown into training to be a Mounted Dutyman and carry out the Queen's Life Guard duties in Whitehall. This of course meant learning to ride a horse. The only horses he had previously seen were the ones belonging to the gypsies in Coventry, who would use Primrose Park as a grazing spot. He had never been within six feet of a horse, following his grandfather's advice that one end kicks and the other bites. The *Riding School* course was six months long with a *Kit Ride* in full ceremonial uniform taking up the last month. It was one of the longest, most physical demanding courses in the British Army and had a high failure and injury rate. But if you took rough kids from the housing estates of Coventry, Hull, Bristol and Glasgow and put them on the back of sixteen hands high cavalry black horses someone is eventually going to get hurt.

The riding school course would take a complete novice rider and turn them into an expert horseman, able to ride a cavalry black horse through the centre of the biggest city in the world and negotiate all the dangers that went with it. Conner remembered on one occasion riding through Paddington railway station, during peak morning rush hour, scattering commuters, train guards and tourists alike. Nothing stood in the way of the Queen's Life Guard.

Conner's natural fitness and ability to learn quickly had made him excel at riding, winning several jumping competitions at the annual summer camp in Thetford. This had only further annoyed his instructors. Well, the ones that hadn't bet on him, anyway.

But there was another side of the Queen's Life Guard. The *Kit* cleaning. It was as relentless as it was unforgiving. Conner and his fellow recruits were expected to be always immaculate. From his coveralls to his ceremonial riding clothing. He would be inspected in the morning before stable duty. He would be inspected before the morning exercise ride. He would be inspected before the first riding lesson of the day. His riding boots were to be not only shiny, but gleaming like black mirrors. This was the everyday standard, despite the boots being trashed by the previous day's riding. His riding jodhpurs would need to be cleaned, shirts pressed, and all the horse's black riding tack were to be as shiny as the boots. This could take anything up to twelve hours work, on top of the riding lessons, and this was before caring for the horses and cleaning the stables. Sleep was a distant memory. The only pleasures in life were cigarettes, coffee laced with *Pro Plus* caffeine tablets, and going for a shit to get left alone for two minutes. Very often he would do all three at once. It all combined into a smell he could never forget. He often wondered if he could keep this up for every day for six months.

Towards the end of the course, more and more of the ceremonial kit was added. Boots. Bandolier, plume, rifle, horse's metal work and leather, including a saddle. The inspections got stricter. Conner now had two or three instructors looking over him and his horse, desperately trying to find something not up to standard. Every morning, at inspection, he would be amongst the line of other recruits, stood to attention in front of his horse and he would hear from somewhere down the line the words everyone dreaded.

"You fucking maggot! You disgusting crow! Provost Corporal, take this piece of filth to jail!"

The poor recruit, who may have simply missed a button on his shirt or scraped his tack whilst fitting it to his horse, would then be marched off at double time to spend a morning being *beasted* in the barrack's guard room. The Provost staff were some of the most sadistic bastards on the planet, so the punishments generally involved pointless physical tasks with toothbrushes and hand bumpers. Occasionally it was a simple, but thorough, kicking. Once patched up and set free the recruit would be marched back for afternoon lessons before running off to clean his kit for a full show parade at 10 pm that night. An almost impossible task. It happened to everyone sooner or later. It happened to Conner more than once. It was a message. Only the very best will do. Get the tiniest thing wrong and you're in a world of pain. And it worked.

By the March of 1990 Private Ryan Conner had passed all his riding tests and inspections and passed off in front of his Granda. The old man had looked so proud of him that Conner kept the hell he'd been through to himself.

"How *did* you get through?" Amber asked, looking in her wing mirror to pull in front of a red London bus.

"I just kept going," Conner said. "I made it through the next hour, the next inspection, the next beating. The next day. Nothing lasts forever," he added. "But that was not the worst of it..."

As soon as Conner walked into Sloane Square Barracks in 1989, he had sensed the constant threat of violence that seemed to seep out of the walls. *Senior privates* ran the stable platoons on behalf of the often-absent sergeants and corporals. Officers were rarely seen in the stables. Senior privates stalked the accommodation block looking for recruits who could be bullied, robbed or exploited. If a recruit was bold enough to talk back to a senior private or displeased them, then, if he was not beaten there and then, he would be visited in the night by a group in balaclavas carrying either knives or large wooden boot trees used as clubs.

The hapless victim would then be beaten with the boot trees or slashed across the chest and back with the knives. These *correctional* beatings were regular occurrences and seemed to happen without any consequence to those responsible.

Fighting was a daily event. In the Mess hall, in the stables, or when there was a short window to get drunk in the nearby Royal Court Tavern pub. Fortunately, he had learnt to fight beneath the underpasses of Coventry, where it was also second nature, so soon the other recruits left him alone. But when he joined his Stable Platoon to complete the Queen's Life Guard duties the terror moved up another level. The senior privates who used to pray on recruits now had full control. There were additional tasks and chores to be done. Forfeits revolved around beatings or buying crates of beer. Most took the latter option unless skint, in which case you took the kicking.

At Whitehall on *QLG,* the new *crows* would be subject to an initiation ceremony, such as eating sandwiches stuffed with insects and washed down with a can of piss. Preferably your own. Conner had witnessed soldiers being tied to chairs and placed in large metal bins used to store the horse manure. The bins were then filled with water via a hose and only kicked over after the water had gone above head height. The water and the man inside would spill out onto the stable yard floor, gasping for air and covered in horse shit. He had once seen a soldier strung up naked in the main stables at Whitehall. His body was covered in horse feed and two horses were feasting on him. He could see the look of terror on the man's face believing his cock and balls could be bitten off at any second.

These type of initiation activities, which would occur every QLG, and would range from being stripped naked and pushed out of a side door into the cold early West End morning in order to steal papers and milk for the NCOs, all the way up to physical assaults. Whitehall being the only guard room in the British Army with a bar, there was always plenty of alcohol to drink. Conner and his fellow crows would often be kept up drinking all night by the games of the senior privates, and allowed to go to bed for only a few hours, before waking up and pouring a mixture of piss and alcohol from out of their boots and going on guard at Whitehall to face the public. The routine repeated itself over and over. Wake up, clean kit, clean horse, ride to QLG for a twenty-four-hour duty, be tortured, ride back, try to eat, try to get some sleep, repeat.

It was no shock for Conner to learn that Sloane Square Barracks had the highest suicide rate in the British Army at the time. Once, after finishing QLG, he had returned to his room and opened the door to see his roommate, a new recruit who had only been with the platoon for three weeks, hanging from the window with a sheet around his neck. The young recruit had clearly been dead some hours, but having never seen anything like this before he had pulled the body down and screamed for help. He remembered how he had felt sick as he looked at the twisted neck, blue tinged lips and vacant eyes of someone he had spoken to only the day before. Help eventually came in the form of the Provost staff who took the body away, took a statement from Conner and dealt with the *CivPol*. Nothing else was ever said.

Conner was immersed in this hostile environment of fear and violence for twelve months. Then one evening he witnessed an incident that would change the course of his career.

In the stable lines there were several extra duties that would need to be completed and these were generally given to the crows of the platoon. One such duty was *Stable Night Guard*, which involved making sure the horses were safe at night and starting the mucking out and stable routine in the morning. The duty was six in the evening till six in the morning and it meant missing a QLG so was technically a break. It was never explained to Conner when you were supposed to sleep before starting the kit cleaning routine for QLG at Whitehall the next day. He had one such duty in the late winter of 1990. At around 11 pm he had finished his checks of the horses and had walked to the balcony to get some air. He looked across Sloane Street and across the rooftops of London, imaging all the life that was going on around him. People with families, having dinner, watching TV. The normality of life, that now seemed like another dimension to him. From the street below he heard the noise of a car pulling up opposite the barracks main gate. Looking down he could see three men illuminated by the streetlights. He recognised them as NCOs from One Platoon. They were staggeringly drunk. One of the men was tall, thin and had a black bushy moustache that was fashionable amongst NCOs in the early eighties. Conner recognised the man as Viv Mason. He had a reputation as being arrogant, violent and extremely well connected within the regiment. The other man was Tom *Ginger* Bailey, Mason's ever-present sidekick. Both men were best avoided, especially when drunk. The third man was paying the taxi driver and Conner suspected it was a senior private called *Scarecrow*, who had been treating Mason and Bailey to a night out in the hope of currying favour. As the taxi pulled off, Conner saw a young soldier that he knew from One Platoon called Steven *Swampy* Taylor, who was walking around the corner, ladened with large shopping bags. The name *Swampy* had been given to him after he had pissed his bed whilst in training in Catterick. It had only happened once, but the army doesn't let that kind of thing go. Taylor had clearly been sent to get cigarettes, *stickies* and bottles of fizzy drinks from the local corner shop for the other members of the platoon who were cleaning kit for QLG. Conner somehow knew this chance encounter was going to be bad news for Taylor.

Viv Mason spotted Taylor first and went over to him, taking one of the bags from his hands and removing all the packets of cigarettes. Bailey followed Mason's lead taking the other bag and rifling through it, chucking items of no interest on to the pavement. The third male just watched on, laughing. Mason threw what was left in the bag at the young private's feet, who, in a moment of absolute madness, appeared to say something back to Mason as he bent down to pick it up. The response was immediate. Mason covered the six feet to the crouched man in seconds, kicking him straight in the face. The young soldier fell backwards and brought his arms up to protect his head as Mason stamped and kicked him repeatedly. Bailey, seeing the vicious nature of the attack, tried to pull at Mason away, but the blows kept raining down on the now unconscious private. Suddenly a police siren sounded, breaking the spell. Mason, Bailey and the senior private looked in the direction of the blue lights that were reflecting off shop windows further up Sloane Street. The group turned and ran towards the guard room's pedestrian gate, leaving a bloodied and unconscious lump on the pavement. Seconds after, Conner saw the three soldiers go through the gate and a red Vauxhall Astra, belonging to the Met Police's *Diplomatic Protection Group*, pulled up next to where Taylor lay unconscious. The police vehicle's lights were still swirling. Two police officers, unused to street policing, scratched their heads and spoke into radios whilst periodically checking that the casualty was still breathing. An elderly woman in a grey business suit walking her dog stopped and pointed to the guard room gate. One officer nodded and walked over and pressed the guard room entrance buzzer. Conner could see that the police officer was now speaking with a provost corporal who was friendly but was also shaking his head. The Met DPG officer seemed to thank the corporal and returned to where a couple of medics were now scooping Steven *Swampy* Taylor up into the back of an ambulance. A minute or so later, the ambulance and the police left the scene and Conner wished he had never gone for some air.

The next day, Downtown was awash with rumours and gossip. Taylor had been arrested, was in a coma, or was dead. There was lots of activity in the Regimental Sergeant Major's office, just off the main parade square, as officers, the Provost Sergeant and the Stable Platoons NCOs filed in and out. At around midday the rumour spread that Mason, Bailey and a Private Tully had been called to see the RSM.

Conner knew what would come. He had been in the cleaning room polishing his brasses when a piece-of-shit senior private called *Browny* had come in the room.

"Private Conner, One Troop Sergeant wants you, now," he spat out.

He placed his brasses on the stand in front of him, wiped some of the metal polish off his hands, took a deep breath, and followed the private down to the One Platoon stable block.

At the entrance to each platoon stable line was an office which should have been used by the Platoon NCO's but was mainly the domain of the senior privates. Conner knocked on the door and as soon as he walked in he knew he was in deep shit. Inside were the Provost Sergeant, a corporal from One Platoon and a staff sergeant from HQ Company. He stood to attention in the middle of the small room and stared dead ahead. The staff sergeant was sitting directly behind the desk staring at him the way a hawk looks at a rabbit. The One Platoon corporal, a large-built black male with the elite blue *Para* wings stitched onto his right shoulder, walked over to him. Conner could feel his breath on his cheek and realised he was now face to face with the Green Mafia's *Top Floor*.

"Private Conner, you are going to get a visit from two police detectives at 3pm today."

"Yes, Corporal," Conner said. "But why me?"

"Don't fuck about boy!" exploded the staff sergeant, raising himself up from the desk. "We know you saw what happened to that fucking crow Swampy last night, and you are going to say fuck all about it to those fucking cops. Understand?"

He closed his eyes and tried to think. Steven Taylor was a good lad. He didn't cause any bother. Why should he stick up for these thugs and protect this twisted system? The Provost Sergeant, *Billy* Bonds, a short balding scouser in his early forties with literally weeks to do before he retired, had been leaning against the wall, smoking. Conner sensed that Bonds knew he was weighing up his options. The Provost Sergeant walked over and stood directly in front of him. Bonds placed the burning cigarette close to Conner's unblinking eye.

"Do you really need to think about this, *crow*?" Bonds said, as he moved the burning ash closer towards Conner's face.

"No, Sergeant. I'll do what I need to do," he replied, as the small but intense circle of heat started to retreat from view.

"Good. Now get out," said the Provost Sergeant.

Two hours later, Regimental Sergeant Major Alan *Buster* Selby called Private Ryan Conner to attention and marched him into a back room of the administration block. He could see two men, clearly police detectives, in plain grey suits sat behind a desk. There were sheets of statement paper in front of them and an empty chair for Conner. The RSM halted him and then stood him at ease.

"You've got him for two hours, then we want him back!" barked the RSM has he slammed the door.

He sat down and relaxed slightly.

"How's Swamp…Taylor?" he asked the detectives.

"He's in an induced coma. Five broken ribs. Possible bleed on the brain," said one of the detective constables, as he organised his papers in front of him.

"Ok, Private Conner, just tell us what you saw," said the other DC, a thin smile on his face.

Conner took a breath, sighed, and then told the police everything he had seen. Absolutely everything.

Things moved fast after Conner had given his statement. Sergeant Mason was arrested that afternoon and was seen being led in handcuffs to an unmarked police car. He was later remanded to a civilian prison. RSM Selby, who despite being as tough as old boots, was an operational man through and through and was no fan of the Green Mafia. He had Conner moved to a HQ accommodation block whilst his fate was being decided. Conner knew this would not keep him safe and he was right.

That night, he was laying down in the darkened room, considering if he should leave the Army, when he heard a key turn in the locked door. Three men in green army coveralls and balaclavas then burst into the room and charged over to his bed and started to thrust knives into the reclined form on the bed. It was at this point that he slipped quietly from underneath the bed opposite, holding a large boot tree. He carefully stood himself up behind the group and raised the hard wooden lump above his head. Judging the distance by the sounds in the darkness. He swung downwards and hit one male across the back of the head with the wooden club. The man slumped straight to floor crying in pain and holding his head. Thanks to the light coming from the corridor Conner could see the terror in the second man's eyes as he turned to face him as the boot tree swung and caught him square in the face. Blood now exploded in the balaclava as the assailant's nose was smashed to pieces. The third male stabbed at him, but he managed to pull his torso out of the way. He brought up the makeshift club with all his might and produced an upper cut that took his attacker off his feet.

There was now a commotion in the corridor as some of the officers came out of their rooms to see what was going on. The three assailants were clutching their injuries, but managed to stagger out of the room and through the double doors that led to the stairwell leading out of the block. Conner moved the green coveralls stuffed with his clothes that had been his stand-in on the bed and sat down, breathing heavily.

The light was switched on in his room and a young officer in blue striped pyjamas looked in astonishment at the pools of blood on the wooden floor. He then stared at Conner in shocked amazement.

"Don't look at me, sir," Conner said. "It's not mine."

An hour later Private Ryan Conner had packed his kit and his personal items and was in a civilian taxi to Catterick Garrison in North Yorkshire. His time as a Mounted Dutyman had ended. He had escaped from *Downtown* and been sent to the Operational Regiment a year ahead of schedule. But at a cost.

Amber drove passed Sloane Square tube station and knew that they were nearly at the barracks. Her eyes had been opened to another world. One which she didn't want to get too close to.

"What happened with the assault investigation?" she asked.

"Steven Taylor was in a coma for a week, but when he came round, he refused to give a statement and left the Army soon after. I was pretty sure the Green Mafia got to him. Mason was released with a caution for Affray. Swampy killed himself by jumping off a carpark roof in '93," Conner added as he looked out of the window. "This is the first time I've been back since that night."

"Will there be anyone there who will remember it? It's been almost seven years."

"There will have been some movement, but the main Green Mafia members will be there, and they never forget."

Amber looked at him with concern as they pulled up to a large metal vehicle gate outside Sloane Square barracks. She hesitated before asking, "Will you be alright?"

Conner didn't reply. Instead, he watched as two soldiers in combats and carrying SA80 rifles looked at them suspiciously through the bars.

She followed his gaze. "They were like you once. Just scared kids... sorry, I didn't mean..."

He looked over and smiled. "It's okay."

He turned his head to look again at the gates and the smile slowly seeped from his face.

"Trouble is the scared ones are often the most dangerous."

Amber was about to say something, when the Provost corporal came out of the pedestrian gate and approached Amber's car window.

"Good morning, Ma'am," the Provost corporal said. "Do you have an appointment?" It was a challenge, not a question.

Chapter 11

Kilburn High Road, Livingston Flats, 1104 hours, Wednesday 12th June 1996.

Simon Gee's eyes sprung open in terror. There was someone else was in the room. A solid black form was leaning over him. Simon looked in horror as arms thrust out towards his throat. He tried to swipe them away but his hands passed straight through. He looked up to see who was attacking him but there was no face, no head. Gee screamed and kicked out at the spectre. Then nothing. Only the darkness of the heavily curtained room. Simon fell back on to the bed clutching his head, a layer of sweat on his shirtless body. He could hear his own breathing, rapid and shallow. Opening his eyes again, he looked down at himself. He was topless but still wearing the bloodied jeans and shoes from the night before. He remembered coming into his bedsit and then he must have collapsed on his bed. His mind started to race as he recalled the murder at Lord North Street. He had almost completely fucked it up and he was angry with himself. He had allowed the target to bully him. To intimidate him. He must move forward, he said to himself.

He sat up on the bed and took off his shoes and socks. He then took off his bloodied jeans and, after carefully removing a half full small popper bottle from the pocket, threw them in a corner. Now naked, he walked over to the bathroom sink in the corner of the small bedsit. Due to his height, it was an effort to bend down and splash cold water on his face. His back ached, an old injury, when he did so. He rinsed the dried blood from his hands. He stole a glimpse of himself in the mirror and through the half-light saw his drawn face and dirty hair. He looked a lot older than his thirty-two years. His body was little more than scrawny muscle and bone. He turned away, disgusted with himself, and sat down at the table. He recognised his father's disappointment in his own reflection.

He thought back to when he had told his father he wanted to join the British Army. His father had wanted him to take over the family livery business in Thetford. Gee had always loved horses, but when it became obvious that he was going to be too tall to be a jockey he looked for something else. He believed he had found it in the soldiers he had seen at the Norfolk Country Show in the summer of 1982. He had been spellbound by the Royal Mounted Rifles' musical ride in their green jackets, elaborate busby hats and black plumes. They were expert horseman, effortlessly wheeling their large cavalry black horses around and intersecting with other lines of fast-moving horses. They were also war heroes, having just returned victorious from the Falklands War. Gee had seen his future. But his father had been opposed.

"You're too sensitive, Simon. You've grown up too protected. You're too intelligent to be another *stupid squaddie*. You're just not cut out for it," his father had said to him.

From that point on he had made up his mind. He would prove his father wrong. He joined the Royal Mounted Rifles at Catterick and within a week the reality hit him square in the face. He did struggle with Army life. He struggled with the shouting, the discipline and the physical challenges. But most of all with the other recruits. He had always been a loner. He had known that, but he was not expecting the claustrophobic conditions he now had to live in. He was never alone, and he hated it. Even worse, everyone else knew it. He was constantly taunted and ridiculed by his peers.

However, the military system works. It turned a shy, intelligent boy into something resembling a soldier in six months. Gee passed out and was not surprised when his father didn't turn up for the parade. His mother had passed away whilst he was in training. It was no loss to him. They had never got on.

But he had made it through, and he would be going to Sloane Square barracks to commence his Mounted Dutyman's riding course. This is what he wanted to do and what he had worked so hard for. He would be back on familiar ground around horses. His dream of wearing the famous midnight green jacket would become a reality. What he didn't know, as he walked through those metal gates in London, was that it would quickly become a living nightmare.

Gee was a good horseman, one of the few on the course. He found the riding easy. Too easy. The horses seemed to know where to go. They were like automatons completing the same moves day after day, just with different people on their backs. He enjoyed the early days of the riding school. He had been placed in a three-man room, which was better than the twelve-man room in Catterick, and although there was still a lot of shouting, he had grown used to it. But there was one big draw back. *The Kit*. He was really struggling to keep up with the kit cleaning. He could not grasp the techniques required for cleaning the horses' tack using polish, water, a tin lid and duster. He had saddle-soaped horses' tack hundreds of times in his father's yard in Thetford, but this was altogether different.

He had been shown how to use beeswax on the knee-high leather riding boots numerous times, but he could not get it right. He had been shown how to put polish on the boot to form a base, and then how to use a silver cloth to get a mirror like surface, over and over again, much to the increasing frustration of his instructors. The whole process could take him six to eight hours and they would still be rubbish. Due to his height he seemed to have twice the amount of leather on his boots to clean than anyone else. This was not how he wanted to spend his time. He wanted to be with the horses. Their warmth, their smell, their affection. As the list of items that he was expected to clean grew, so did his feelings of terror at every inspection. He started to fall down the pecking order once again. He was now a dirty *maggot,* a disgusting *crow.*

He was jailed on three inspections in a row and on the third he was beaten by two Provost Corporals in an exercise which they called an *attitude adjustment.* The assailants were careful not leave any bruising to the face. Anywhere else on the body could be explained away by a fall from a horse. After his obligatory punishment of a *show parade* that night he went to his room in pain and cried like a child.

The next day he went to the stables for mucking out as normal, but on the way to the canteen for a breakfast he was approached by a ginger-haired corporal he had seen around the platoons but never spoken to before.

"Private Gee?" the corporal had said with a smile and thick Scottish accent.

"Yes, Corporal," he replied instinctively, standing to attention.

"Come with me."

The corporal led him out of the Mess block and down into the depths of the barracks. Simon's heart was racing as he feared another beating. But the corporal seemed relaxed. Whistling and cracking jokes with the other soldiers he met. Eventually they went into a cleaning room and the ginger corporal jumped onto a work bench and sat looking at him.

"Do you know who I am?" the corporal said.

"No, Corporal," he replied.

"Well, I'm Tom Bailey, but most people call me Ginger. So, when we're alone you can call me that, ok?"

He nodded and felt more relaxed.

"Now I understand your struggle, Simon. I do, I've been there. It's the horse's kit, the boots, the lack of sleep, the beatings?"

He looked down.

"Listen, I can help. I can show you some tricks to help with the tack. I can have a pair of gleaming boots appear at the bottom of your bed every morning. I can speak with the corporals, see if they can go easy on you."

Gee looked up at Ginger who was smiling at him like the Cheshire cat from Alice in Wonderland.

"Why would you do this? What do you want?" he asked suspiciously.

"Well, one day I will come to you with a proposition, and you will be expected to say *Yes*. This proposition will not be illegal and you will get paid. So, it's a win, win."

Again, the Cheshire cat smile.

He thought about it and, as desperate as he was, he agreed almost immediately.

From the next day, as promised, the boots started to appear at the bottom of his bed or in a cleaning room with his name on them. The inspections, although still thorough, became less about him. This continued, and he was passed out as a Mounted Dutyman and was sent to One Platoon under the watchful eye of Ginger Bailey. He was extremely proud when he completed his first Queen's Life Guard at Whitehall. On the night of the guard, he watched in horror as the other recruits were made to perform some terrible acts for the senior privates' amusement whilst he was treated to an initiation of his own. This involved being placed on a window ledge and shown a metal bin four storeys down. He was told he had to jump into the bin and if he missed, he would probably break his legs or die. To make it harder he was told by a senior private he would be blindfolded. After being told to take one last good look, a hood was placed over his head, and he was spun around until dizzy and forced to stand up on the ledge. He could feel the sweat forming on his forehead. The sheer terror was causing his lips and legs to tremble.

"Jump, you fucking crow!" came a chorus of voices from behind him. "Jump!"

Gee had backed away, trying to get off the ledge to find hands pushing him forward. One of the hands gave him a huge push and he dropped forward screaming, expecting to die. He hit something soft like a mattress a split second later. He ripped off his hood to see a group of senior privates and other members of the QLG looking down from a few feet above him and laughing hysterically. He then realised that when he had been spun around, he had been moved to an adjacent window that had a balcony directly underneath. He fell down onto the mattress and turned his head to throw up. The so-called *Boxman's window* was one of the oldest and gentlest initiation ceremonies he could have done. He considered himself lucky.

After he had completed several QLGs, Ginger came to his room one evening after stables had finished. It was late and he had the room to himself. He lay on his bed watching a very small portable TV a roommate had bought from the NAAFI.

Ginger burst in. "Simon, get some decent clothes on, mate. We are going to a party."

He looked at him quizzically.

"Come *on!*" said Ginger as he walked over to his locker and started to take out his suit and choose a tie. The corporal threw the clothing at him. "You've got 10 minutes to meet me outside the guard room. Oh, and have a shave."

Gee realised he had no choice in the matter.

Ten minutes later, he was standing in front of the guard room gate with four other soldiers. He noticed how they were all similar. White, young, tall, slim and articulate. No one spoke, but one or two shared cigarettes. A minibus drove up to the pavement and Ginger leant out of the passenger window.

"Come on, boys!" Ginger shouted, and they all got inside.

Gee sat near the front and asked the lad in front of him where they were going. The lad remained silent and stared straight ahead.

Ginger, overhearing, answered, "To a party, Simon, I've said, haven't I."

Gee sat back in his seat.

Around twenty minutes later, the minibus was travelling up Charing Cross Road when it turned left into Soho, before parking up in a cul-de-sac which had an old-fashioned looking pub at the end.

As he sat now in his darkened room, just thinking about the pub's name brought a sickness into his stomach. The name of the pub was The Rutting Stag.

He remembered following Ginger Bailey and the other soldiers up to the pub and noticing how rough it looked from the outside. There were two large bouncers on the door, but on seeing Ginger they just nodded them all through. The ground floor was like any other London boozer. Old wooden panels, large mirrors and men smoking, laughing or crying into their beers. The group looked around the pub and no one gave them a second glance. They went through a door next to the bar marked "PRIVATE".

Gee followed the group upstairs and it opened up into a much more lavish bar. The wooden panels were new and stained a deep brown. The mirrors were large and ornate, missing the normal advertisements across the middle. The black painted windows were covered in crimson drapes. Light music was being played from a record player and groups of men were standing around talking and laughing. Some of the men that had come with him went to join the groups, who greeted them with great drunken excitement.

Ginger slapped him on the back. "Go and get a drink," he said. "Tell them to put it on the *Tyking* account."

He had done as was told and ordered a gin and tonic. He looked around and recognised the type of people in the bar. Other than one or two older-looking women it was exclusively male. Bankers, lawyers and media types, he thought. The sort of people who would ride their horses at his father's stable on a weekend. He felt he would be familiar and comfortable mixing here.

He could see Ginger talking with a large built man with a shaved head. A bit like a bouncer but better dressed. They shook hands and then Ginger walked back to him.

"Right, finish your drink, Simon, you're on."

He put his drink down and, intrigued, had followed Ginger back to the stairs and up another floor. This level contained lots of doorways into rooms that were each the size of a large bedroom. There were numbers on the door.

Ginger stopped outside number six and turned to look at him. Suddenly very serious.

"Simon. Here's that proposition. You are going to go in that room and you're going to be fucked. You're going to suck cock. You're going to get shat or pissed on. You're basically going to do or have done to you whatever the gentleman wants, ok?"

He had gone into shock. The feelings of terror, sickness, revolution erupted in him all at once.

"What! No! I'm not gay!" he exclaimed. "I've never even been with a woman."

"Oh no, this is not being gay. This is men who have sex with men. Very different. Now you will get a cut of the money. Normally around thirty quid, so in you go."

"What? No fucking way. I'm not doing it, Ginger."

Wallop! A hard, sudden smack to his head sent his senses swimming. Ginger now had him by his throat. The violence that had always been simmering under Ginger's surface clearly in control.

"Listen, you fucking crow, you fucking owe the Green Mafia!" Another whack. "We didn't get you through training for the good of your health. You are going to fucking pay us back. If you don't, the next QLG will be your last. All sorts of accidents happen, you know that, don't you? Don't you?" Another slap to the head.

He nodded. "Yeah, yes!"

His brain squirmed. Maybe this was just another wind-up. An initiation, with it being his first time at the party. Maybe he'd just get jumped and a kicking. Then entry to the club. Surely that must be it. But why the violence. Why the sincerity in Ginger's words.

"And if you fuck off," Ginger said, bringing him back to a harsh reality, "you'll go down as AWOL and then when you're caught you go to the Provost staff. They will make this seem like a NAAFI break."

Ginger released him, composed himself, then straightened his tie.

"Now go in there. When its finished, clean yourself up in the bogs at the end of the corridor and come back to the bar and we'll see if there are any more punters. Well, go on!"

Gee remembered he went into a trance, realising there was no escape. He opened the door and stepped into a pitch-black room.

He had thought about what happened next every day for the last twelve years. He had been punched in the face almost immediately, and two men, one of which he suspected was the large male he had seen with Ginger earlier, took off his clothes. He was punched in the stomach causing him to fall to the floor before being lifted up and tied to a bed. Even then a part of him had thought it would stop and the light put on to reveal lots of laughing faces. Just like the Boxman's window. But then any hope was extinguished as his legs were spread and attached to the bed posts and his arms tied in front of him and stretched out.

Horror. Screaming burning horror flooded his body.

He was bent over and just as he started to recover from the stomach blow, he felt a sharp painful kick between his legs causing him to cry out in pain. The sickness rose up into his stomach. He stood, bent in two, crying and wailing. His mind in turmoil. He heard a door open and shut and then other than his own pitiful cries there was silence. But the atmosphere had changed. The noises of the floorboards had lessened and there was now only one man in the room, a different man. He had sensed the man walking around him with light and balanced bare-footed steps. The room was almost completely dark other than the light from the corridor coming in through a small gap at the bottom of the door. He had felt the man's eyes staring at him. Admiring him and loathing him in equal measure.

"What's the matter, *Crow*?" the man said.

The voice was of an educated male, perhaps ten years older than Simon. He had a London or home counties accent. And that word, *crow,* was said with real meaning. Disgust.

"What *have* they done to you? Well, I will make it better. For both of us."

He had sensed the male closing in behind him and smelt the fiend's aftershave. Sweet, complex, expensive. The rest he blanked out, until he passed out. When he came round, he was travelling in the minibus. He had felt drunk and had a bottle of scotch in one hand and thirty pounds in the other.

The same abuse, by the same mysterious man, carried on once every week for the next three months. Until he had not been able to take it anymore. He had drunk a tin of metal polish to poison himself. When that failed, he was placed in the Provost jail for his own safety. There he tried to hang himself from his cell's window bars. Cut down close to death, he survived, although he had caused himself serious injuries to his back and neck muscles in the process. This meant he was now unable to ride without being in agony. He was medically discharged from the Army shortly after with the label of "*medically unfit and mentally unstable.*" His Army career was over.

He had returned home to his father in shame. His father had been right, but they never spoke about his time in the Army. The family business collapsed shortly after he returned. His father was never the same, as the business limped on selling horse feeds, and retired a broken man. He became a gamekeeper on a local estate. Although his love of horses was now curtailed by his injuries, which hurt him every day, he learned about watching and tracking his prey, shooting and gutting animals. He was alone, with a lot of time to think. In time, thinking turned to hatred, hatred into action. Then his father had died two months ago. The reason for stopping him bringing any further shame to the family had gone.

Back in the darkened room, sunlight streaming in through gaps in the makeshift curtains, he lightly fingered a single piece of A4 paper in front of him. Behind it were the Yellow Pages, a collection of society magazines, a London A-Z and a copy of Who's Who. But a special place had been reserved for his special weapon. A large computer linked to the fledgling internet by the telephone line. This was his oracle. The A4 piece of paper contained a list of seven names and the phrase "*Persons of interest who had frequented The Rutting Stag Tyking Parties 1982-1984.*"

It had arrived in an unmarked package with the small *popper* bottle, which to his surprise contained aftershave. The package had been posted to his Thetford address and appeared the day after his father had died. After opening the bottle of aftershave, he recognised it as the type worn by his first abuser. It was sweet, delicate, expensive. He stared intently at the list of names. One of these names on the list was his first abuser, he knew it. One of these names had ruined his life and deserved to die along with his family. But surely, they all deserved to die. He had started at the beginning of the list with West. Then onto Bale, then Granger.

He put a red line through Granger. But it was too random, he thought to himself. No real thought had gone into the names. That needed to change.

He had not learned anything from the murder of Granger other than the fat sack of shit was not his primary target. Smell is one of the foremost ways the mind remembers events. Burning leaves can take your mind back to bonfire night. The smell of chalk and damp can take you to a classroom. A perfume or an aftershave can remind you of a relative, a lover, or the man who first raped you. But it was not always that simple. The odour could be affected by age and environment or the physical state the wearer was in. The aftershave would smell slightly different on each individual in different circumstances. If they were in a state of sexual arousal, for example. This fact, he had figured, would lead him to his ultimate target.

He had managed to splash a couple of drops onto Granger, and this confirmed his suspicions that it was not him. He cursed himself as he remembered he had spilt some of the liquid whilst leaving the flat. He read the list again for the hundredth time. Three names had been crossed off. Four remained. He realised he needed to work smarter. He could not just keep murdering his way through the list hoping to get lucky. He was running out of the aftershave. He had been driven to the first murders by anger, hatred, excitement. He needed to focus on cold, calculated revenge. He needed to prioritise the list. Work out the individuals most likely to be his primary target, balanced against the threat and risk they presented.

I have a just cause, he reassured himself, just as he had done a thousand times before. My abuser must pay for his sins. What I do is not sinful, if it is in a just cause.

Once he had found this evil man, he would not only kill him, but tell his story in front of the world's media on the steps of the Old Bailey and bring the whole rotten system down. Right under the inscription in stone, "DEFEND THE CHILDREN OF THE POOR AND PUNISH THE WRONGDOER". He had seen the stone inscription on TV following a high-profile court case and it had struck a chord with him and what he must do.

Yes, a new approach, he thought, as he studied the names. What have I *missed?* He bit into his hand to try to get some focus. Cold, calculated revenge, he thought to himself. He would bring Ginger Bailey and the Green Mafia down, but he would kill his sexual abuser first. Think. Think back. What did he know about this vile man? His nemesis.

He was certain he was a white male, probably now around forty years of age. He was very well-educated, middle to upper class. He originated from southeast England and had some ongoing contact with the Green Mafia. He was athletic without being physically imposing; hence the ropes. If his first abuser had thought of himself as a man who had sex with men, a sado-masochist, he would not class himself as homosexual and was likely to be married with a family. With children, who deserved to have their innocence taken just as he had. His abuser had influence and money even at a young age. He was able to pay to have men look after his security, as well as to arrange and prepare Gee for the twisted abuse. His abuser could also afford designer aftershave.

For hours, he looked at the names on the sheet. He poured over his magazines, books and the internet. At the end of his research, he had allocated each name on the list, each target, a codename. He would deal with them in a strict order. Risk versus reward.

Mr. Deer, Mr. Vixen, Mr. Fox, Mr. Wolf. The codenames indicating the level of risk to him.

And now he had a *Trigger plan* for how to kill each of them.

During his days as a Gamekeeper, he would often be called on to dispatch a diseased animal. His list of *animals* all had a disease. A disease whose symptoms included abusing young men. He would despatch them all in turn and would not stop until he had found his primary prey.

Chapter 12

Sloane Square Barracks, HQ block, 1145 hours, Wednesday 12th June 1996.

Temporary Detective Constable Ryan Conner and *Temporary* Detective Constable Amber Mills sat in a waiting room outside the Regimental Sergeant Major's office, to which they had been unceremoniously escorted forty-five minutes earlier. Conner sensed that Amber was getting agitated. The oak-panelled room was full of paintings of old colonels and identical-looking modern photos of companies of men sat in long rows. The lines of white faces looked like a string of pearls on a green velvet cloth.

He looked to see if he was in any. He wasn't.

The name plaque on the door opposite read: "RSM GIBBS". Not a name that he recognised, but that was to be expected. The regiment had soldiers around the world as well as Catterick and London. In the time they had waited, a few NCOs had come in and out of the RSM's office. No one offered them a drink or even looked at them. Suddenly, the door was unexpectedly thrown open and a deep commanding voice rang out. "Come in, come in!"

Conner and Amber looked at each other, then stood up, adjusted their attire and walked in. The office was almost identical to the waiting room, other than a large desk in front of a bay window which overlooked the main parade square. RSM Gibbs, a slim, balding man in his early forties, with half-moon reading glasses perched on a long nose, busied himself with pieces of paper on his desk, and without looking up said, "Morning, Officers. Sorry for the delay. How can I help you?" They were not offered a seat.

"Thank you for your time, Sir. And, oh, I am going to need your *full* attention," Conner said pleasantly.

RSM Gibbs slowly laid his papers on his desk and looked up at Conner's smiling face over his half-moon glasses.

"Detective Mills and I are from the Metropolitan Police's One Area Major Investigations Team. We are investigating a murder that occurred yesterday in the City of Westminster. We believe that the suspect may have a connection with the Royal Mounted Rifles, so we would like to speak with some of your staff."

"What is this *connection*?" RSM Gibbs said.

"The suspect used the word *crow* during the assault, which leads me to suspect some connection to the RMR. The victimology would suggest the suspect was early middle-aged and is likely have previously served with the regiment. Someone might know who it is."

"You're basing your enquiries on one word? Seems a bit thin, doesn't it?"

"Well, it's one of a number of enquiries," Amber said with a smile.

RSM Gibbs looked at her and thought for a few seconds before looking back at his papers.

"There's a Mess meeting here tonight at 7.30pm. You can address the NCOs before the meeting starts. Good day."

"Thank you, Sir… and at least now I know where to find you. You know, if I need to speak with you again," Conner added and nodded an approval at Amber before leaving the office.

The RSM's door was slammed shut a few seconds later.

As they walked down a series of concrete steps that led to the guard room gate and back to the car, Conner could smell the horse manure and burning hooves from the farriers' workshop. The smell took him right back to his time *Downtown*. He looked across the parade square as young soldiers busied themselves carrying bits of shiny metal and leather or leading horses, often two at time. He took a deep breath and slowly released his dark memories as he breathed out.

Conner drove the car to the vehicle gate. A face appeared at the guard room window and without smiling pushed a button, allowing the gate to swing open. He drove out and was aware that the Provost Sergeant was staring at him. He thought he recognised the man but could not be sure.

Once they turned out into traffic Amber let out a long tight breath that she had been holding on to for an hour or more.

"What an oppressive, dour place," she said, ruffling her hair as if to shake out the gloom that had landed on her, whilst checking her phone.

"I think we got away lightly, and we have an in," Conner said.

"I've had a message from the AMIT Int. Cell," she said. "Locals have been to the address Mimi gave to Immigration and she's not there. In fact, the hostel said she never turned up. What do we do now until the briefing at six?"

"We try to find Mimi, and I know just the place to start." He drove on with purpose.

At the same time, Provost Sergeant *Scarecrow* Tully picked up the phone in the Sloane Square guard room and rang through to the NCO's Mess where Sergeant Ginger Bailey was taking tea and toast.

"I need to speak to Sergeant Bailey urgently."

There was a gap of about a minute. Then a voice full of food said, "What?"

"Ginger, it's Scarecrow. We have a problem. An old crow who's now a fucking cop. And you'll never guess who it is!"

****

Conner parked the Corsa at the back of King's Cross Police station. Amber looked around.

"I've been to this nick before, it's a shit hole."

He laughed and agreed.

"But," he said, "we're not going inside there, we're going inside there."

He pointed to an innocuous black metal door in an outer wall. It had a keypad next to it.

Getting out of the car and walking over, Amber observed, "Isn't that just a back gate?"

He smiled as he entered a number onto the keypad and the door clicked open.

They walked down a series of poorly lit steps. Here they met another heavy metal door which required a card key which he produced and swiped for entry. Once inside, Amber could see a huge bank of CCTV screens in front of her, covering King's Cross railway station and the surrounding streets. The room was over air-conditioned and there was a sickly electronic buzz in the atmosphere. Sitting at desks were CCTV operators zooming into the pictures on the screens. Two males fighting in Birkenhead Street. A uniformed police officer searching an Afro Caribbean male in an alley off St. Chad's. A young girl, no more than sixteen, getting into a dark saloon in York Way. Radio chatter squawked out of a speaker on the wall.

"Welcome to Op. Garden City," Conner said, as he signed into a logbook. "Come on."

To the right of the screens was another door that opened onto a long corridor with rooms off each side. He looked for a room number whilst speaking to Amber.

"Op. Garden was set up in the mid-eighties to try to deal with the drugs and prostitution in King's Cross which was at epidemic levels. London Borough Council have big plans for the railway station, fresh investment, new transport links, but it can't do anything whilst it's a moral cesspit. So they put in one of the largest collection of CCTV cameras in London. Then they created a multi-force, multi-departmental specialised team to police it. Uniformed cops from The Met, The City of London Police and British Transport Police. Supported by intel cells, detectives, photographic imaging units and SO10. Hence my access. It's all very secret squirrel. Oh, here we are."

He opened a door to a room that contained a few desks and filing cabinets, but its most striking features were two huge walls all covered in photographs. One wall had a sign that said, "OP GARDEN CITY DRUG DEALERS" and another that said, "OP GARDEN CITY SEX WORKERS". Amber looked open mouthed at the walls. Conner noticed how in contrast to the photos of the mainly white men in the RSM's waiting room, the *dealers* wall was a sea of black male faces whilst the *sex workers* wall was mainly white women. He felt there was a deep social message here about race, poverty and the choices people are forced to make. But he couldn't quite grasp it.

Amber moved over to the *sex workers* wall and started looking at the custody photos and still CCTV images of the girls. Each one had a real name or operational nickname, date of birth, and last known address typed underneath.

"Most *Toms* pass through King's Cross at some point in their career," he said, looking at the *dealer* board to see who was still around. "If you see Mimi, let me know and we'll see if we can get her picked up. If she's not on the board, there are tons of albums in the cabinets." Amber nodded, staring at the rows of pictures.

Twenty minutes later, she tapped on a grainy night-time picture of a young, slim African girl leaning towards a car passenger window but facing the camera. The female figure was wearing a short light-coloured dress and dark high heels. Amber could see the scar on the woman's otherwise perfect features. Conner came over to have a look.

Frenchie he said reading the name tag. There were no other details other than the day the photo was taken, which was last week. He took the picture from the board. "Let's go speak to the *Int. Cell.*"

A minute or so later, they were both standing in a dimly lit air-conditioned office.

"We don't know that much about her, Ryan," said a pretty, blonde female analyst sitting behind a computer screen. There was a pot plant, nail file and a Tom Cruise calendar on her desk. "She was picked up on CCTV, but uniform can't get close. I could put a tasking out for the plain clothes teams on nights?"

"Could you? That would be amazing. She's an Immigration absconder so nick her for that and ring me anytime and we'll come and sort the prisoner. Thanks Emma," Conner said, leaning on the desk and smiling.

Emma smiled back. "Been to any more house parties in Hammersmith recently?"

He looked down to the floor sheepishly. "No, no. I've been run off my feet recently."

"Well, we can't have that, can we. All work…" Emma said, placing a pen to the corner of her mouth. "Give me a call when you have some time."

"Ok, will do," Conner said, rather too matter of factly, as he turned away.

Amber had already walked off.

****

At exactly 6 pm that day, Detective Inspector Hanson placed a cup of coffee on the lectern in the AMIT briefing room as "Operation Pulse" appeared on the screen.

"Ok, ladies and gentlemen, your attention, please."

The chatter in the room dwindled down.

"Now, a few updates. SOCO have been to the scene and the early updates are that all the blood belongs to the victim. There have been several unknown fingerprints recovered and these are being put through the prints database and the Police National Computer, but so far, they are all *No Trace*. The SIO and I are visiting the scene this evening before it is closed down. The CCTV and traffic cameras from the surrounding area have been checked and a group of males were seen walking away from the area shortly after the murder, but they look like the football fans who had been fighting earlier. We are trying to trace this group, but as they are likely to be Croatian or Turkish it may be a *challenge*."

Challenge was police speak for nigh on impossible.

DI Tony Hanson continued. "The post-mortem has shown that the victim sustained a head injury prior to being stabbed. The mechanism of the head injury was likely to be falling back and hitting his head on the bathroom wall. There were also defence injuries. This suggests a dispute before the fatal assault."

Hanson flicked through a report on the lectern.

"Nothing else of note. Traces of alcohol. A concentration of chemicals consistent with aftershave on his neck and chest. Ok, DSs, can I have the results of your tasking please?" He looked up from the papers.

The AMIT DSs gave an overview of what their teams had done and highlighted any new actions that had come out of it. When it was DS Parsons' turn to speak, he added on, almost as an afterthought, that Conner and Amber were going back to the barracks to talk to the Army and that local police units had been tasked with finding *Mimi*. The meeting broke up and the detectives went back to their desks. There were overtime pizzas paid for by the SIO to be had. Conner and Amber went back to the car. They ate their pack up sandwiches and listened to the radio. Neither said anything. They then drove to Sloane Square barracks in anticipation.

****

At the barracks, Amber found herself sitting in a large room not unlike the RSM's waiting room but ten times the size. The same wood panelling and, as far as she could tell, the same paintings and pictures on the walls. In the far corner there was a bar with beer pumps packed on to it.

Optics hung in rows at the back. The room smelt like a pub which had been bathed in brass polish. It was packed full of soldiers sitting on smart wooden dining chairs, all facing towards a large, highly polished table at one end of the room. Conner was sitting behind the large table next to RSM Gibbs. Either side of both men were two middle-aged white males with three stripes and crown on their *rank slides*. All four men stared poker-faced at the packed room.

Amber was at the side of the room, about halfway down from the top table. Every now and then she would look at the rows of men and see a wink here and kiss blown there. She chose to hold the individual's stare long enough for them to become uncomfortable and then ignore them completely.

The low noise of chatter and laughter immediately came to a stop as RSM Gibbs stood up and addressed the room.

"Gentlemen, thank you for attending this month's Mess meeting. In a slight change to the agenda, we have *Temporary* Detective Constable Ryan Conner from the Metropolitan Police, who would like to speak with you regarding an investigation he is working on. Now, I have been told that the officer is ex-RMR, so I'm sure you will all be as helpful as you can."

A light laughter went around the room as the RSM sat down and Conner stood up.

"Good evening, gentlemen," Conner said, clearing his throat. "And thank you for your time."

He felt it was hot and stuffy. The large Mess windows amplifying the sun's evening heat.

"We didn't get a choice!" someone shouted from the back of the room. Again, laughter.

"Yes, perhaps not," he smiled, but continued. "On the eleventh of June this year, in Lord North Street, Westminster, the body of a fifty-year-old male was found stabbed to death in his flat. Before the victim died, he told police that his attacker called him a *crow*. Now, we all know that that term is used in the RMR as a derogatory one for a recruit. From our suspect profile we suspect the killer was male, in his thirties, of a slim build but muscular, with a deep hatred of homosexuals…" There was an audible groan from the room.

Conner ignored it and pushed on.

"The suspect may have served in the regiment or been here on an attachment."

At that point one of his many job phones audibly beeped as a text message arrived.

"Switch your fucking phone off in the Mess!" shouted a voice from the back row, which was met with raucous laughter.

Conner went silent. Amber could sense that something was building inside of him.

Quietly, Conner said, "My phone, yes, of course." He took a deep breath. Trying unsuccessfully to contain himself. He looked up from his paper. "Your Mess, your rules. Your stupid, arcane rules!"

This was louder than he intended, and there was a collective gasp in the room, followed by silence.

Conner looked at the RSM whilst resting his notes back on the table.

"Mr. Gibbs is right. I served here. Saw all the shit you pull." He looked around at the soldiers. His hands clasped at his waist. His voice calm, but authoritative. "Drugs lying about. The beatings. Betting scams at the horse races. Red diesel taken for private vehicles. Young girls picked up in Hyde Park and smuggled into the barracks, then given money to be quiet. Rock stars visiting the floors at strange times of the night. I know it all."

He moved his eyes from one man in the audience to another. The intensity in his stare drilling into each man's conscience.

"So, you have rules, we need rules. But, gentlemen…" He addressed the whole Mess. "You are now playing by my fucking rules!"

His calmness had dissipated.

"I can have ten cops a day in this barracks. Walking the floors, searching every car, inspecting your bar stock, checking your bank accounts. Reporting assault."

He looked around the room, waiting for his threat to sink in.

"A man has been murdered. His sexual preferences are not important. What is important is that the killer may have murdered other people and is likely to kill again."

He briefly looked at Amber. She could see the serious look on his face, but his eyes were glistening. Smiling even. And for the tiniest moment she felt they were solely engaged on her.

He returned his attention to the room.

"The killer probably has links to the regiment. And that means you are all potential witnesses in *my* murder enquiry. Until the investigation is complete, I own you. All of you."

The men remained silent. Some looked to their RSM for him to say something meaningful, but he just stared at his papers.

"Please contact me via RSM Gibbs if you have any information. Good evening, gentlemen."

Conner gathered up his papers and nodded at Amber. She picked up her coat and then they walked out of the Mess to complete silence and made their way back to the car.

In the very back row of the Mess, Staff Sergeant Viv Mason was seething with hate.

A few minutes later, Conner and Amber were sitting in traffic at the edge of the barracks. It was now grey and raining but still humid. He was driving and gripping the steering wheel. She noticed his hand was trembling ever so slightly.

"Are you ok?" Amber asked. No reply. "Ryan?"

"Yeah, I'm fine. I just got sick of their bullshit. Their fucked-up little world that doesn't realise there is another one outside it."

Just then there was a rap on the passenger window. Startled, they both turned to see a large white man with swept-back, dark hair and a neat, thin moustache. He looked agitated in the rain and had a three-quarter length leather jacket pulled over his head. Conner could now see he was wearing army greens. He reached over and lifted the lock on the rear passenger door as the man got in, wiping the rain from his face and hair.

"I've got ten minutes while they have a smoke break," the man said. "Drive around the block and I'll tell you what I know."

Conner turned the car left on to Eaton Gate into solid traffic and looked into the rear-view mirror at his new passenger. He recognised the man as Tim Hallam, but did not let on. Sergeant Hallam had been in Two Platoon when Conner was Downtown, but from his *rank slides* it now appeared that *Lance Corporal* Hallam had fallen from grace.

"Right… oh, fuck. Look, this is all going to be off the record, kid, isn't it?" Hallam asked.

"Well, we'd like you to give a statement, but if not, we can class you as a confidential contact and everything you tell us will be just that. *Confidential*," Conner said.

"Ok, well… er, here goes. I don't know who your man is, your killer, but I do know what might have made him kill. If he was Downtown in the early eighties that was the height of the *Company Tyking*."

Conner and Amber looked at each other, confused.

"You've not heard of it?" said Hallam, incredulous. "What type of cops are you?"

"Busy ones," Amber said, impatiently.

Hallam cleared his throat.

"Right, so, fuck, I can't believe I'm telling you this… but in the eighties, the Green Mafia were moving into prostitution in a big way. Large companies from the City and the West End used to hold parties to win favour with their wealthiest clients. The company fixers would bring in some pretty girls to the parties as, well, you know… *decoration*. But as tastes changed, they started to want tall, attractive-looking men as well. The Green Mafia were only too happy to help. After all, Downtown had a never-ending supply. It started as a good gig. No funny business if you get my meaning. But something changed and there was a split off group of high-profile men who liked the macho side of sex with other men. The violence, the pain, the challenge. I don't know. It's all fucking sick if you ask me."

Hallam looked out of the car window. The world outside seemed very big to him.

"Go on," Conner said, as he turned on to Belgrave Square.

"What...yeah, so, these sex parties were set up for exclusive clients and the Green Mafia provided the men. Some out of choice, others didn't have one. I heard some terrible stories of bad beatings, gang rapes followed by suicides."

"Why didn't they go to the police?" Amber asked.

Both Hallam and Conner shared a knowing look.

"The culture, the threats," Hallam said, leaning forward. "The whole place was... is built on violence and intimidation. If you grassed anyone up you'd be in hospital within a week. But bollocks to it. I'm out of the Army and this shit hole in two months. I'm going to Cornwall. Run a tea shop or some shit. Look at the sea and get pissed every day."

"Can you think of anything else? Names? Locations? Any dates?" Conner asked.

"That fucking ginger prick Tom Bailey was involved. As for the boys, I don't know, these crows... sorry, recruits came and went quickly. I remember one kid. Loved the horses but a maggot. Shit at the kit. Quite bright, educated. But I can't remember his name or his face other than he was white. Oh, and he was tall. Yeah, a lanky streak of piss. He tried to hang himself, I think. Rumour was he was abused, but there were a hundred like that."

"What about the clients, the abusers?" Amber asked.

"Well, that's the rub, isn't it, love," Hallam said, sitting back into the seat. "This thing went up to royalty, it was said. I'm sure it did, judging by the money it made. So, you won't get anywhere near them bastards."

Amber and Conner looked at each.

"Why did it stop?" Conner looked into the rear-view mirror at Hallam.

"Military Police got a whisper. Something was leaked to the press. Too much heat. It collapsed as far as I know in the late eighties. At the Stag anyway."

"The Stag?" Amber enquired.

"The Rutting Stag Pub. Some dive in Soho where all the fucking queers hang out."

"Why are you helping us?" Conner said, shifting uncomfortably in his seat at the mention of The Rutting Stag.

"Because I'm sick of the whole fucking lot of 'em, that's why!" Hallam put his hand through his hair. "When you're on the inside, it's fucking amazing. The money, the girls. The trips abroad. But when you're out, you're right out. I fucked up and I was lucky I wasn't killed for it. But now I'm going to punish them. Why am I doing this, you ask? Revenge, detective. Straight forward revenge."

The car was now back on Sloane Square. Conner pulled up out of sight of the barracks gate.

"Look," Hallam said. "I've told you what I know. Please don't bother me again." And with that, he jumped out of the car and ran through the rain to the rear pedestrian gate.

Amber turned to Conner as the traffic moved on. "What do you make of that?"

"It seems to ring true. I'd heard the rumours, of course. Soldiers going into the officers' Mess late at night. Pop stars and TV personalities on the accommodation floors at strange times, but I didn't realise the scale of it."

"What now?"

"Well, we can get in contact with Army Manning and Records in Glasgow for the names of any soldiers that were discharged following suicide attempts from Sloane Square barracks between 1980 and 1990, but it's going to be a lengthy list. We need to get the Royal Military Police file on *Company Tyking* from Colly... sorry, Colchester, where the RMP are based."

"I don't suppose they are just going to hand that over if there is a royal link."

"Nope, probably not."

"Right, well, I'll update the action sheet and we'll look at it again in the morning. It's been a long couple of days already," Amber said, stretching her arms out as best as she could in the small Corsa.

"The Rutting Stag in Soho," Conner said to himself. "You go to the briefing in the morning. I'm going to get my piss stinking clothes back on and pay it another visit."

Chapter 13

A Fire Exit Doorway, The Hippodrome Nightclub, Leicester Square, 1430 hours, Thursday 13th June 1996.

The smell from the nightclub fire exit doorway was overwhelming. A heady cocktail of urine, alcohol and rotting food. In fact, it was beaten only by the smell of Conner himself. He was slumped in the back of the doorway with an empty can of special brew, half of which he had poured over himself, the other half he had used as a mouth wash. He pulled his sky-blue baseball cap down over his eyes and enjoyed the cool shade, momentarily escaping from the West End heat. He also thought of Amber. She had gone into Paddington Green police station to work on the Immigration Service and Royal Military Police leads.

Nash had arranged a deployment late last night with DI York, who was only too happy to get *his* asset back on the ground. A foot team had been scraped together from the local proactive unit and now *Mark* was back up and running. He had told Nash his real reasons for the deployment, which was to gain more intel on The Rutting Stag pub. And, as it fitted under the SO10's guidance for an intelligence-gathering deployment, it had been begrudgingly sanctioned by the DI. But it had been made very clear that Mark was expected to *score* as well. The key to both outcomes was Peter. He had been seen by the Local Intelligence Officer plying his trade around this fire exit for the last few days. He just needed to wait and try not to vomit. After an hour or so he felt a kick to the sole of his foot and someone treading on his ankle. He looked up to see a startled-looking, slim male in cut-off jeans, standing over him and clearly shocked that he had trod on a pile of rubbish that turned out to be a man.

"What the fuck!" exclaimed the male.

Conner went into defence mode, acting stoned and drunk. He curled up in a ball and started to shout gibberish. Just then a hand grabbed his shoulder, pulling him into the sunlight.

"Calm down, honey," said a familiar voice to the male. "This is Mark. He's cool, man. Mark, it's Peter. What the fuck has happened to you?"

Ten minutes later, Conner was guided into a chair at a greasy spoon café on Leicester Place. He had been given a large mug of hot coffee and was slowly sipping it, as if coming round after a bender. It was a convincing act, partly through experience. Peter had disappeared with his male for fifteen minutes and then had come back and was now sitting opposite him in the Café.

"Mate, you looked fucked. What have you been doing?" Peter asked, stirring his mug of tea.

"I don't remember much," Conner said, rubbing his eyes. "From the custody tracky bottoms, it looks like I was nicked." He pulled at the grey joggers issued to Met Police prisoners.

"I must have lost it, until I was woken up by being trod on by your *John*."

"You nearly cost me money, Mark," Peter said, in a mock serious tone. "But I always win them round in the end. Got an extra five notes on top of the usual fifteen. So, what do you want to do now, Mark?" he added, with a knowing smile.

Conner pulled out a battered old twenty-pound note and slammed it on the table.

"Score, brother, I want to score."

Having convinced Peter that trying to get a deal on the street was too risky due to the number of new dealers, most of which were likely to be selling brick dust, they made their way to The Rutting Stag. On the way, they hatched a plan to put a call into the dealer known as White

Boy. Conner's police brain also had a plan. He wanted Intel about the infamous pub and needed to find out more about the man wearing the military special forces grade watch. Was there a link to the Green Mafia? Why were they becoming were more active?

Conner decided he liked Peter as they walked up Shaftesbury Avenue. Sure, Peter's life choices had led him onto the path of drugs and prostitution, which was far from *ideal*. But Conner knew Peter could be earning money doing far worse things. He had a tinge of guilt, as he was conscious that he was manipulating the young rent boy for his own ends. But this thin young man wasn't doing anything he didn't want to. He was not that type of character, and he would be using drugs whether Conner was with him or not. Even so, Conner decided that when this was all over, he would point Peter in the direction of some help. Whether he would use that help was another question altogether.

They turned onto Duck Lane and the pub building loomed up ahead of them. Conner could see the old building must have seen some wild times. If only it could speak, he thought to himself. But of course, it couldn't, so the next best thing would be to talk to some of the older punters and have a look around.

Four bouncers were on the door, which seemed a lot. One of them recognised Peter and nodded them in. The bar was busier than Conner had previously seen it. The tables were all full and there was a crush at the bar. The sound of bar orders and the clinking of drinking glasses rang out in the smoke-filled air. He noticed that not many of the orders were in English. It sounded Russian or Polish. In the corner of the room an old TV appeared to have been hastily set up on a spare table. There were two groups of men sat around the TV with a clear dividing line between them. On one side were some balding, thick set, leather-jacketed bruisers and on the other side some slimmer and older-looking men in colourful track suits and slicked back hair. He saw the TV show, the Euro 96 logo, and then *"Bulgaria V Romania. Live from St James Park, Newcastle. Kick Off 16:30 hours"* appeared on the screen. A cheer sounded from both groups as Des Lynam reassuringly welcomed the viewers.

Then the scene made sense to him, along with the extra bouncers. The local criminal ex-pats from the relevant nationalities had gathered together and put their quarrels and feuds on hold. Or at least moved their focus. The Bulgarians had a grip on the blossoming Eastern European prostitution business and, it was said, the firearms trade, whilst the Romanians ran the pickpocket rings throughout most of central London. Organised, ruthless and very secretive, both groups were masters of their respective areas of criminality, but despite the clear division of interests, they still hated each other.

Peter managed to find space in a small alcove near the main door and squeezed himself in. He busied himself rolling a smoke and looking around at the faces in the pub. Conner pushed his way to the bar, eventually ordering two lagers. Whilst waiting he noticed an interesting character sat on his own at a corner table, chain smoking and staring at a copy of the *Racing Post.* The man looked in his early seventies but could have been younger, with a hard life to blame for his elderly appearance. He was skinny, as opposed to slim, and had thinning, slicked back grey hair on top of a rodent-looking face. Despite the heat outside and the claustrophobic atmosphere of the pub, he wore a large suede wool-lined coat. Conner figured he had been around the scene for some time and may be able to give a bit of background to The Rutting Stag's shady past. Conner handed Peter his pint, who swore at the phone he held in his other hand.

"What's wrong?" Conner asked.

"White boy's not picking up," Peter replied.

"Text him again and give him a bit longer, mate."

"I'm clucking, Mark, I've not scored for two fucking days."

"Chill, star. He'll come through. Listen, who's the geezer with BO sat at the table in the corner?"

Peter strained to look.

"*Two Time Tony*, that old queen! Why ya interested in him? He's been drinking here for years. No other pub would have him on account that he's a lying, thieving, child-molesting wanker."

"It's not him I'm interested in, it's his racing tips. A few notes on the horses could sort me out for the weekend. Stay here and keep trying to get hold of White Boy," Conner said, before heading off to the old lag's table.

Pulling up a stool opposite Two Time Tony, Conner noticed that only thing he was wearing under the large coat was a white string vest and couple of cheap gold chains. Tony's trousers were from an old suit and were held up by a snake belt popular in the seventies. He decided he would play on Tony's clearly battered ego.

"Can I sit here mate?" he asked Tony, pulling his stool up anyway. "I'm Mark. A friend of Peter."

Tony slowly looked up from his paper and on seeing Conner's boyish face, a wicked grin slowly appeared revealing yellow, rotten teeth.

"Of course, my son. I'm Anthony. Nice to have a bit of company for a change." Tony smoothed his hair back, figuring Mark was a new rent boy on the scene.

"Got a horse running?" Conner said, nodding at the racing post.

"Got my eye on few. Get tips from a stable boy in Newbury," Tony replied, appearing to grow a few inches taller in his chair.

"Sound, sound. Care to share?"

"I could do my son, if you're willing to, well... help me out."

Conner laughed, then said in a softer tone, "Have you been drinking here long?"

"Oh yeah. I am a proper face around here. Been in and around the pub for years. Going back to the early eighties. Yeah, I'm well known in the manor, and you know... feared," Tony said with an overdramatic snarl.

"The eighties, cool. What was it like then, in the good old bad old days?" Conner said, trying to sound impressed. He also noticed that the door marked "PRIVATE" was just to the left of where Tony was sitting.

"Crazy, my son, fucking crazy. Charlie everywhere. Blow. All the cock I could handle until *The Aids* fucked it all up. So much money around you could get a fortune for the right *specialist* video. I still have some if you're interested. Why don't you come back to my flat and have a gander, it's not far."

"Maybe, yeah... but not today, I'm looking to score, you know how it is. What about the parties here? I bet they were crazy,"

Tony, sensing he was on to a good thing, wrongly as it happened, hushed his voice and lent closer to Conner.

"They were unbelievable. Toffs from *Up West*, businessmen, TV stars, rock stars, government types. The aristocracy. All upstairs drinking, using, fucking. Well, there was money to be made, if you're a resourceful fella like me. A few bits of fanny, but mostly it was a meat rack.

Runaways from Piccadilly. Men from the Army it was said. Fucking brilliant."

Then Tony snarled. "But nothing good lasts forever. People got hurt and word got out. It was in the papers and that was the end of it. All gone, almost overnight. Had to stop before the *Filth* turned up you see. Too many important reputations to be damaged."

"And what happened those who ran it?"

Conner glanced at the TV and noticed that game had kicked off. He made a mental note to add *Tony* to the intel board and he would make sure the local sex offender team paid him a visit to see if these videos breached his licence conditions, which he was in no doubt they would.

"Nobody had any names of course. Certainly not of the squaddies. They went back to kicking the shit out of the Irish or whatever the fuck they do. The suits went back to their high-flying, highly paid business jobs in the City, I guess. Or it moved on elsewhere. Fuck knows. Anyway, about these videos…"

Just then all the Bulgarians jumped up as one and started to bounce around the pub.

Hristo Stoichkov, the old Bulgarian war horse of a striker, had put his team one-nil up within three minutes. The pub was a sea of black leather, as the fans rebounded around the bar catapulting everyone, especially the Romanians, in different directions to screams of joy and outrage. Three bouncers burst in through the pub entrance and waded in.

Even Tony stood up to look at the ruckus. Conner realised this was an opportunity and casually walked to the black door marked "PRIVATE". Amazingly, it just swung open when he pushed it. It led to a corridor with stacks of empty crisp boxes and beer crates laying abandoned on a dusty grey carpet. At the end of the corridor, a set of stairs led up to the first floor, which he carefully climbed. A short landing led to a large function room, that had seen better days. The windows were painted black and had old burgundy drapes handing forlornly across them. There was a mismatch of tables and chairs piled up like deserted islands. On the right side of the room was a dusty bar in front of a large cracked and faded mirror. Empty optics hung like glass bats, waiting to be woken from a long slumber. The room smelt of must and decay. The stairs continued up to another floor and stopped at a long corridor with what appeared be a number of bedrooms down both sides. He walked along and tried a few handles, but the rooms were locked and many looked like they had not been opened in years.

Conner took in all that he had seen and heard over the last few days. The large disused function room, the bedrooms in this pub. Granger's dying words. Tony's account. Hallam's information about Company Tyking. There was now no doubt in his mind that it was all true. London's elite had been having sex parties at The Rutting Stag and young men were being beaten and sexually abused for their warped pleasure. And then a sudden realisation of what Granger's last words, "He called me a *crow*," had meant. His killer, the Tall Man from Mimi's description, was taking some form of revenge. The Green Mafia, the criminal elements in another wise fine regiment, had used the Tall Man to facilitate this depravity. Now, years later, this killer was stalking the streets of London. Hell bent on revenge against those who had abused him. Right here. In this pub. Likely this corridor. Conner slumped with his back against the wall. He felt sick. He felt ashamed. But most of all, he felt he needed to put things right.

****

Temporary Detective Constable Amber Mills sat at her computer screen, in an otherwise quiet Operation Pulse incident room, at Paddington Green police station. There had been a gangland shooting at a Chelsea nightclub overnight leaving one fatality and a number injured. AMIT's Team One had been called into help with the initial forty-eight hours. The world does not stop because there is a serial killer on the loose and neither does the Met. She had carried out several intelligence searches on Lance Corporal Tim Hallam from the RMR. Other than an affray in Catterick in 1986, there was nothing remarkable on him. Or more likely he had not been caught. She had then drafted a letter to the *Army Manning and Records Office* in Glasgow, requesting details of all soldiers who had left the RMR following suicide attempts between 1980 and 1990. She figured this would be an extensive list and wouldn't be arriving anytime soon. Finally, she sent an email to The Royal Military Police HQ at Circular Road Barracks, Colchester, requesting to speak to someone regarding an investigation into *Company Tyking* by the RMP Special Investigation Branch during the late eighties. She had immediately received a standard email reply, stating that someone would deal with her request within twenty-four hours. This had made her feel more hopeful.

Amber stood up from her desk and sipped some flavoured water from her sports bottle. She studied the three victimology boards in front of her. What was it that connected them? The males were all gay and middle-aged, but after that there was nothing more to it. If they were connected, how was the killer choosing his victims and why? She decided she would spend some time going back through the files from all three murders. Was there something that had been missed?

****

Conner walked back down the staircase and the noise from the earlier excitement had died down. He narrowly opened the door and could see that there was now a line of large-built bouncers sitting on stools between the Bulgarians and the Romanians. The bouncers looked like naughty adults sat on school chairs. A thirty-yard shot towards the Bulgarian goal was enough to cause some commotion and he slipped back into the room. He noticed that Two Time Tony was counting out pennies at the bar to get a drink and so he walked over to Peter, who was texting.

"White Boy's coming in ten minutes. Meeting us at the Brewer's Street car park, across the road," Peter said, without looking up from the phone.

"Grand," Conner said, taking a last look at the TV screen. "Let's go."

Five minutes later they were sitting on the grey concrete steps that led up to the first floor of the car park. Conner took a drag on Peter's Marlborough Light and passed it back to him. Peter was sweating, agitated. He went between standing up and kicking the metal banister and sitting down swearing to himself. Conner thought he would try to take his mind off it.

"What's the *men who have sex with men* scene all about?"

Peter looked up from kicking at a particular railing. "Why, *interested?*"

"Nope, just curious."

"Crazy shit man. Part of the sado-masochist scene. All that leather and metal studs. Some of those bitches just do it for the pain. They don't see a nice-looking guy and feel horny. They just want to give or receive violence. They don't love one another, like me and Ken. Ok, we are no fairy tale, but we do love each other." Peter went back to kicking the railing.

Conner heard a screech of tyres and could see White Boy's Blue BMW driving into the car park. It completed a *J turn* and reversed into one of the many empty spaces. A thousand specks of light from smashed car quarter lights glistened in the sun on the grey concrete next to the now parked car.

Conner and Peter peered from the stairwell. Conner made a point of staying behind Peter to keep out of line of sight.

"Listen, Peter, I want to see who we are dealing with. Make a fuss about the size of the wrap or something,"

"Fuck that, brother. I just want to score a rock and fucking forget."

"Mate, please, for me."

Peter nodded his head in resignation. They approached the front driver's window with Peter in the lead. Having handed over the money, White Boy reached into the central console, picked up a white wrap, and handed it to him.

"Fucking twenty notes for that, it's tiny bruv..." Peter started to argue.

Conner, seeing through the tinted windows of the car that there was another male sat behind the driver, pulled his cap down over his eyes and ducked down low, scrambling to the rear of the car. Taking a cubed piece of the smashed glass laying on the floor, he unscrewed the dust cap from the rear offside tyre valve, placed the glass cube into the valve and screwed it back on. The foreign object in the cap forced the value to release the air pressure within the tyre. The noise of the engine covered up the sound of the air rushing out. When the tyre was flat, Conner tapped Peter on the back.

Peter grabbed the cocaine he was being offered and walked off. Conner kept his head low, acted stoned, handed over the money and took the first wrap given. Both men then walked at speed back to the stairwell. Conner went down the steps, then turned around and lay down with eyes just above the top step. He could hear Peter charging down the steps, no doubt to have his fix. The Blue BMW drove off, then stopped as the rim of the flat tyre scrapped along the concrete floor. The vehicle's red brake lights came on and then the driver door was flung open. White Boy got out and walked around to the flat tyre. He stood looking and swearing at it, as the rear passenger door opened and out stepped a tall, muscular, white male wearing dark jeans and a baggy red Kappa jacket. Both men from the car stared and kicked at the tyre. *Kappa Jacket* knelt to inspect it and Conner could see the large military type watch on the man's wrist, reflecting the sunlight. He also recognised the man. He'd seen this man in the window of the Sloane Square guard room. It had been playing on his mind. But now he remembered. The night Taylor had been beaten up. He was the third man present. It was *Scarecrow* Tully from the Royal Mounted Rifles. A member of the Green Mafia, dealing drugs, and now he had him in his sights.

Chapter 14

Great Eastern Mainline Train to Colchester, 1017 hours, Saturday 15th June 1996.

The train shuffled from side to side as Conner looked out of the window at the flat Essex countryside, resplendent in the bright morning summer sun. He and Amber had spent Friday at the Operation Pulse incident room in Paddington Green Police Station, updating the Detective Sergeant on their actions, and planning what to do next. The investigation had not moved forward. No direct witnesses to the any of the murders. No useful CCTV, which was taking an age to go through anyway, and no forensics. It boiled down to *no face, no case.* A media appeal had been launched, but as ever, this had been a double-edged sword. For every bit of useful information, there were thousands of pieces of crap. It ranged from people who were sure they saw the whole thing, to others who wanted to put the police off track just for a laugh. The murders had also caught the attention of gay rights activists who were convinced that the whole of the gay community was at risk, and opinions ranged from a reasoned view that the police were trying, but not doing enough, through to the police were facilitating the murders. He left such sensitive matters in the hands of the Senior Investigating Officer, who was clearly better suited to that sort of thing. But shit rolls downhill and the DSs were now demanding more information and better results from the DCs.

The drug dealer he had tagged *Kappa Jacket* played on his mind. He knew it was *Scarecrow,* the Provost Sergeant from Sloane Square Barracks, but the test purchase operation, Operation Atlantic, didn't. He wanted to keep it that way for the moment. Yesterday he had considered getting a buy from Kappa Jacket on camera, using another TPO to prevent his cover being burnt. But, whilst in the incident room, Amber had received an email from the Royal Military Police HQ. It had informed her that Brigadier Sir Hugh Fairfax, the Provost Marshall, and the most senior military policeman in the country, would see them tomorrow at 1pm, in his office at Cavalry Barracks in Colchester. Conner thought this unusual, with it being a Saturday, and it would also mean him missing the England V Scotland game which was due to kick off at 3 pm, but it was an opportunity he could not turn down.

Then, just before finishing work for that day, he had received a phone call from Emma at Op. Garden City. When he saw the name appear, and it being a Friday evening, he was half expecting her to ask him to take her out for the night, but he was thankful when it out to be work-related. She had phoned to say that Mimi or *Frenchie*, as the Intel Cell knew her, had been nicked for soliciting whilst drunk outside King's Cross railway station. She had been bedded down at Islington Police Station and could not be interviewed until the next morning. Conner had thanked Emma, then quickly hung up, preventing any evening proposals being made. After speaking with Amber, they formed a plan for the next day. Amber would deal with Mimi in custody, while he spoke with the Brigadier in Colchester.

****

As he had suspected, the barracks were almost empty when he arrived. Like most other jobs the Army is predominantly Monday to Friday, unless on exercise, on an operational tour or at war. The officers go to their cottages in the

Cotswolds, the married men go home to their wives and kids in the married quarters and the *singleys* go back to their girlfriends in their hometowns. This leaves just a handful of squaddies left to do guard duties and go out drinking locally.

Conner arrived at the guard room and spoke to the orderly RMP Corporal, who then signed him in and handed him a letter. It was from the Provost Marshall, and it gave him directions to his office. He was requested to enter, take a seat and help himself to coffee. The Provost Marshall would join him shortly, the letter read.

Ten minutes later, he was sitting in an almost identical room to RSM Gibbs's office in Sloane Square Barracks, except it had nicer chairs and a nicer desk. He lent back into a rigid leather armchair and looked around at the eloquence of the office. He then poured himself a cup of coffee from a silver decanter into a patterned fine china cup, which was situated on a low round table, and took a sip of expensive tasting coffee. He was shaken out of his admiration of his surroundings when the door opened and in walked a man in his late fifties, clean shaven, with a full head of grey hair, cut in the typical military *number two* back and sides style. The man wore a blue and white checked shirt, open at the collar, red corduroy trousers and expensive Italian leather shoes. covering brightly patterned socks. Conner sensed the man was bursting with energy.

"Good afternoon, Hugh Fairfax… thanks for meeting me in the afternoon, I had to catch the early tide." The man offered Conner his hand and he stood up to shake it.

"DC Conner, Metropolitan Police. No problem, thanks for seeing me, Sir."

"Call me Hugh. Please sit down." The Provost Marshall gestured him back to the leather chair. "How can I help?" he added as he sat down.

"I'm part of a team investigating the murder of a man in his flat in Lord North Street in the City of Westminster on the 11th of June this year. We suspect the murder is linked to at least two other murders of middle-aged men. The men may or may not have been homosexual, but it is known they had sex with other men,"

"Good lord, that's terrible. So, what is the Army connection?"

"The victim from Lord North Street said he had been called a *crow* by his killer shortly before he died. I… we believe that this could indicate a link to the Royal Mounted Rifles. A regiment I served with for six years. I've also been told that the RMR, or at least certain elements of it, have been involved in facilitating male prostitution in the past,"

"You mean the Green Mafia," Fairfax said in a matter-of-fact tone.

"Yes, Sir," Conner said, rather surprised at the acknowledgement, "I believe they were involved in the prostitution of young men, so-called *Company Tyking*. My understanding is that the RMP's Special Investigation Branch completed their own investigation into this activity, and I would like to see the file as part of my enquiry."

Conner watched Sir Hugh Fairfax's reaction carefully. After a few seconds, the Brigadier lent forward and poured himself a cup of coffee before leaning back in his leather chair. Clearly buying himself thinking time, Conner observed. Fairfax took a deep breath through his nose.

"Do you have a court order or warrant instructing us to release the file?" he said before taking a sip of coffee.

"No, I don't. But I can get one," Conner said, with a casual smile.

"Detective Conner," Fairfax said, placing his cup and saucer on the table, his tone lightening. "This was all dealt with in '87. There were a few reports that a couple of low-grade soldiers had been selling sex at some illicit parties during the late seventies and early eighties. We investigated it, but there were no credible allegations, and the reports seem to stop shortly after. It's an unfortunate and rather unsavoury fact of life, but these types of practices have been going on for years. The *Perils of Piccadilly*, as it was called, has a long and dubious history and yes, the Army turned an occasional blind eye. If the Royal Military Police had arrested every serviceman who had sold his backside during the 1930s, we would have had no one to fight the Second World War!"

Fairfax laughed, pleased at his own joke.

"Then came National Service in the fifties, when the Army let anyone in, and some individuals brought their *unnatural* behaviours into the barrack rooms. During the seventies we moved a few regiments we suspected were involved out of London for the summer months and this put a stop to any further *indiscretions*. But an organised prostitution ring? That is pure fantasy, I'm afraid."

Conner looked sternly at Fairfax. "We think it's more serious than that and it has led to at least one murder and who knows how many more. You mentioned the Green Mafia earlier. Is there any evidence they were involved?"

"The Green Mafia are a fairy story, Detective," Fairfax said, with a relaxed laugh. "The Royal Mounted Rifles play on it to frighten other squaddies out of the

NAAFI and local pubs. Don't get me wrong, there are bad apples everywhere, but a so-called *Organised Crime Group* within the British Army? Well, it's absurd."

Conner realised he wasn't getting anywhere. Fairfax was either naive or sticking to the party line.

"What about any tyking links to royalty?"

Again, the relaxed laugh. "Detective Conner, have you really come all this way to engage in this charade? No, there were no links to royalty."

"Can I get a copy of the SIB file?" Conner asked, more in hope than expectation.

"With a court order, of course," Fairfax said, opening his hands wide as if there was nothing to hide.

"If it was all a storm in a *China* teacup, why can't I see the file?"

Conner sensed that Fairfax was now having trouble staying calm.

"Because, *Constable*, this was an Army matter, not a *CivPol* one," Fairfax replied curtly. "If the Metropolitan Police were that interested, they should have carried out their own investigation at the time."

The Brigadier, perhaps remembering his senior position, composed himself. He flicked an imaginary speck of fluff off his red trousers and continued.

"I suggest that you move your enquiries elsewhere. Now, if that is all, I would like to get back to my boat. I wish we could help you more, Detective. I really do. I'm sure you can make your own way back to the guard room."

Conner picked up his bag and nodded at the table.

"Thanks for the coffee, Sir. But can I have tea next time. You know… when I come back with a court order and collect your file."

Brigadier Sir Hugh Fairfax watched DC Conner walk back to the guard room from his office window. He went to his desk and opened a drawer, at the back of which, was an unregistered pay-as-you-go Nokia mobile phone. He switched it on and pressed the number three on the speed dial. It rang and was answered within two rings. He spoke into it.

"Yes, it's me. Yes, he's been. Just like you said, a gobby little *shit*. He's not going to give up. Send him a clear message, today."

Then Fairfax hung up.

At the same time on the top floor of the accommodation block in Sloane Square barracks, Viv Mason closed his flip phone and smiled widely to himself. He'd been waiting to get even with Ryan Conner for five long years and he was going to make the best of it.

****

One of Conner's many phones rang in his briefcase. He lifted out the Operation Pulse phone and saw "Amber" on the call screen. He lent back in his train seat, looked at the passing greenery and answered.

"Are you free to speak?" Amber asked.

"Yes, yes," he said, looking around a deserted carriage, no doubt due to the England versus Scotland game, he thought.

"So, how did it go?"

"Rubbish. The Brigadier played it all down and wouldn't let me have the SIB file without a court order which, we both know, we're not likely to get. But I'll try anyway. I think he's just trying to keep the Army out of it as much as he can. How'd you get on with Mimi?"

"Well, better than you it appears. We talked as part of an intelligence interview before she was carted off to another asylum hostel. She went over her account of the attack on the South Bank. She even signed a statement. But there were no other new details. The attacker was probably white, tall and slim, but that's all she could see in the rain. She mentioned again the suspect inhaled poppers and that he dropped some on the victim's head. I mean, why do that?"

"I don't know… to show dominance. The smell maybe. Wait a minute," Conner said, sitting forward in his chair. "What if it wasn't poppers? What if it was something else? You said that at the scene of the beheading, the flat smelt strongly of aftershave."

"Yeah," Amber said, growing curious. "It was expensive as well. It was not from a duty-free bargain bucket. It was bespoke, designer."

"At Lord North Street the bathroom had a strong smell of aftershave, but again the victim didn't seem the type… because the suspect brought the aftershave with him!" Conner said excitedly. "That's the link to the three murders. The killer is using aftershave to distinguish his victims."

"But why?" Amber asked.

"Memory. The killer is re-living an event. Smell is one of the strongest ways to trigger a memory. The smell of your old school classroom. Burning leaves in autumn. The perfume or aftershave of a lover."

"Or an abuser," Amber said. "An aftershave's odour can be affected by a person's temperature, their hormones or feelings."

"Or if they are having sex," he added.

"Yeah, yes, of course."

There was silence between them. Just the static on the line.

Conner spoke first.

"Can you use your old contacts to find out how many designer perfumeries there are in Central London. We can then try to narrow it down to those who produce aftershaves popular amongst city types, army officers, politicians, that lot. And I'm not asking you to do this just because you're a woman…"

"Oh, you had noticed then," Amber said, a smile in her voice.

"But… you know, you used work in health and beauty and… right, I'm going to stop digging a hole now. When I get back, I'll speak with the SIO and tell him our *hypothesis*. It's what… 4 pm now. I'll be back at Paddington for about 5.30 pm."

"Ok, see you then. But one more thing, get this… Mimi says that she has been working with a few other call girls at Sloane Square barracks. Offering *services* to some squaddies!"

"No way!" Conner replied. "I'll have to think this through, you know, how it can help us?"

"I thought you'd be pleased," Amber said, still smiling. "And Ryan," she added, "well, just be careful."

Then she hung up.

****

Thirty minutes later, the ticket barrier let Conner through and he walked quickly across Liverpool Street Station's foyer, under its high glass ceiling and ring of shops. The station was quiet, as it often was at the weekend. The big advertisement screen was showing the England V Scotland game and a few tourists gawped up at it. England were two-nil up with six minutes to go and he made a mental note to catch the highlights later. He quickly walked into the open-fronted entrance to the tube station and flashed his warrant card at the Underground staff, who tapped a card and let him through a gate. His mind started to race. The aftershave could be the key to investigation. Find the aftershave, find the next victim.

He stepped off the downward escalator and turned right towards the westbound Central line. Here there was a short staircase and just before he got to the bottom, for a split second, he was aware of someone behind him. Suddenly he felt a sickening blow to the back of his head. He bent double immediately, only then to receive several punches to his kidneys and kicks to his stomach. He curled up in a ball and could hear shouts of "You English bastard!" and "Fucking English scum!" between the blows raining down on him. He managed to open his eyes to see four men in blue football shirts and bucket hats. One man wore a Scottish team shirt and Conner thought he recognised the face underneath a pulled-up tartan scarf. His attackers continued to kick and punch at him. Conner wrapped his arms around his head and crawled so his back was against the staircase wall. This had at least stopped the assailants surrounding him. He knew if he didn't fight back they could kill him.

He started to kick out with his legs, catching one of his attackers in the inside of the knee which resulted in a yelp of pain and one attacker falling over. From his sitting position he manged to get some power in an upper cut which caught another attacker under the jaw sending him back reeling. Conner continued to kick and punch out when the blows suddenly stopped. He opened his eyes just in time to see the man in the Scotland shirt and tartan scarf pull out a semi-automatic pistol from his waist band and point the gun two inches from Conner's face. He stared down the barrel wondering if this was the end.

The barrel moved towards the right side of his head and he saw that the hand holding the gun wore a green and white *Celtic FC* wrist band. The pistol fired right next to Conner's right ear which sent a splitting pain through his brain, before a hard metallic blow impacted the crown of his head and he passed out into blackness, slumped and bleeding on the staircase.

Chapter 15

Terri's Wine bar, Roof Top Terrance, Maiden Lane, Westminster, 2008 hours, Monday 17th June 1996.

A young Mediterranean man brought Simon Gee his drink and placed it on the table in front of him with a smile. Taking a sip of the gin and tonic, Gee looked over the London roof tops towards the Thames. The sun was just about going down, but the warmth of the day continued, even up at the second-floor level. He had been busy since the Lord North Street debacle. He had assessed the risk of getting caught for each of the four remaining targets, cross-referenced with the likelihood of them being his first abuser, based on what he knew about the names he had been given, and from this produced a list. Lowest risk of being caught first, highest risk last. Gee had given each name on the list a code name and produced a *trigger plan* of how he could capture, interrogate and kill each one in turn. *Man trailing,* he called it. It was an expression borrowed from his days as a Gamekeeper. Rich businessmen would get their pampered pooches to try to find them in the woods around Thetford. They rarely did. His Gamekeeping trade had taught him to be patient, cunning and ruthless, when he needed to be. He had felt his confidence growing since Lord North Street. It had been a disaster, but he had survived, and had not been caught. It was his destiny to complete his task.

And now it was time to put the first trigger plan for *Mr. Deer* into action. It was the reason why he was sitting up on the roof top bar at Terri's, which just happened to be at the back of the Adelphi Theatre on The

Strand. Looking at his watch, Gee knew that Mr. Deer would have his throat cut within the next two minutes. How did he know that? Because it had happened every night for the last three weeks, except for Sundays. Mr. Deer was an actor playing the role of Adolfo Pirelli in the musical version of *Sweeney Todd* at the Adelphi Theatre. A small supporting role for the former soap opera star, and a brief one. The demon barber would be strangling him and slitting his throat halfway through the first act. Effectively giving Mr. Deer the rest of the night off. It was then the actor's routine to wait in his rather small dressing room for the next two hours, until he was called for the bows at the final curtain. Not something an aging actor was going to turn down.

Gee finished his drink. It was time.

Moving to the rear of the terrace, he stood next to a low wall and looked down towards the ground floor roof of Terri's. Behind that there was a short yard, full of crates and barrels. A wooden fence, with barbed wire along the top, was at the rear of the Adelphi Theatre. From his position, Gee could see a crack of fluorescent light emanating from a rear fire door. That door should have been shut, but Mr. Deer had a habit of smoking a joint after each of his nightly demises, so he needed the ventilation to dissipate the sickly-sweet odour. This had unwittingly become a signal to Gee. After a quick look around, he checked his tools for the job. Paracord, alcohol-soaked cloth, balaclava, knife and aftershave bottle, all were secure in his cargo trousers. He quickly dropped down onto the ground floor roof. From there he dropped into the yard, and at the wooden fence made a couple of snips with wire cutters, which was enough to make a small gap that he could fit through. He pulled himself over the fence and dropped again into the rear vehicle yard of the theatre. The whole entrance had taken less than two minutes. Ignoring the pain in his back and neck, he walked into the back of the theatre, through the open fire exit door, put on his balaclava and gloves and then stood silently looking into a small dressing room on the left.

****

Taking another big draw on his cannabis joint Cyril Holloway looked into the small dressing room mirror which was illuminated by a series of bright lightbulbs. A gay S&M pornographic magazine was open on his dressing table. This period between his stage death and the final curtain was what he enjoyed the most. Despite the small dressing room, he had this end of the theatre to himself. He had slipped off his nineteenth century brass-buckled shoes, taken off his wig and beard and sat staring at his drawn face, with its dark hollow eyes, in the mirror. In the eighties this face had once been the toast of the BBC, he thought to himself. Its first openly gay soap star! Standing up for equality, for the gay community, and attending all the rallies. Talk of a political career abounded. Well, that's what the PR department would like to have the public believe. He knew it wasn't true, of course. He liked having sex with men. He liked men having sex with women. But what he really liked was the violence. The beatings. Giving and receiving.

Looking into the mirror and seeing himself in the costume of Adolfo Pirelli, he could not ignore the similarities with his character. His critical self-conscious told him he was just another *over the hill* fraud. He took another draw on the joint and distracted himself with fantasies about picking up a boy from the Soho meat rack after the show. It was all very seedy nowadays. Not like when he was a star, and he had his *fun* delivered to him. Those were great days. The whole bondage and sadomasochistic scene had taken hold of Soho with its studded leather glove and was squeezing its bollocks. Different parties every night. The pubs and the nightclubs all welcoming him, craving him. It was an open secret amongst his tribe. Cyril Holloway, the gay rights activist, was one of them. A *leather man,* as sado-masochists were known in the gay scene.

Holloway was suddenly thrown out of his daydream when he heard gentle footsteps coming down the hallway. He quickly extinguished his joint, putting the roach in his shoe, and vigorously wafted away at the smoke, fearing another ticking off by the theatre manager. He turned to his open dressing room doorway to see a tall figure wearing a balaclava and before he could shout out, a wet cloth was forced into his mouth and a rope was wrapped around his neck, shoulders and arms. In his stoned state, his struggling was little more than a token effort and he realised it was futile. He was now bound to his chair. The figure bent down to face him while taking a few heavy breaths. Spittle forming on the woollen hood, where a mouth should be.

"Good evening, Mr. Deer," the figure said. "Shall we begin?"

Simon Gee walked around the tied-up man and stared into the terrified eyes that were watching his every move. He wondered to himself. Was this him, his first abuser and ultimate target? He was the right sort of age. A bit too thin, but the right height. Certainly, an arrogance and contempt radiated off him. There was only one way to be sure. The smell of the aftershave that accompanied the abuse for the months it went on. Gee smiled to himself now he was back in control.

"Mr. Deer," he said, to muffled objections. "No, no, it's Ok. I know your real name, but for my purposes you have a code name, *Mr. Deer*. No doubt your squirming, depraved brain is probably screaming, *Why me?* Well, it might not be you, or your family, I want. Your partner is Brian and you have a stepson, Carl, I believe?"

Gee circled his prey and went on speaking.

"But before that can be decided, I need to do a test. And oh, it will be painful, but I think you like that, don't you?" Gee said, nodding at the open magazine on the table.

Gee stopped behind the figure, who was desperately trying to shake free from his bonds and placed his hands on the actor's shoulders.

"Steady now, steady," he said, whispering into his captive's ear. "Why are you trying to get away? I'm going to do you a favour, Mr. Deer. For my test to be complete, I need to have you sexually aroused, and you of all people should know, one of the best ways to elicit sexual excitement is by strangulation."

The chair started to rock around even more violently as Holloway desperately tried to get free. Gee placed two leather gloved hands around his captive's neck and started to squeeze. He whispered in the actor's ear.

"You will probably know that erotic asphyxiation occurs when the oxygen supply returns to the brain after a period of strangulation. Yes? But what you don't know is… when I'm going to stop."

Gee gripped tighter and tighter around the man's Adam's apple, pushing back onto the windpipe. His helpless victim struggled in his chair, trying to get his hands free. Gee held on tightly, pushing him down. The sounds of stocking feet kicking on the ground echoed around the near empty building. The occasional noise of applause wafting through the air vents. Gee felt the man's body starting to go limp. The head lopped to one side. He released his grip and removed the small poppers bottle from his cargo pant pocket. This allowed time for the feelings of euphoria to envelope his captive. He unscrewed the bottle and dropped a tiny amount of the aftershave on to Holloway's sweat-covered neck and inhaled.

It was not him. He had believed it was. Gee stepped back and took off his balaclava. Sweat poured from his face. His hair ruffled. He had been convinced he had found his first abuser in Holloway. But it wasn't him. The smell of the aftershave pervaded his mind. The memories of the pain and humiliation returned. Then disappointment that the killing would continue. The sight of the pornography, the heady smell of cannabis filled his senses. The man in the chair slowly came around. Gee could see an erection through the man's silk costume trousers. He made up his mind.

He took the cloth out of the actor's mouth.

"Now, you can redeem yourself. What do you know about the Green Mafia's sex parties in The Rutting Stag in the eighties?"

Holloway coughed and gasped. Gee slapped his face to help him regain focus.

"I don't know, honestly, I don't know."

Holloway gasped for breath. His face white, drained of blood.

"I've not heard of the Green Mafia. I went to lots of parties," he spluttered.

Gee slapped him again, harder. "Think!"

"I went to The Rutting Stag parties. Lots of people did," Holloway wheezed. "You know, celebrities, businessmen. We just wanted to keep our kinks private." He started to sob. "But honestly, I've never seen you before. Please, please just let me go. I won't say anything about this... just let me go home."

"What about the soldiers? Did you fuck any soldiers?"

"I don't know, I don't know. They were there, so probably, yes." Holloway had started to cry. "I'm sorry. I'm sorry. I need help," he whined.

Gee pinched Holloway's nose and as his mouth opened he stuffed the alcohol-soaked cloth back into the actor's mouth.

"The irony of the situation cannot have escaped you, *Mr. Deer*. Here you are portraying a charlatan, who gets strangled to death, whilst here you are, a despicable perverted charlatan who..." Gee started to take deep breaths while shaking out his arms and hands. "Well, let us face reality, *Mr. Deer*. There is only one way this scene ends."

Chapter 16

"Search Team! You're up!" came a cry from over young Private Ryan Conner's shoulder.

He was sitting on a grass bank by the side of a road that led up to an old farmhouse less than 600 metres from the Southern Irish border. He and the rest of his Counter Terrorist Search Team had been waiting just off the *plot* while the Royal Ulster Constabulary and soldiers from The Royal Mounted Rifles had put in an inner and outer cordon and, unusually, the Garda Siochana, the Irish Police, did the same on the southern side of the border. Whether the Garda's involvement was out of duty or a morbid curiosity, Conner could not work out. The briefing given by his corporal had told him that *Information had been received,* which was how briefings always started, that the farmhouse contained weapons and ammunition for an Irish Republican Army cell that had been crossing over from County Leitrim to attack British Army patrols. This type of activity was not unusual for Fermanagh, surrounded as it was by the Republic of Ireland on three sides. It was the Search Team's job to find the cache of weapons now that the premises had been confirmed as empty and the surrounding area secured.

Conner extinguished his cigarette into the wet, boggy Fermanagh grass, stood up and adjusted the straps on his permanently soaked British Army issue helmet. He picked up the green canvas bag which contained his search equipment and joined the others on the road. The sun was shining on the beautiful Irish hills and, not for the first time, he had to remind himself that he was in a warzone.

On one of those beautiful hills there could be an IRA sniper with a Barrett rifle, capable of killing him from over a kilometre away. Indeed, sniper shootings had already happened more than once on this tour.

The Search Team walked up the stone-chipped road in single file with the corporal at the front. Conner could see soldiers he recognised from his platoon laying down and facing out towards the border. One or two turned to him the *V's* or 'wanker' sign before smiling and returning to their arcs. They had been there for two hours already and were likely to be there a few hours more. The two-storey farmhouse had an overgrown garden inside a low stone wall with a short path leading up to the front door, which was ajar. The house certainly looked abandoned. Nobody had been in the premises yet, but hours of observations had shown no movement or noise. The corporal returned to the team after speaking to the captain in charge of the cordon who, after a brief conversation on his radio, gave him the thumbs up.

"Ok, right," the corporal said, "the cordons are secure. There has been nothing to suggest the house is occupied. But as no one has been inside the house we're going to do a drop and drag along the path and a full examination of the front door."

There was a low moan from the Search Team. A drop and drag involved having a wooden pole with a block of wood on the end, making it look like a giant broom, and, as the name suggested, dropping it forward from a pivot on a stand and then dragging it back to catch any trip wires or mines. It was a slow and tedious process.

"Shut the fuck up," the corporal hissed. "I don't want to have to tell your mummies you've been blown up because you're a bunch of lazy bastards."

The corporal's strong Welsh accent was exaggerated for effect. He then turned to look at Private Hall, the youngest and newest to the team.

"I would tell your mum Hall, then give her a good sympathy shagging."

Hall smiled and looked down self-consciously as laughter went around the rest of the team.

"We drag and drop and then, Conner, you go first, and check the front door. Jones, Baylis, you're next, weapons up, remember to check the floor for pressure pads, light sensors, all that good shit. Hall, you bring up the rear. We'll search the bottom floor and then move on to the top. Ok, lads, let's get it done."

The team set up the drag and drop and meticulously lifted the *broom,* which was attached to a rope, and allowed it to drop a couple of metres in from its original position before they dragged it back along the path, taking cover behind the low wall. The path to the front door was only twenty metres long but very overgrown, so the whole process took thirty minutes and, although nothing was found, it was time well spent. The team walked up the now clear path to the front door. Conner resisted the temptation to take off his damp helmet and instead pushed it back on his head, so he could get a proper look at the door hinges to see if they were new or recently oiled, which they weren't. He looked all around the doorway for any wires or pieces of metal that could make an electric circuit if moved but could not find any. Finally, he placed a thin endoscope through the letter box and rotated it around to see if there were any copper wires. The IRA had a neat trick of having one wire horizontally across the door and another hanging vertically on a weight a few centimetres apart. When the door was opened the vertical wire would swing and touch the horizontal wire. Hey presto, an electrical circuit that would donate a bomb.

Not finding anything suspicious, he carefully opened the door as Private Jones and Private Baylis stepped into a dusty hallway. The soldiers lifted their SA80 rifles and carefully looked for pressure pads on the floor. Nothing was found. The entrance being clear, the team assembled in the hallway and started to look around. The walls were covered in damp, with a leafed pattern wallpaper peeling off. The smell of decay was everywhere. To their right was a blue door with cracking flaky paint, which was shut. To their left was a kitchen with a rusty sink and battered old wooden wall cupboards. Straight in front of the soldiers was a wooden staircase with a hole in the fifth and seventh step. The corporal squeezed into the hallway.

"For fuck's sake, it's tight. Conner, Baylis, go to the room on the right. Hall, Jones, take the kitchen. I'll wait here and start the search log. If you find anything you know the drill. Stop and tell me."

Conner started to look at the old blue door just as he had done with the entrance. Private Baylis stood behind him.

Private Baylis cast his glance behind him, just in time to see Private Hall grab a handle of one of the kitchen cupboard doors.

Conner just about heard Baylis shout, "No, stop!"

Boom! An explosion ripped through the downstairs of the building.

The blast flung Baylis and Conner through the blue door. The almighty explosion sent bricks, wood, glass, and body parts in all directions. White dust mixed with a pink mist. Conner felt an impact as what was left of Baylis's skull hit his head. The force of the blast and the impact knocked him unconscious.

When Conner came round, his head throbbed like it was being hit with a mallet from the inside. His ears felt like they were being drilled out, the painful sound of the drill pushing through his eardrums. He screamed and put his hand to his right ear in a vain attempt stop the terrible pain and ringing. He forced open his eyes to see white walls, a shocked-looking nurse and an attractive redhead in jeans and t-shirt. *What was going on?*

And then he remembered. Amber. The kicking in the tube station. A shot fired. He fell back into the bed sweating and put his arms across his eyes.

"It's ok, Ryan, you're going to be fine," Amber said, as she lightly took his hand.

****

Private Ward 2, St, Bartholomew's Hospital, Smithfield, The City of London, 1900 hours, Tuesday 18th June 1996.

Amber had passed Ryan Conner a glass of water. He took a sip and passed it back to her. He laid back against the upright pillow and turned his neck to look at her on the chair next to him. She could see he was in real pain.

"Well, I leave you for one day and this is how you come back," she said with a grin.

He tried to laugh, but it was clear that it hurt to do so.

"You've been out for two days," she said.

Now he looked startled.

"You had a suspected bleed on the brain, broken ribs and a perforated ear drum. They put you in an induced coma. It seems you were lucky. No long-term damage."

Amber was holding his hand.

"Bastards," he said in a hoarse voice. "The shooter. Scotland football shirt. Celtic wristband. Never happen." Conner was slowly shaking his head. "Green Mafia."

"Yes, I know," she replied.

Amber felt it a bit odd to be holding his hand. But it felt good in so many ways. Real good. But then there was that memory. Her being the one in the hospital bed. Badly beaten up. All the *Officer Protection Training* in the world could not protect you from a violent bully who lives with you. You have to sleep sometime. Her boyfriend had shown remorse of course. Tears. More for his police career than for her, she knew. He had tried to hold her hand as she lay in traction. She had pulled hers away, despite her injuries. Turned her battered and bruised face away from him to the window and never looked at him again. She had felt nothing but shame since.

But she knew Conner was a different type of man. Tough certainly, but also kind. A good heart. She had been reluctant to show her true feelings for fear of being wrong again. Fear of having to blame herself all over again. But she found she could not keep her feelings for him to herself much longer. She trusted him. It felt right to be holding his hand. She started to smooth the skin above his thumb with hers. It felt wonderful to her.

"BTP checked the CCTV," Amber said, still stroking his hand, "The suspects were all masked up with scarves and wearing hats. We did track them to a stolen Focus ST near Old Street. It was later found burnt out in Wood Green. Not what your average soccer hooligan would do. The round was a blank by the way."

Conner nodded slowly.

"Did you recognise any of them?" she asked.

Conner shrugged. Then thought for a bit. "One maybe. Ginger… Bailey… Tom Bailey? But so long ago. Can't be sure."

He closed his eyes, then said, with considerable effort, "FDR?"

"FDR?" she repeated. "Oh, Firearms Discharge Residue. There is less cordite in a blank round to get on clothing but, yeah, it's possible."

"The wristband?" he whispered.

"Could have been overlooked. A mass spectrometer would pick up the residue from a blank firer. And we have your clothes for comparison. It was a setup, but by who?"

"The Provost Marshall."

"That high up?!" she said incredulously. "Anyway, we'd never prove it."

Conner opened his eyes again and she looked into the two dazzling blue pools. He then nodded in agreement.

"We need to get back into the *Top Floor,*" he said after a pause.

"Ryan," Amber looked at him, suddenly very serious. "There's been another murder, probably by our suspect."

Conner shut his eyes again. "Go on."

"Cyril Holloway, actor. Forty-four years old and openly homosexual. He was found strangled and his throat cut in his dressing room yesterday. The stage runner who found him described a sweet unknown smell in the room. He thought it was a mixture of cannabis and an expensive aftershave."

Conner tried to get out of bed, but she stopped him.

"No, you don't, Ryan. You need to rest. The Op. Pulse SIO has linked it to the Bale and Granger murders and it's caused mayhem. The press is now saying there is another *Gay Slayer* on the loose. The gay community are calling for protests at New Scotland Yard. Stonewall have held a meeting with the Commissioner, which has bought us some time, but it's still a shitstorm. Just for tonight, you need to rest, and tomorrow we will go back to the incident room and speak with the SIO about your theory."

"What about the aftershave?" Conner asked, as he reached for another drink of water with his free hand.

"If we are setting a parameter of the West End there are only three elite perfumery producers. I have the details and one has been closed since the New Year. So that leaves just two to visit."

Just then the door opened and she saw a male hospital orderly in a blue uniform wheeling in an old box-shaped TV on a hospital stand.

"Couldn't have you missing the big game," the orderly said, as he plugged in the set and attached an aerial from the wall. "My brother is a cop up north. He'd be livid if he missed it."

She looked at Conner, confused.

"England versus Holland. It kicks off in ten minutes," the orderly said, placing a small paper cup containing tablets by the side of the bed.

Conner gave a big smile. Amber resigned herself.

"Budge up," she said, as she made herself comfortable on his hospital bed. Amber knew she was dropping her guard. But she'd been waiting by his bed for two days, as the empty cans of coke, rolled up crisp packets and magazines lying on the floor were testament to.

Conner moved to the side of his bed, then looked at her with a smile, before saying, "If we are watching the game, the Green Mafia will be watching it in their Mess on the Top Floor. If England win, they will have a party."

The two police officers stared at the TV for a few minutes thinking, as the national anthems were played. Then they both looked at each other and said, "Mimi!"

England won four-one, in what was probably the greatest display by an England football team since they won the World Cup in 1966. Conner and Amber had however busied themselves with more intimate things and despite Conner's injuries, and the cramped conditions in the bed, they missed the last half hour of the match.

****

A small pedestrian door in the rear vehicle gate for Sloane Square Barracks opened and Mimi lifted up one of her long smooth legs and stepped into the vehicle yard. She stood next to four other girls, all of whom were scantily dressed. She clutched a small purse bag and ran her fingers through her long black wig, as she waited for the last of the girls to come in.

"This way ladies," said a chubby man wearing designer glasses and jeans with a striped, collared shirt. The girls followed him to the entrance of a lift.

Mimi had received a call from PC Amber Mills an hour ago, asking her if she had been invited to the *Barracks Party*. Mimi told her she had. The England football team won a game or something, she recalled, and the escort agency she was working for had asked her to go, as she was now a regular.

PC Mills had asked her if she could look out for some blue football shirts and a white and green wristband while in there. In return, PC Mills promised she would get her an upgrade in her bail accommodation. This seemed fair to Mimi, as she would be there anyway, and she hated the women's hostel the Immigration Service had put her in while they processed her asylum claim. No status, no benefits, no official work. She was lucky she had a face and body she could make money from.

After the lift came to a halt at the top floor, the doors slid open and drunken chants of "It's coming home!"

rang out against a backdrop of clinking beer glasses and a TV turned up too loud. Mimi sensed that the party had already started. Groups of men, some still in green army uniforms, stood around. There were beer cans and spirit bottles strewn all over the floor. The air was heavy with smoke. No sooner than she stepped into the room, the man she knew as Ginger came straight for her and put his arm around her waist before putting his hand on her arse. Ginger was very drunk and mumbled something in her ear before leading her off to the usual bedroom. It was going to be a long, but profitable, night, she thought.

On the balcony of the top floor flat, Viv Mason looked out over South Kensington. The lights of Harrods dominated the skyline. The unregistered mobile phone in his hand rang and he answered it.

"Yes, Grand Master, it's done," he said. "That little *crow* cop won't be sticking his nose into anything again. He'll know the next time he does it will be a live round into his head. Yes, no issues with the *Stag*. We'll have full control by the end of the month. Thank you, Grand Master."

He threw the phone from the balcony. Put out his cigarette and decided it was time to leave the party and let the boys have their fun.

By four in the morning the noise of the party had died down and Mimi lay in a bed in a darkened room. Other than half an hour with a large black male, she had been with Ginger most of the night. He lay naked, facing away from her, unconscious with drink. The normal routine was that she would be gathered up by the man who had first met them and then they'd be taken out of the barracks the same way they went in. Mimi figured she had twenty minutes to have a look around the top floor apartment for the blue shirts and the wristbands. She quietly stood up and slipped on her underwear and the electric blue silk dress she had worn for the evening. There were drab military issue wardrobes and a chest of drawers in the room which she carefully opened, but they all were empty. She slipped out of the room, into the darkened corridor where a group of men were drunk, unconscious on the floor. She tiptoed into the bathroom and, whilst taking a pee, looked around the room. This was hopeless, she thought to herself. After cleaning herself with toilet tissue, that reminded her of greaseproof paper, she went back into the corridor. There she saw the chubby man who had let her in. He was pushing white sheeting down into a laundry chute.

"Are you and your little friends ready to go?" he said, feeding dirty sheets and towels into the chute.

"Oui, er, yes," she smiled. "I just need my purse."

She crept back into the room and retrieved her clutch bag from the floor, scooping up several unused condoms as she did so. The laundry chutes, she suddenly thought to herself. Surely, that's where dirty clothes would go? She decided that once back in the yard on the ground floor, she would take a look.

First out of the lift, Mimi went straight around to the right of the building. At the bottom of the building, near a fire escape, was a large metal flap. As the other girls made their way to the gate, Mimi pushed open the metal flap and leaned in. She could see that just underneath her was a large metal bin and on top were the dirty white sheets and towels from the top floor flat. The bin was just within her arm's distance. She pulled away at a few dirty white sheets. Then smiled broadly to herself.

"Are you all here?" she heard the chubby man ask.

She came from around the corner. "Pardon, I needed to piss," she said, and joined the group.

"For fuck's sake," the chubby man said, as he looked her up and down disapprovingly.

Mimi stepped out of the gate and picked her phone out of her bag.

"THE CLOTHES YOU WANT ARE IN THE LAUNDRY CHUTE IN THE YARD OF THE TALL BLOCK IN THE BARRACKS," she texted to PC Mills and then set off back to her hostel to pack.

Chapter 17

**Weymouth Street, London W1A, 1824 hours,
Wednesday 19ᵗʰ June 1996.**

A blacked-out Ford Granada sat, with its engine idling, at
the junction of Portland Place. Simon Gee looked into the
rear-view mirror, adjusted his tie and wiped a small speck
of blood from his right cheek. It wasn't his. The blood
belonged to the vehicle's driver who was tied up,
unconscious, in a large cylindrical metal bin two streets
away. The original driver of the vehicle had a habit of
screwing some of the residents of the nearby YMCA when
they were down on cash. Gee had been in the foyer of the
YMCA, given the driver a wink and gestured to follow him
into the alley. He had then smashed the driver's head off a
brick wall before incapacitating him. He was amazed how
easily violence came to him now. A firewall in his head had
been breached and the years of abuse, shame and disgust
had fermented into pure unadulterated violence. The
deranged but brilliant lead singer of the seventies punk
band the *Sex Pistols*, John Lydon, had once sung, *Anger is
an energy.* At that moment Gee could not have agreed
more.

He knew intimately the routine for his next target.
Mr. Vixen would come out of the rear of BBC's
Broadcasting House at 6.30 pm after commenting on the
previous night's football game on the flagship drive-time
radio show. After a football career that had seen Mr. Vixen
become England's top striker, with a host of domestic
trophies, he was now being groomed to be the face of
football for the BBC. Gee had to admit he had been
surprised when his name appeared on the list, but looking
at Mr. Vixen in his heyday, the perm, the expensive
clothes, the string of failed marriages, a double life in the

male sadomasochistic sex scene sort of made sense. Tonight's drive-time show would have been especially important following England's emphatic win against Holland, and they had rolled out the big guns. One would image that Mr. Vixen would be in a good mood. In fact, Gee was relying on it. He placed the hunting knife and masking tape in the driver's side door compartment and slowly moved the car off to the pick-up point just outside the marble columns and steel bollards of Broadcasting House.

****

Inside the BBC building, the lift doors opened, allowing Jason Kemble to step into the lift, and he immediately checked his reflection in the mirrored walls. He pressed the button for the basement level and then turned back to his reflection. The drive-time show had gone well, although he did feel that he had been cut off towards the end, just as he was about to explain the complex interplay between Gascoigne, Sheringham and Shearer for England's third goal. After all, he had scored more England goals than any other player since Jimmy Greaves.

But no matter, he thought, as he smoothed down a straggling eyebrow, he had got what he wanted. The meeting with producer of Football Tonight, a Wednesday evening football magazine show, had gone very well and he had been promised the regular pundit spot from September. From there it was only a hop, skip and a jump to the big one, *Match of the Day*. Jason looked at himself. He was good-looking in an executive car salesman sort of way. The *New Face* of the game, his agent had said. That reminded him. Dennis had agreed to call Sarah, his wife, and say something had come up and he was needed in London for another night. This would give him the chance to visit a young Moroccan footballer who, thanks to him, was now on the books at a Second Division club. They had struck up a relationship and Kemble felt it was time the debt was repaid.

The lift doors opened, and he stepped out into the front lobby. The BBC security guard in his dark suit and cap saluted him with a cheery "Good evening, Sir." Kemble forced a smile. It might well be, he thought to himself.

Seeing his normal dark saloon courtesy car parked in its usual place, in front of the bollards, Kemble walked over and went to open the rear door. It was locked. The blacked-out electric front passenger window smoothly came down.

"Sorry, sir, it's jammed, can you sit in the front, please?" the driver said. It wasn't his normal driver, but they did change frequently.

Kemble was quietly furious and made a mental note to tell Dennis about it. He opened the passenger door and sat inside. The new driver was a man in his early thirties. Slim, toned in fact, in a grey suit and blue tie. Not good-looking, but pleasant. An outdoor type, Kemble thought to himself. The driver locked the door remotely.

"Where's Toby?" Kemble asked.

"Taken the rest of the night off, sir. Celebrating the football too much, by the smell of it. Could you put your seat belt on? I don't want you to get a ticket," the driver said, keeping his eyes on the road.

They drove in silence for some time in the stop-start traffic.

"Did you listen to the show?" Kemble asked, adjusting his suit jacket.

"Oh yes. Brilliant as ever."

Kemble laughed at the flattery.

"I'll be honest. I'm a big fan," the driver said, stealing a quick glance towards him. "I followed you all the time you were at the top of the game. All through your England career. There was no number nine like you. Strong, fast, good with both feet. The perfect striker."

"Well, that's very kind of you to say," Kemble said, warming to his new driver.

"I do have to ask why you went to the old Second Division when you did?"

"Well, eh… I wanted a club in London that had a real connection with fans, you know…"

The driver nodded. "Yes, of course, a man of the people. A man's man." The driver turned to look directly at him.

Simon Gee was enjoying toying with his next victim. He had control of the car and the situation. This was going to be textbook. Gee placed his left hand on Kemble's right thigh and moved his hand up towards his crotch.

"That's right, isn't it. You're a man's man. You went to men's sex parties in the eighties, after you moved clubs. The Chairman used to go as well, didn't he?"

"Well, look, I'm not sure who you think…" Kemble muttered, sounding agitated.

"Gordon James, the football scout. Convicted of seven accounts of *Gross Indecency* with a child. He went there as well. Or so I read online in the court report. This internet is a wonderful thing."

Kemble looked like he was going into shock. His world crumbling in an instant.

Gee removed his left hand from Kemble's thigh and then took hold of the steering wheel. The traffic had stopped. Gee took hold of the knife in the driver's door compartment with his right hand and swung it across his body with all the force he could muster and into the side of Jason Kemble. Gee followed this up immediately a further three quick stabs to the abdomen. A spurt of deep red blood arced into the air and landed on the dashboard. Kemble let out a sharp burst of air from his lungs. His diaphragm froze, his mouth opened, but he was unable to scream. This gave Gee just enough time to shove a cloth soaked in alcohol into Kemble's mouth and slap over it some prepared masking tape to ensure his victim would be completely silent. Gee placed another piece of masking tape across the largest stab wound. He didn't want Kemble to die too soon. Kemble's hands automatically went to his side. His eyes bulging. Gee turned to him and smiled.

"Time for a chat about old times, *Mr. Vixen.*"

****

The Operation Pulse incident room in Paddington Green police station was now a hive of activity despite it being well after 6 pm. Phones rang, detectives waited to fight for car keys as soon as they were returned, so they could go out and complete their actions. Admin staff typed furiously into HOLMES terminals. The murder of Cyril Holloway in his dressing room had changed everything overnight. Holloway had been a high-profile member of the gay community. Stonewall and the Soho Community Action Group had gone to the press and now the Met could no longer deny they had a serial killer on their hands. Press conferences had been called. The Home Secretary had to field off questions in Parliament. The Commissioner had been called in to Marsham Street and given a rollocking. Shit does indeed roll downhill and DI Tony Hanson was now under a pile of it. No CCTV or forensics. All the investigation had to go on for a suspect was a composite electronic description of a *Tall Man*.

Ryan Conner and Amber Mills sat opposite each other, amazed by the sudden commotion in an office that had been empty four days ago. He raised an eyebrow, which was partly obscured by a gauze patch, towards the bustle. Amber stifled a laugh.

Conner had spent the morning giving his statement to the British Transport Police regarding his assault. He was lucky it had occurred on tube property rather than the railway station. This meant the investigation had gone to *BTP* London Underground, who were much more effective than their overland cousins. In fact, even more luckily, it had gone to an experienced Detective Sergeant, someone Conner knew very well.

DS Shelia Dean had sought his help when her daughter had gone missing in Camden. Conner had negotiated a release by the girl's captors, local low-level drug dealers, outside of normal channels and the child had been returned soon after in one piece. Shelia was eternally grateful. She worked for the *LU*'s Robbery Squad, an elite unit within the BTP, who were used to dealing with the worst that London's Organised Crime Gangs could offer. DS Dean had already recovered the CCTV from around the area of Conner's assault. Forensics had been to the steps and pretty soon, thanks to PC Roger Kelly from 1 Area TSG, a bag of Scottish football clothing and Celtic wristband had been recovered in a routine stop of a laundry vehicle in Sloane Square. These items were now winging their way to the BTP LU Robbery Squad offices above Great Portland Street Tube Station. DS Shelia Dean had set in motion a Firearms Discharge Residue comparison between Conner's clothing and the recovered clothing. If there was a DNA and FDR match, she was confident that she could get a Section 8 PACE police arrest and search warrant on the back of it.

In the afternoon, Conner and Amber had gone to the perfumeries on their list. The first, Santa Maria of London based on The Strand, only dealt in female perfumes. The second, Sergio Firenze in Regent Street, was much more productive. Situated on the second to sixth floors of an office block above an Italian furniture shop, the perfumery was a picture of Florentine chic. The entrance consisted of exposed Tuscany stone walling, with a grand welcome desk and a young dark-haired female receptionist that Conner, if he had not now been intimately linked to Amber, could have looked at all day. Despite the *on-spec* nature of the call they had been welcomed in and given Italian coffee. After fifteen minutes, a slim and elegant lady in her late fifties, who introduced herself as Yvette, had come to the waiting area and showed them into her large, open plan office. The noise from the street below was muffled by expensive glass and the view of Westminster was superb. Yvette sat relaxed behind a glass desk and Conner and Amber were offered two high-back black leather chairs, no doubt purchased from the ground floor.

"How can I help you, Detectives?" Yvette said in perfect English, with just a hint of a continental accent.

Conner told Yvette about his theory that a serial killer was using the smell of a bespoke aftershave to identify his abuser from perhaps ten years previously. In order to do this, the killer had to get his victims sexually aroused, which in turn fired his anger and hatred and inevitably resulted in him killing his victims.

"It's possible," Yvette said. "Without getting too technical it's called the *Proust Effect*. Odours get into the limbic system of the brain very quickly and do not degrade over time, hence the vivid recollection when the odour is smelt again."

She sat forward in her leather office chair.

"Making a good perfume or aftershave is like composing good music. Different scents are like different notes, high and lows, allegro and adagio, yes? People get different memories, feelings, emotions from different pieces of music. It's the same way with a scent. It can smell differently on everyone. Their age, their metabolism, their level of sexual arousal, as you say, can all affect the scent."

She leaned back and continued, "It is likely that the same aftershave on your suspect's abuser will have changed in odour over time but the core scent, the melody if you like, will be the same. Perfumes and music both have magical properties when it comes to memory."

Conner nodded. "We think the killer's abuser could be one of your most long-standing customers and perhaps one of ,your most wealthy, willing to pay a thousand pounds for an aftershave, probably more. Now, I know this would affect your business, but this is a dangerous man."

Yvette sat back in her chair and looked out the window. The summer sun was high in the sky. Then turned to the detectives and spoke in a remorseful tone.

"Sergio Firenze, my father, came to England in 1965. He had grown up a poor boy in Tuscany, but he loved music and flowers. He was also a brilliant chemist. He set up his first perfumery in Florence in 1951 on the Via de Badri. He lived with his family above the laboratories. After a few years, he became successful, producing subtle perfumes and distinctive aftershaves, each with over a hundred ingredients. This eventually, of course, attracted the attention of the local Cosa Nostra. They visited a few times and asked for protection money. This was routine, no? So, he paid. Then they asked for more and for his family, he paid. Then they asked for too much and he refused."

Yvette took a sip of water from an expensive-looking glass on her desk and stared deep inside him.

"The fire in the laboratory ripped through the building in seconds. It destroyed a lifetime's work. It also destroyed his family. A wife, a son and baby daughter died in the inferno. My mother and siblings."

She gazed out of the window. Then a few seconds later she looked back at him.

"My father moved with me to London a year later to get away from the disgusting smell of crime, corruption and evil. Detective Conner, you be sent everything you need."

Conner and Amber sat stunned and nodded their heads in thanks.

Back in the incident room, Conner looked at the typed list that had been given to him by Yvette Firenze. It contained around fifty names. He had set the parameters of male customers regularly buying bespoke aftershave costing over five hundred pounds from the company since 1975. A cursory glance had not revealed anything or anyone of note. Amber was spending time doing what research she could on the names on the Met's very basic and heavily regulated fledgling internet. Conner was watching the DI's office door and waiting for the Intel analysts to come out. He just wanted to catch the DI for five minutes to explain his theory. The door opened and a gaggle of young female analysts, armed with large patterned books and decorated pencil cases, filed out.

"Right, I'm going in," he said to Amber. "Can I have a quick word, *Guv* ?" he shouted in the direction of the closing door.

Amber looked at the list and then looked at Conner scarpering off. She smiled to herself. Perhaps it was because she could still feel his hand in hers, or the intimacy they had shared in the hospital bed. Or because they had gone to an exclusive perfumery. A romantic place, full of exciting scents, hand-crafted with the very purpose of eliciting desire and attraction. They had been together in the perfumery surrounded by the sweet smells of orange blossom, lily and musk. Like a two-minute holiday on the Cinque Terre coastline. She knew they would have not been there if he had not seen the link. The link no one else had seen. But what mattered most to her was his kindness. Sure, he could play the tough street cop around the report writing room. But so could she. Everyone had their own personal suit of armour. The thick skin they didn't issue you with at police stores. It was earned and grown. However, she understood that underneath he wasn't like that. He was something and someone else. The thought made her heart beat faster. She was starting to admit to herself that she was beginning to have real feelings for this man.

Her thoughts were rudely interrupted by the DI shouting from his office.

"PC Conner, stop wasting my fucking time with fucking conspiracy theories! Either do the actions you're given or fuck off back to pushing a panda around Camden!"

There was a loud slam of the door.

Conner slunk back to the desk.

"Could have gone better?" Amber asked.

"Yeah..."

Suddenly the door to the incident room was thrown open and an out of breath, uniformed policeman burst in.

"They've got him," he said through panting breath, the man's large body heaving under his black body armour. Everyone in the room looked at him, bemused.

"The Tall Man. A limo driver from the BBC has just been fished out of a bin at the back of the YMCA. Says a slim, tall man took his car. The driver was due to pick up the footballer Jason Kemble."

Another deep breath. Faces stared at him.

"Well, everyone in football knows Kemble is as gay as a maypole. The stolen car hit a number plate reader at a traffic light one minute ago. It went into a car park on Brookes Street."

There was a second of silence as everyone looked at each other, then bedlam. The DI, who had heard everything, came out of the office.

"Right, I want everyone down there looking for this car. You," he said pointing at the uniformed cop. "Put it out over the air I want every unit in the West End looking for this prick."

The cop nodded and turned to go back down the stairs, talking on the radio whilst still panting. In the incident room there was a mad scramble for car keys.

Conner looked at the car key board. He noticed a set had fallen off and were lying on the floor. He quickly went over and picked them up just DS Parsons got there.

"I'll have them, PC Conner," Parsons said, holding his hand out. Conner dropped them into his open palm.

"Stay here and write up your actions," Parsons said, throwing the keys up into the air and catching them. "Oh Amber, you can come with me, if you like?"

Amber shook her head.

"Oh well, keep out of trouble, you two!" Parsons shouted as he walked out of the office.

They both looked at one another.

"Come on!" Conner said excitedly.

They ran down the stairs and stopped at the first floor. They turned into the nick proper, past the custody block and storerooms into an open plan office which was used by uniform officers as a writing room. The place was a tip as normal. There were piles of paper, cans of fizzy drinks and sweaty stab vests. A sign on the printer said, "BROKEN AGAIN".

Two cops were writing up Incident Report Booklets. They must have a prisoner, thought Conner. He approached the older one.

"Mate, can I borrow your motor, if you're going to be stuck in with a body? It's just a quick suspect on call."

The older officer, a middle-aged man obviously tutoring a proby, looked up and seemed to be sussing him out. All cops have this innate ability to recognise an *arsehole*. This of course was most people, but the trick was establishing the level of arsehole in front of you. The cop threw him the keys, adding, "All right mate, just do the mileage and don't prang it. It's out on the street."

Conner nodded thanks, Amber grabbed a police radio, and they both ran out.

****

Thirty seconds later, Conner was driving on *blues and twos* along George Street in one of the Met's ubiquitous marked-up white Vauxhall Astras. Amber was in the passenger seat, listening in to the talk group on the police radio. The world and his dog were making their way to the car park on Brooke Street. The first car on the scene was a local uniformed unit. A young female voice came over the air.

"Charlie X-ray, Two One,"

"Go ahead, Two One," the control room replied.

"We are in the car park. The car is here. Standby."

Silence.

"Yeah, Two One here, we need an ambulance please. I have a male with serious stab wounds in the vehicle. Unconscious but breathing."

"Received," replied the controller.

"I'm also going to need officers to cordon the scene. The suspect is not here but is likely to be nearby."

Amber started to look at a battered A-Z street guide left in the door cavity.

"He could have gone anywhere," she said.

Conner continued to weave in and out of traffic, the sirens doing their job of getting everyone out of the way. Shops and people were blurs of colour in the passenger windows. They were at least five minutes ahead of the unmarked vehicles as he turned onto Grosvenor Square and started to look for something out of place. He knocked off the blues and twos.

Conner had learned by looking for terrorists in Northern Ireland that there were three things that made people stand out in an area. Their clothing, their behaviour and the fact that they look out of place for a specific location. This is often referred to as *stereotyping*. He liked to call it his *spidey sense*.

There were lots of people about. It was a nice evening, and people were dressed in t-shirts and jeans. A few *suits* were having a drink after work in groups. Groups of tourists. Male and female. Black and White. But it was a young hip crowd. They drove down on to St. George's Street. His head on a swivel like a fighter pilot. Looking for someone who didn't fit.

Then Conner saw him.

At the junction with Maddox Street stood a tall man in his early thirties, though he looked and dressed older. He was panting slowly. Trying to catch his breath. He kept opening and shutting his eyes as if blocking something out. Conner noticed he was in a dark suit, but it was too small for him. Too warm for the city. Too tight across the chest. Too threadbare. The man didn't have a briefcase or bag. Bingo. That's him. Conner was now about thirty metres away. People passed in front of the tall man, but he had locked on.

"Look over there, geezer on the corner of Maddox," he said to Amber.

"Worth a stop," she said, after assessing the male as a proper arsehole.

Conner continued to drive up to the junction. They would park up and, as they were in plain clothes, get closer on foot. As he got out of the car, he could see that the tall man was still on the corner, but was now looking more composed. He had taken off his tie and stuffed it into his suit jacket pocket. The tall man felt for another heaver item in the other pocket and reassured himself it was there. He undid his top button and, as he did so, he looked straight at Conner, who was now only around twenty metres away. There was a split second of acknowledgement and then the man was turning and running as fast as he could away from Conner.

Amber called into the radio as they both burst into a sprint.

"Runner, Maddox Street. Possible suspect for the driver of the car involved in a stabbing."

"Units to Maddox Street, please. Possible suspect for an earlier stabbing," the control room echoed.

Units started to call up over the air and the sound of their own sirens drowned out their shouted callsigns. Conner and Amber gave chase, pushing their way through the crowds of people who, realising this was a police matter from Amber's radio blurting out, were now parting naturally. Conner was still nursing his broken ribs and he could see Amber pulling away from him.

Amber could see the tall man running in long strides down Maddox Street, past the designer clothing stores and towards Grosvenor Street. She was making ground on him and could feel the reassuring weight of her handcuffs and pepper spray in her back jeans pocket.

Her feet thundered on the pavement. Her target up ahead, getting closer. The public diving out of the way. Jumping back into shop doorways.

She was going to get this *bastard*. She would eradicate the shame she had felt of being a *victim*. Put it all right. Conner was a distance behind her. He was shouting and gesturing, but she couldn't make it out. On the corner of the street junction, a shopkeeper was putting out copies of the Evening Standard. The tall man clattered into him, then ran into his newspaper shop. Amber caught sight of her suspect entering the shop. She reached the store seconds later and went in to see knocked over displays of magazines and greeting cards. A terrified-looking, elderly Asian lady was standing behind the counter, pointing to the storeroom to her left. Amber took out her spray and ran in.

Conner arrived at the shop around ten seconds later. The male shopkeeper was looking down at something on the floor of the storeroom. The elderly female was crying and hiding her eyes with her brown patterned scarf. He skidded to halt in the storeroom. A fire exit door was open at the back of the room. Looking down he saw that behind a stack of cardboard boxes there was a body.

Amber's body.

He collapsed down beside her. She was on her back, eyes open. A thin wheezing noise was coming from her mouth. He looked to see red blood coming from her neck and seeping through her t-shirt around her stomach and chest.

"Don't just stand there, call a fucking ambulance!" he shouted at the shopkeeper.

Conner applied pressure to the side of her neck and fumbled for the police radio that was at her side.

"Control. I require urgent assistance. Officer down. Stab wounds to the neck and chest. Casualty conscious, but barely breathing."

The control room acknowledged, followed by the radio bursting into urgent police chatter which he didn't hear.

"Amber, it's Ryan," he whispered into her ear. "Come on now, baby, don't do this. Stay awake."

Conner put his hands on her neck and chest, trying to stem the flow of blood. He looked around for anything to use as a bandage. There was a roll of blue tissue paper on top of one of the boxes and he quickly unreeled it and stuffed it onto Amber's chest wound and pressed it into place. He then put tissue on her neck wound. Her blood bubbled out between his fingers.

"No, Amber, no. Come on now, hold on."

It looked like she was trying to say something, but instead a wretched noise came out of her mouth.

"Don't speak. It's ok, it's going to be ok."

He was urgently looking around for medical help. His heart beat so fast he could feel it in his throat. He looked back at her, his eyes moist. Tears running down his face. Everything running in fast forward. His thoughts racing.

He leaned close to her. The thinnest wisps of her breath on his cheek.

"I'll be here for you. When you're better. I can't… I can't lose you, now I've found you." A tear fell onto her soft cheek. "We'll go somewhere nice. Italy perhaps."

He tried to laugh. He failed.

Sirens wailed all around. But he could not hear them. He stared at Amber, wanting her to live. All that mattered was her.

Again, she tried to speak. He shook his head.

"Don't… don't. Save your energy."

And then, she squeezed his hand, which was holding the paper tissue to her bloodied neck. He leaned in, so his face was millimetres away from hers. She opened her mouth. He didn't expect anything, but somehow, somehow, she spoke in the faintest of whispers.

"Italy…ice cream."

Her brief strength vanished. Her eyes screwed up tighter. Her breathing even fainter.

Conner looked up and saw two firearms officers storm into the small room. At that moment he might as well have been a young squaddie in the Irish bandit country, cradling a dying soldier. These officers were basically heavily armed paramedics. He bellowed at the cops.

"Help, please, help. She's my girl! My girl."

Chapter 18

Hall Street, London W1A, 2113 hours, Wednesday 19th June 1996.

The early evening light was beginning to fade as Simon Gee rolled out from under a white Toyota Corolla that had been parked at the dead end of Hall Street. The vehicle had a blue pass in the window, no doubt connected with Great Portland Street Hospital which overshadowed the short road. From his position under the car, looking back down towards Weymouth Street, he had seen the black boots of police officers running around, putting up police tape, shouting instructions and getting shouted at. He could hear sirens blaring and dogs barking. At one point he could hear two radios chattering as two male police officers walked down the cul de sac past the car he was lying under. Desperately holding his breath, the cops realised it was a dead end and turned around and walked away. That had been three hours ago. When the light started to fade, and he thought the coast was clear, he ran to an alleyway opposite where he had been lying. Now, other than the cordon officers around the newsagents, London had moved on and the police were busy dealing with more sadness and pain elsewhere.

      The alleyway led to a service area for the hospital and, half way down as he was, Gee felt safe in the shadows. He brushed himself off and in the half-light could see his jacket was covered in blood. Some of it Kemble's, some of it the female officer's. It was obvious now to him that's what she was. He had expected the male officer, who had noticed him on the street and had gained ground on him, to walk into the shop. Gee had figured a quick stab to the gut would slow him down. But it had been a female that had burst in on him. A fighter too. She had refused to go down and so he had stabbed again and again. He had gotten away, but at what cost? This was not part of the plan. He had regretted his actions, especially seeing her lying there, bleeding to death. But he knew it had been a necessary evil. His job, his mission, must come first.

Kemble, it turned out, was not particularly good with real pain. He was a footballer after all. Within seconds, Gee had discovered that Kemble was very susceptible to torture. A twist of his fingers in the stomach wound. A punch to the columella of the nose and he had started to talk. Kemble had recognised the aftershave in the popper bottle as belonging to a man he knew from The Rutting Stag parties back in the eighties. He was an important man, an army officer, Kemble believed. Well connected. Powerful, had his own personal security team to ensure everything went smoothly. Yes, Kemble admitted that they had talked, screwed on occasion, but the violence, the beatings were too much for him. They had parted ways. Kemble had not seen him again, as The Rutting Stag parties folded soon after.

"A name, give me a name!" Gee had said, sticking his fingers into a stomach wound whilst turning the knife in another. A name was given, and Gee recognised it from the list.

The last but one name. Codename *Mr. Fox.*

"Where is he now?"

Another twist of the knife.

"I don't know where he lives. He left the Army suddenly. Went into politics. That's all I know, please, please ... help... me."

Kemble's voice had started to become slurred as he went into shock. Gee took the knife out of the stab wound.

Gee had let Kemble go unconscious and with five stab wounds to his stomach, he was slowly, but surely, bleeding out. Kemble was going to die. Gee had left the car in Brooke Street car park and walked out on to Maddox Street. He had stood on the corner of the street, feeling elated that he had identified his first abuser. His ultimate target. He had not recognised the name when he had seen it on the list. His research for his trigger plan had not shown that he had been an army officer. If true, it seemed to have been omitted from *Who's Who* and the internet.

Had it been covered up? But why?

The information about him going into politics was correct. Gee had discovered that Mr. Fox had gone into politics after a short spell trading in the City of London. He was the MP for Southwood East and a junior minister in the Ministry of Defence. Married to Veronica, two children both under ten, no doubt a dog, Range Rover and Volvo in the basement garage of a three-storey town house. Outwardly respectable, but Gee knew different. He just needed the address, the time and an opportunity.

However, at this moment, he was in an alleyway under the hospital and he had work to do. He took off his jacket, curled it up in a ball, and stuffed it with the bloodied knife into the bottom of metal bin situated just before the alley became the service area. The police search teams would find them in a few days, but by then it would be too late. The first part of his mission would have been accomplished and any evidence that was found would help fast-track him to the steps of the Old Bailey. Once there he would bring down the whole rotten system. Yes, the young male police officer had seen him, but it would take days to identify him, if at all. The female officer would likely die. The thought of which gave him no pleasure.

He rolled up his white sleeves to hide some of the blood stains that the jacket had not absorbed, scooped out some rainwater that had gathered in an upturned bin lid and rinsed his hands and face before smoothing back his hair. He knew Regent Park tube was a short walk away and once on the Underground he would be invisible amongst the masses. He would make his way back to his flat in Kilburn and put the last details together for his *Mr. Fox* trigger plan.

Standing in the alley, looking out into the light cast by the street lights, he believed he could hear the chants of football fans in the distance. Never a big fan of the so-called *beautiful game,* nevertheless, he imagined he was a footballer walking out of the tunnel into one of the great stadiums – Old Trafford, St. James Park, Wembley. He thought he could hear the distant fans chanting his name. Encouraging him on to complete his vital task. A modern gladiator taking on the lions. He was changing. He had changed. He had become an accomplished killer. Despite his reservations, he allowed himself to feel a sort of pride. He walked out of the alleyway, ready for the game to be concluded. An angel of vengeance.

As he walked calmly past the cordoned-off newsagent, the scene of the female officer's stabbing, Gee reflected that he was almost sad he wouldn't get to carry out the last trigger plan for *Mr. Wolf.* He had recognised the name immediately on reading it for the first time on the list, but could scarcely believe it. It would have been a challenge; hence the reason Mr. Wolf was last on the list. It's never easy to get close to *royalty.* But he had developed his trigger plan. The large house near Windsor, a little-known access route for the Gamekeeper. He had the outfit, the equipment and the patter. He was confident he would have killed Mr. Wolf if it had been required of him, although he himself would have probably died in the process. But that was not to be. Gee smiled to himself. He had the name of his first abuser. *Mr. Fox* and his family would now get his full attention.

****

Looking out of the top floor canteen window at New Scotland Yard, Ryan Conner could just about make out the Centre Point building that marked the boundary between the City of Westminster and the City of London. The two entities were worlds apart. The drugs, vice and violence seemed to know to stop at the City's *ring of steel*. Thanks to recent IRA bombings, the City of London Police had close to a thousand police officers covering a square mile with 24/7 armed response units and CCTV cameras covering every inch of pavement. It was basically a police state. Serious crime was almost zero. Meanwhile the understaffed, under-resourced, underappreciated Met Police lurched from one disaster to the next, of which this evening's horror show had been just the latest. Conner threw the plastic spoon that he had been absent-mindedly stirring a cold cup of tea with onto the table. He thought about the incident again. He had thought about nothing else since it happened three hours ago. Had it been his fault? Was he to blame for Amber being stabbed? The Professional Standards Department detectives had certainly implied that it was. But that was their job. Who knew what they really thought?

They had gone over the incident a dozen times.

Why had he taken the marked car?

"It was the only one available."

Why didn't they have full Personal Protective Equipment?

"There wasn't time."

Why had he let PC Mills go into the shop on her own?

"I thought she would hold the front of the newsagents, as I went around the back. But before I could get there, she went in."

Why had he not called for backup immediately?

"Because I was trying to save her life, you fucking prick!"

They had decided to stop after that. He had been served misconduct papers, par for the course, and told he would be doing admin duties in AMIT while the SIO decided what to do with him.

He had spoken with the Police Federation Welfare Officer.

"How do you feel, Ryan?"

"Fine."

That was it.

An electronic face reconstruction of the suspect had been done with a SOCO and he'd been sent for a hot drink, while a car was found to take him home. He had been sitting waiting ever since.

Amber may die.

The thought made him sick to his stomach, his head erupting in sharp pains. His eyesight phasing in and out. She was lying in the University College Hospital's Intensive Care Unit. The stab wounds to her neck, chest and stomach had caused her to lose nearly four pints of blood. Her injuries were life-threatening in the truest sense of the word. She was to go into surgery in the next few hours. It was not looking hopeful. Roger Kelly, her partner from the TSG, had gone to the hospital as soon as he heard, He had been at her bedside ever since. No one was going to tell an extremely large and sorrowful Jamaican TSG Officer that he couldn't stay with her. In the basement of the same hospital, Jason Kemble was laid out in the morgue awaiting a post-mortem examination. He had died while in theatre, from multiple stab wounds to the abdomen. He was the Tall Man's fifth victim. Would Amber be his sixth?

It was clear to Conner that the Tall Man was gaining in cunning, confidence and ruthlessness. A dangerous mix. How many more must this bastard kill? Would he ever stop? God, this was awful, but somehow he had to dig deep, focus on stopping this monster. For Amber. Yes, for Amber. He looked at his shaking hands. Focus on controlling his thoughts. Breathe, breathe, breathe. He imagined Amber talking to him. Telling him it would be all right. His hands stopped shaking. He dug deep. Deep into his past. The dark experiences of his past must harden him for what was to come. In that moment, he found a renewed sense of purpose. He started to become more than just who he was before Amber was stabbed. He became something else altogether. An angel of vengeance.

Just then one of the double doors swung open and a middle-aged woman in a smart white shirt and blue cravat came in. A member of the control room team he thought. She was holding two pieces of paper.

"TDC Conner?" She asked.

"Yeah."

"This has been faxed over from the Operation Pulse incident room. Something about, waste your own time not ours! Now that's not nice, is it?" she laughed.

Conner took the pieces of paper from her before she bustled out. The sheets were blurry from the number of times they had been re-faxed but he could make out the British Army Manning and Records, Glasgow emblem in the top right-hand corner. Underneath was the heading, "Members of the Royal Mounted Rifles discharged for reasons other than End of Service 1980-1990."

There was a list of twenty-five names with each individual's date of birth, height, National Insurance Number, blood group, reason for discharge and a small photo. He ravenously looked down the list and about two-thirds down his heart went cold. There was the man he had seen on Weymouth Street. He was about fifteen years younger in the photo, but it was him. The long face. The piercing tragic eyes. Conner looked at the name.

"Gee, Simon Oliver, 17/04/ 1964, 6' 3" CO65 53 21 A, O Neg, Attempted Suicide resulting in injury to spine and neck. Mental Abnormality. Medically discharged. Sloane Square Barracks 26/06/84."

Simon Gee was the *Tall Man*.

Conner was sure of it. Inspiration took him and it all started to fall into place. Very likely Gee had been involved in *Company Tyking* and had been driven to a suicide attempt because of the abuse. The Army had then got rid of Gee as quickly as possible whilst he was still vulnerable. Conner now had a suspect name and a picture of the killer's face. He just needed to find him.

At the bottom of the last page, there was another name that he had nearly missed. The ink had been badly blurred as it had come out of the fax machine, but he could just about make it out.

The title said, "Additional – Officer Ranks". He looked at the one name on the list and its details: "De Lacey, Sylvester Henry, The Lord, 15th Earl of Medbrook, 04/09/1960, NH 24 81 36 D". The reason for discharge and date were difficult to read, but to him it looked like "Required to Resign 05/09/92". The recruit picture was nothing, a black ink blob.

De Lacey, De Lacey, Conner said to himself. Sylvester De Lacey.

An electric pulse went through his body. It was the same feeling he had just before he made a good arrest, a dangerous drugs buy or solved a crime. It was what Ryan

Conner lived for. He pulled out the list of clients from the Sergio Firenze perfumery that had been folded up and stuffed into his back jean pocket. He frantically unfolded it and there on the third page near the top was what he was looking for. A client's name, who, the information said, had been buying the same bespoke bottle of aftershave for nearly twenty years, now costing a thousand pounds for a twenty-five millilitre bottle. The name, Sly De Lacey. The ex-Royal Mounted Rifles Officer. Gee's first abuser. The next victim.

Ryan Conner looked out of the New Scotland Yard canteen window as the last of the reflected sunlight began to fade from the City skyscrapers. He forced himself to breathe, slowly, steadily. He had his suspect. He had his next probable victim and a motive. He had a plan. What he needed was a group of people to put it into action. Not just the police, who were the biggest and meanest tribe in London, but a tribe within a tribe. His tribe.

Chapter 19

Ministry of Defence Main Building, Room 237, 2nd Floor, Westminster, 0834 hours, Friday 21st June 1996.

As the door opened to his private office, The Lord Sylvester De Lacey, 15th Earl of Medbrook, looked up from his alcohol-induced slumber to see his plump secretary waddle over to place a large cup of coffee and a copy of The Times on his functional office desk. The tippy-tap of keyboards, ringing phones and general office chatter pierced his ears and his hangover. Being only a *junior* minister meant he did have an office to himself, but it was among the general rabble.

"Morning, sir!" his secretary said, rather too cheerfully for his liking.

"Morning, Ann," he replied, through a bleary-eyed forced grin. "Please, call me Sly."

She giggled and waddled out with a stack of signed letters to post. The door shut, bringing some tranquillity to his office once more.

Thanks to the threat of Tony Blair's New Labour, everyone had to be more approachable these days. So, in response, he had dropped his titles and shortened his first name. Sly D L was how he was generally known now, which he didn't mind, because it sounded a bit like *Sly Devil,* which he knew he was. He took a sip of coffee and leaned back in his chair before swivelling around to look at the view over Whitehall and onto Horse Guards Parade through a large, security, blast-proof window. The sun was shining, picking out the intricate details of the stately buildings and reflecting off countless office windows. He could see commuters walking to work, already carrying their jackets over their arms due to the heat, and attractive young female secretaries in white sleeveless blouses and black pencil skirts striding along in high heels, enjoying the morning heat. At least he presumed they were attractive. Girls weren't really his area of expertise.

Taking another sip of coffee, the sun's heat radiating through the glass, he fell into a daydream. If he was honest with himself, he did miss the titles. After all an ancestor of his had earned them at Waterloo by holding a key farmhouse against the French onslaught. A mention in dispatches by The Duke of Wellington himself. Lands and deeds had followed. The family set for eternity. Sure, the family home had been saved by the National Trust in the forties, but the money had still rolled in from rents, bonds, stocks and shares. This was thanks to his father in the main. He grimaced when he thought of his father. The disapproving looks, the shouts of exasperation, the look of disappointment on his face the day he died. Sylvester was still a teenager at the time. Whoever said you only remember the good times was talking bullshit. Negative thoughts always have the upper hand in a bitter mind.

He had liked the kudos of being called The *Lord* Sylvester. When he was just fifteen years old, at Marlborough School, even the richest and most popular boys didn't have *The Lord* as a prefix. Despite his modest exam results, Belvedere College in Oxford had welcomed him. A fine college, good reputation, excellent social scene. The only drawback was the express instruction from his mother that he must join the Officer Training Corps like his forefathers before him. And, as it was a condition of his inheritance, he did as he was told for a change. Although never sporty, he was naturally fit, like a lightweight boxer. The physical element of military life had not phased him.

But what Sylvester had really enjoyed was the dominance he could exert over others in the unit. He adapted well and had moved up in seniority quickly. He was cunning, naturally authoritative, and was happy to let others do the heavy lifting, reporting to him how it went. He covered his laziness by encouraging an *Empowerment and Trust* strategy. It was bullshit of course. He generally didn't trust anyone, but was often too lazy to care.

Sylvester had never found the appeal of the fairer sex. They were soft, humble creatures in his experience. Easily swayed by money and charm. He had slept with a few, and it had left him cold. Although he'd had sex with other boys whilst being a boarder, he didn't think of himself as gay either. All that phoney camping it up made him sick. Why would you want to portray yourself as a weak woman? Pathetic. In either activity, there was no challenge, no excitement, no threat. It was all too clean. But then he happened upon a man who would change his life. Howard Linnet-Boyd had shown him a new world.

The son of a media baron, Howard was rude, arrogant and aggressive. Sylvester had first met him when they were both summoned to see the head porter after they had tried to slip back into *Halls* after lights out. Howard was a big guy, but he looked like he had taken a proper beating. A fact that he repeatedly denied to the head porter, despite the overwhelming evidence to the contrary. It had made Sylvester laugh, as Howard ran verbal rings around this poor little man in his ridiculous blue coat and hat. After being told they would be reported to the Master, they had gone for a drink in Howard's room. Although there were two beds, no one else had stayed in the room for long.

"It's a mystery," he said, with a wicked smile. "I'm very friendly."

Howard explained to Sly the reason for his appearance. He had gone to rob one of the queers down by the boathouse on the riverbank, a known cruising haunt. He would generally ask to be the giver and then beat the poor urchin up after and take all his money. He said it all in a very matter-of-fact tone. However, on this occasion one of the queers was a Thai boxer and was quite handy, as it turned out. Howard laughed and Sylvester nervously laughed along, amazed at how open he was being about his sordid exploits.

"You should come along next time, we'll get that bastard!" Howard suggested.

Sly had thought about it for a bit. It was risky, but exciting. It was getting him aroused just thinking about the violence. The pain. The control of a body before the sex act itself. He decided to take up the offer.

The next night, Sylvester had enticed the same male to the bushes near the boathouse. In Sly's first time as a *honey trap*, he proved a natural. Little did the man know that Howard was waiting for him. Sylvester had gotten in the first punch, breaking the man's nose. He had never felt so alive. Before his victim could retaliate, Howard had punched him in the kidneys and hooded him. They had beaten the man senseless, before taking turns to rape him. They did so, safe in the knowledge that the general distaste around homosexuality in the organisations of authority would mean it would never be believed, even if it were reported.

Howard picked up the victim's battered old wallet from the muddy ground, breathing heavily as he looked through it. He then took out the cash and then threw it back at the recumbent figure lying in the dirt.

"No hard feelings, old man," he had said, as Sylvester looked on with bulging, excited eyes.

The sadomasochistic clubs and parties in Oxford and London followed. De Lacey knew his tastes were a sexual and mental disorder of course. It was listed in the Diagnostic Manual of Mental Disorders. He could only be sexually aroused by the feeling of distress in others. He had tried being the person who was subjected to the domination, but it was not for him, although he knew he had started from the bottom up, as it were. He loved the tight leather, the sharp steel promising pain at any moment. The anticipation of the act of violence. Then the physical release. It was all these elements that turned him on. He was an addict. He knew it.

University flew by and he effortlessly walked out with a 2:1 in Medieval History. As per his inheritance instructions, the Army now followed and after an uneventful year at Sandhurst he was given a Commission. His final report had not been glowing.

"Too arrogant, too willing to let others take the risks and do the work. Calm under pressure, even if on the verge of being nonchalant in his decision-making. I recommend a line infantry regiment or even The Royal Mounted Rifles, bearing in mind his inherited titles."

In May 1980, The Lord, 2nd Lieutenant, Sylvester De Lacey, 15th Earl of Medbrook, Royal Mounted Rifles, arrived at Sloane Square barracks. Just in time for the summer party season.

After finding a private, known as his *man*, who would be paid to clean his ceremonial kit and look after his horse, 2nd Lieutenant De Lacey found that he had quite a lot of time on his hands. He had of course ridden horses before, so riding school was an enjoyable pastime. After the morning's watering order and two hours in the ménage, the rest of the day was his own. After four months of Riding School, he completed the Ceremonial Kit ride comfortably with the assistance of his man. Sylvester was generally in bed by midnight each night. Meanwhile, everyone else on his intake would get little more than two hours sleep before waking up to muck out the horses at 5.30 am. He would appear pristine at around eight in the morning.

He *passed off* seven months later, in front of his tearful mother. Howard had also attended and had spent the whole time laughing at the weird outfits, the strange shouting and complex formations. He told Sly how ridiculous it was that this strange pantomime was being taken so seriously by these crusty old men. Sylvester had to agree with him.

But it was when Lieutenant De Lacey was assigned to the mounted platoons that things got interesting. He had been assigned to 3 Platoon, which already had two very experienced sergeants. They knew how to run the stables, get the soldiers out to their duties on time and in good order. They also kept any complaints in-house. Some of their methods could be described as brutal. Sylvester occasionally saw privates with black eyes and what would look like cigarette burns on their arms or faces. But his deep belief in *Empowerment and Trust* would win the day and he didn't inquire too deeply into issues that didn't really concern him. With the sergeants running the show, he was only really required at the weekly platoon meeting or when he was on Queen's Life Guard. All the QLG duty meant to him was that he slept in the Officers' Mess at Horse Guards Parade rather than in his military flat. His daily routine didn't really change. He didn't ask too many questions about the laughter and screams that came from the Other Ranks Mess in the basement of the guard room. "Just a bit of fun with the *crows*, sir," was all he was ever told and that suited him.

All this free time meant he and Howard could seek out the sadomasochistic flesh pots of London. Having previously sought his thrills in robbing rent-boys, male prostitutes or men at cruising haunts, Sylvester could not now risk the adverse publicity if caught. So, he now threw himself into the gay club scene in Camden, Clapham and of course Soho. But he found what was to become his very favourite party, right under his very nose. It was organised by the Green Mafia, the criminal arm of the Royal Mounted Rifles.

Sylvester had heard of the Green Mafia of course. The stories had started at Sandhurst. One of his Physical Training instructors, Corporal Mason, was from the Royal Mounted Rifles and he was the meanest bastard of the lot. The sense of menace that radiated from him as he walked into the gym in razor-sharp green lightweight trousers and a bright white PTI vest was enough to make some of the other officer cadets feel physically sick. It was said that Mason was arrested for an armed robbery in Germany linked to the Green Mafia and, although nothing was proved, he'd been moved back to the UK at the earliest convenience.

The stories about the Green Mafia's exploits swirled around like magpies feeding off roadkill. However, when De Lacey got to Sloane Square Barracks, he realised the stories were just the tip of a criminal iceberg. Every week, the Colonel of the Royal Mounted Rifles at Sloane Square would issue a bulletin around regimental activity, upcoming events and, unusually for a British Army regiment, a criminal intelligence report around suspected Green Mafia activities. Individuals were never mentioned. That information was held by the Regimental Adjutant until there was definite proof, which rarely came. There were reports of drug dealing in the Mess staff's accommodation, prostitutes being arranged for junior NCOs, a break-in at a NAAFI shop, and burglaries at nearby supermarkets of alcohol and cigarettes. The list went on. Everyone would, of course, shake their heads in despair, but they knew deep down that the culture of the Green Mafia in the RMR had been around for a hundred and fifty years and there was no getting rid of it. It was down to the Provost staff to deal with. Who, unbeknown to most of the people in the room, were responsible for a large amount of the crime. Sylvester ignored the stories and the whole ruddy mess for the most part.

Then one day he was waiting for his horse to be brought forward to the mounting block by his man, when he noticed that it was a ginger-haired corporal leading his ride. Sylvester had seen the NCO around the stables, but being from another troop never had much interaction with him.

"Morning, Sir, you've got *Hector* this morning. A wee bit twitchy but a beautiful-looking creature," the corporal said, his ginger hair covered by the khaki stable cap perched way back on his head. One hand was on the rein, the other in his green coverall pocket.

"But I believe you're known to like a challenge, Sir. Like to control beautiful creatures?" he said, looking straight at him.

Sylvester mounted the horse and took hold of the reins.

"We all have our vices, Corporal," Sylvester replied, tightening the reins in his left hand and gripping his polished rifle in his right.

"We do that, Sir. We do that."

The corporal then turned, put both hands into his pockets and walked away laughing quietly to himself.

When Sylvester got back from Queen's Life Guard, he found a small note under his room door that read, "Exclusive Party Tonight - 1st Floor, The Rutting Stag, 9 pm. Black Tie, No Medals."

Intrigued, Sylvester decided to go along. He gave his kit to his man to clean, dug out his dinner suit, showered and shaved, before splashing on a generous drop of his favourite aftershave from Sergio Firenze. It was made bespoke for him. His own musical fanfare, the Italian perfumer had told him. A hint of oak, copper and the wet grass on an autumnal morning. It was how a man should smell. A mixture of scents that announced his arrival. He loved it. It cost around seven hundred pounds a bottle, but for Sylvester it was worth every penny.

The Rutting Stag was situated at the end of a short, dark cul-de-sac. It had a dirty red brick exterior with brown flaking paint on its blacked-out windows. Sylvester wondered if he was in the right place, as he walked into a smoky and unremarkable London pub. But having been looked up and down by the barmaid, he was directed through a door marked "PRIVATE" and followed the sound of excited chatter and the clinking of glasses up a set of scruffy stairs. At the top of the stairs, he turned into a large and very grand ballroom. The wallpaper was gold with a luxurious green ivy pattern swirling to the roof. Heavy burgundy velvet curtains covered the windows. Artfully crafted tables and chairs were placed in neat patterns. The most striking feature was the long bar at the far end of the room. It was glass fronted with a rich oak top and was in front of a large ornate mirror, which gave the impression the room was twice its size. Sylvester looked around as he walked up to the bar. He recognised a few faces from the Sloane Square social scene, a few businessmen from *The City*, apparently a footballer, and a few actors and rock stars of course. Also, rather surprisingly, yet reassuringly, a few faces from his *specialist* club scene. All were rich by either new or old money. At the bar he was met by the ginger corporal, now dressed in black tie.

"Good evening, Mr. De Lacey, please, call me *Ginger*, everyone does," he said, holding out his hand.

"Well, thank you for the invite, Ginger," Sylvester said, signalling to the barman, before shaking the offered hand. "I presume it came from you,"

Ginger laughed, but did not answer the question.

"Have a wee drink and mingle. If you would excuse me, I need to collect tonight's entertainment."

Sylvester circulated and had the normal chit chat, but the purpose of the party was not discussed. Then at 9.30pm there was the noise of feet clattering upstairs and in came around fifteen young men dressed in suits, shirts and ties. Sylvester recognised a few young faces from his regiment. Some went straight into the groups and were met like long-lost friends. Others stood around awkwardly before being approached and pulled into a black tie group. Soon the suits and the black ties were going out of the room and up to another set of stairs. It dawned on Sylvester what was happening. The party was effectively a male brothel.

Ginger reappeared. "Anyone grab your attention?" he said with a grin.

"Good Lord, man, are you mad?" Sylvester said, sounding incredulous. "I can't be involved in this, in my position. Not least because the men, some of whom I presume are RMR, will recognise me. No, thank you. I'll finish my drink and bid you goodnight."

"Of course, you are free to leave. But we do have special arrangements for those who want to be even more discreet. Perhaps you would like to follow me?"

Ginger walked towards the edge of the bar where there was a barely noticeable door cut into the mirror and wall. Sylvester finished his drink and then, against his better judgement, followed Ginger as he went through and up a flight of stairs. The opulence of the ballroom had been replaced by cold, stark chipboard and lightbulbs swinging from open wires. Ginger turned on to a landing and walked to another door which opened out into a large bedroom in keeping with the downstairs ballroom. Both men moved to the middle of the room.

"So, we have a service where we can bring a young gentleman to you in any state you desire," Ginger said, smoking, and picking a piece of loose tobacco from his lips.

"He can be dressed, stripped, tied up or already beaten. They can be hooded, or if you like to hear the screams of pain the room can be darkened. You will always have some security with you. They are very discreet of course. Yes, you're at the party, but no one sees you leave with anyone. It works very well, and you are not the first of our clients to take this service. We also offer young women at some of our other establishments. We're very *highly* recommended."

Ginger stood patiently as Sylvester decided what to do. He liked the vibe of the place, the thrill and the idea of giving some squaddie a good battering before buggering them.

"How much?" Sylvester said lighting a cigarette.

"A thousand pounds a night, free drinks and as many *encounters* as you like. Discretion is assured. We shut at 7 am and we drive you back to your lodgings."

Ginger spoke as if he had made the offer a hundred times, which of course he had.

Sylvester took a long drag on his cigarette, then wiped some smoke out of his eye. It was very tempting. No fuss. Just enough risk to satisfy him. He could pick and choose his victims. But let someone else do the initial dirty work.

"When can it start?" he asked.

"Why tonight of course. The night is young. Now let's discuss your requirements…"

Sylvester had chosen men that he thought would fight. Ideally tall, dark-haired and wiry. Sometimes he would have them bound and ready, other times they would just be thrown into the room. He would sneak around in the darkness with the advantage. He loved the thought of his aftershave catching his prey's nostrils before he moved in. His security had done all the fetching and carrying. They also got involved once or twice. A safety word would be used to restore the balance in his favour. He had his favourites, for whom he would ask several times, but would get bored after a few months and move on. The *Tykes*, as the men were called, would be recirculated around the party, or sometimes they would just disappear. It had all gone so well. Occasionally Sly would be asked for a signature for some exotic military kit Ginger and his *friends* would require and he'd be happy to oblige. It was a mutually beneficial arrangement. That was until the day he received his orders to move on.

Lieutenant De Lacey was to be given an *opportunity* to develop. Twelve months as a Training Officer at The School of Infantry in Warminster, then real command. He would be the Royal Mounted Rifles' liaison officer for Northern Ireland ahead of a regimental tour. Overall, a two-year posting out of London. Sylvester had gotten very drunk when he was given the news and cried himself to sleep. It was the beginning of the end for Sylvester De Lacey's military career.

Things did not go well from the start. He found his new role consisted of tedious yet demanding work. He spent hours in meetings, praising and berating in equal measure. Warminster was just too far away from London, although he did manage to make it back occasionally. But by then, the parties at The Rutting Stag had stopped. Apparently, the press had got a sniff that royalty was involved, and this had fizzled out the client base. The link to royalty was never proved, of course, and Sylvester sometimes wondered if they mistakenly meant him. Then terrible news came, when he read in the paper that Howard Linnet-Boyd, the son of the media tycoon Mozart Boyd, had been killed in a motorbike crash in Marrakech. He had been chased by the police shortly before the accident and his father was crying foul play. Sylvester suspected that Howard had earned his police attention, but was still devastated at the news. It had taught him how cruel yet precious life could be. He decided he would not be one of life's cruel victims. He would be crueller still. The giver, not the taker.

The year at Warminster passed slowly and Sylvester learnt a lot about infantry tactics, though probably not as much as he should have. He did learn how to conduct a meeting so he never came out with any extra work. How to get others to believe that you were the smartest in the room and follow your advice. How to task out large pieces of work to lower ranks and then sell them to the higher ranks as his own labours. He learnt how spreadsheets and lavish documents could deflect a lot of scrutiny around his work. Then on 1st February 1992, he was deployed to Fermanagh in Northern Ireland. The Royal Mounted Rifles were taking over from 2 Para in June, so he was attached to their A Company, as an observer before the main party arrived. He found the Paras to be a bunch of Neanderthals. Even the officers came from comprehensive schools, with not a title amongst them. He would be called *Boss* rather than *Sir* and he would rarely get a salute. True, they were shit hot in the field and tough, but he was glad to see the back of them as the Green Mafia moved into St. Angelo barracks in Enniskillen.

Captain De Lacey occupied himself with long meetings with the Colonel, the Intelligence Officer, the Company Commanders and the Platoon Commanders. He had secured the training officer role, which meant no *bog trotting* for him. He would patrol a carpeted corridor for six months, with a soft bed and occasional trips to Belfast for seminars and conferences. Then one day, his lack of real soldiering caught up with him.

The first four months of the tour had taken a toll on the Royal Mounted Rifles. So far, two RMR privates had been killed by a culvert bomb in West Fermanagh, with two more injured in the same explosion including a lieutenant. A captain was injured when a sniper had killed a Royal Ulster Constabulary officer at a check point and the bullet had gone through the policeman, hitting the RMR officer in the thigh. The operational teams were running short of officers and so Captain De Lacey had been sent out from his warm office to oversee the inner and outer cordons for an arms search at a disused farmhouse just five hundred metres from the border with the Republic of Ireland. This had meant liaison with the *Garda Siochana,* the Irish civilian police. He had met with a Chief Inspector Seamus Callahan at a road junction near to where the borders touched. The Chief Inspector had been cheerful enough. They had exchanged pleasantries and Sylvester was assured that the house had been watched by a Garda surveillance team for at least a week and no one had been in or out in that time. There was also no intelligence to suggest that the premises was booby trapped.

"Why blow up your own guns?" the Chief inspector had said cheerfully.

Empower and Trust, Sylvester had thought to himself and left it at that. He had returned to the RVP and spoken to the other Platoon Commanders overseeing the cordons on the British side of the border. The inner and outer cordons were in place, he was told. Captain De Lacey had assessed the risk as low, so no need for Explosive Ordnance Demolition officers. Counter Terrorist Search Team soldiers could enter the building taking normal precautions. Let's crack on. He gave a thumbs up to the Search Team corporal.

Captain De Lacey was just lighting his third cigarette when the explosion ripped through the building and machine gun fire started thumping into the ground and into the soldiers around him.

The after-action enquiry that followed the bomb and machine gun attack at Roslaw Farmhouse did not go well for Sylvester. Four soldiers dead, twelve injured. A major coup for the IRA, who not only detonated a bomb on British soil but had broken through the Garda cordon to give accurate fire on the RMR troops. The enquiry discovered that in all likelihood the bomb had been placed in the farmhouse three to four days before the search. The Garda had only been watching the house for forty-eight hours. The real Chief Inspector Seamus Callahan had been found two hundred metres away from the meeting place with De Lacey. He had been stripped to his underwear, his hands bound, mouth gagged. The questions had then started flying at Sylvester like a swarm of angry bees.

Had he not noticed that the uniform didn't fit or was not correctly worn?

Had the radio been switched off? Was this not suspicious?

Why didn't they sit in the vehicle?

Did he ask to see observation logs? Intel reports?

It was unrelenting.

He had taken the blame and was asked to resign his commission. In return, his name would be kept out of the papers. His so-called friends in the regiment distanced themselves from him. They had always felt he had a whiff of unpleasantness about him, but they could not deal with him being incompetent as well. He was a civilian within three months. An outcast, not even allowed to be seen at the military funerals. Sylvester burned with fury, with injustice that he had been made the scapegoat. He had been called sloppy, unprofessional and lazy when the inquiry published their findings. He faded into oblivion and for a time his life was in utter turmoil.

He moved back to Essex and into his mother's smart Georgian house in the countryside. He started to rebuild his life and took responsibility for Roslaw, on the surface anyway. Deep down he still seethed about how he had been sacrificed by the regiment. He joined the local Conservatory Party. Not needing to work, he threw himself into the running of the local party. His accent, organisation skills and ability to bend people to his will resulted in increasing importance at the local branch. He met a girl and got married. Some children followed, although the marriage was a pretence for respectability purposes. After the sitting MP for Southwood East died suddenly, he was convinced to stand and won a tight by-election. He was now The Lord Sylvester De Lacey, 5th Earl of Medbrook, MP. Once at Westminster, his skills and competent, relaxed manner were in demand. These qualities often outweighed the rumours of a mishap in Northern Ireland amongst his colleagues. It was combat after all. Who knows what goes on in the fog of war? Then there was the over-friendliness with the young male interns. "He's married. He just wants to inspire them to greater things," his allies would say. Minor committees and the chair of a working group followed, until he was installed as a Junior Minister for the Ministry of Defence with a single portfolio.

Now turning back to his desk, he looked at the green paper laid out in front of him. It spelled out his single portfolio, and it was entitled, "The reduction and amalgamation of line regiments in the British Army."

He turned the front page and the first point read: "The efficiency savings to be made by the disbandment of the Royal Mounted Rifles, both armoured and mounted regiments, and the redeployment of existing troops to the two remaining Household Cavalry Regiments."

Sylvester smiled to himself as there was a knock on the door.

"Your attendees for the 10 am are here, sir," Ann said, as she ushered in a series of grumpy-looking, purple-faced old men in Army uniforms, the heads of the Royal Mounted Rifles among them.

"Gentlemen," Sylvester De Lacey said. "So pleased you could make it – to discuss our shared future."

Chapter 20

London, 0900 hours, Saturday 22nd June 1996.

An average day in the Metropolitan Police is still a relatively busy day by normal standards. Even so, there are small days and there are big days. A small day could be a Tuesday at the end of January. No murders, no large protests and only one or two serious incidents. Today was not going to be one of those days. Today was a big day. Maybe the biggest in thirty years.

Wembley Stadium had seen its fair share of big days since it was built in 1928 but today could see the England national football team reach a European Cup semi-final for the first time ever. Standing in their way was an impressive Spanish team, who were their opponents at today's quarter-final. Kick-off was scheduled for 3 pm in front of a packed Wembley and a global TV audience of billions. The Met's policing response to the event had started as soon as the England team had qualified. The eleven thousand extra officers on duty had either been briefed at their home stations and were now patrolling in vans around Wembley, the West End, Camden, Islington, Brixton or Clapham, or they were on their way to an event briefing.

In Piccadilly, England fans were decked out in red and white shirts and bucket hats and had started to drink their first of many lagers of the day. It was a beautiful morning, sunny, bright and already getting hot. Supporters from both teams had gathered in loose knots in front of the pubs and bars. Giant St. George's flags were draped on walls and metal barriers. The singing of football songs and the now omnipresent "It's coming home!!" rang out from every corner. Police officers patrolled the *hot spots* on foot in pairs or vanned up, peering out of blacked-out Mercedes van windows. It continued to get hot and by 10.30 am the cops were queuing up for free ice creams.

Around five thousand of the extra officers had made their way to a non-descript trading estate just south of Wembley Way. Here, they had been given an English breakfast and received a briefing from the Operational Bronze Commander. Officers were told to be alert to the terrorist threat, not only from the IRA, but also ETA, the Basque Separatist Organisation. Any suspicious vehicles or packages must be reported to *Event Control* immediately. The Football Intelligence Unit had deemed the threat of crowd violence low. There was no trouble expected between the rival fans. The Spanish crowd tended to turn on their own team before the opposing fans, but there was always the prospect of a small but determined gang of English hooligans wanting to steal the show. Nowadays, thankfully, football had changed for the better and the thugs would be vastly outnumbered by well-meaning supporters, including families. The purpose-built custody suites, which were just big metal cages in a separate lock-up, had been swilled out with white spirit and were open for business.

Full of sausage sandwiches and banter, the Met officers then travelled to Wembley in their respective vans and stepped out into the morning sunshine. They put on thin reflective jackets over their crisp, white shirts and adjusted their custodial helmets to shade their eyes. It was going to be a big, but enjoyable day.

Ten miles south of Wembley, sitting in the back of a battered old Vauxhall Corsa in Soho, Ryan Conner had also planned a big day. He had spent the last forty-eight hours planning, when he should have been cataloguing the Operation Pulse unviewed CCTV. He had called in favours, mustered some charm to secure staff, circulated a briefing pack to those involved, booked custody space at Paddington Green, and had been allocated an operation name, Op. Midway. This at least made it all legit. He had even managed to get an overtime code. With most of the Met tied up with the football, he knew this was a good day to turn his plans into action. But despite all his hard work, he was missing a few vital elements. The most important of all for him personally was Amber. She was still in intensive care and her life was in the balance. She was due another operation today and her family were now at her bedside in case the worst should happen. He was petrified that this would be the case. He had hardly slept in days, thinking about what could have been and what would be.

He was exhausted, but he had to push on. Live off his adrenaline and channel his nervous energy into positive actions. He was also still missing a private address for Sylvester De Lacey MP, but he had Emma, his favourite analyst from Op. Garden City, working on it with the Parliamentary and constituency offices.

He checked his personal phone again, still no text from Emma about the address. He checked his Op. Atlantic drug dealing phone. Still no text from Peter saying he had got hold of the drug dealer known as White Boy. Conner ran his hand through his unkempt hair and rubbed his unshaven chin. He picked up a handheld radio and broadcast, "No Change, No Change," over the back-to-back channel.

Two members of the Brixton Crime squad, who were sitting in the front of the car in their scruffs, passed the time by smoking and talking about girls. Conner needed things to happen and fast.

The Met had not sorted out the murders by the Tall Man. But he now knew the suspect to be an ex-Royal Mounted Rifles private called Simon Gee. He also knew that his likely next victim and first abuser was Sylvester De Lacey MP. Conner had experienced a *Eureka* moment when he had recognised the face of De Lacey from the British Army Manning and Records report. It had also not been lost on him that De Lacey had been the RMR officer in charge of the search at Roslaw Farm, which had nearly cost him his life, and had claimed the lives of four of his comrades. Conner had remembered how *Captain* De Lacey had disappeared shortly after the military inquiry into the bombing. The inquiry was a whitewash. Nothing more was ever said. Now Sly De Lacey MP was in the news as a defence minister wanting to disband several British Army regiments, starting with the Royal Mounted Rifles. It was all too much of a coincidence and he had been a cop long enough to know there was no such thing.

But what or who was behind it all? Certainly, he had been sent a very clear message, in the form of a beating, that he was getting too close, after visiting Sir Hugh Fairfax, the Provost Marshal. But could the most senior military policeman in the land really be involved?

The Met would not listen to his *wild* theories, so he would have to sort this out himself. After all, the thing that everyone had always said about Ryan Conner, whether fighting in the sink estates of Coventry or in the fields of the Irish Badlands or on the mean streets of London, was that if he believed he was right, he would never give up.

He would start by giving the Green Mafia a couple of *distraction strikes*. Two black eyes. He looked at his personal phone. It was ten to eleven in the morning. It was almost time for the first blow to be struck.

****

In the still, summer air, the rattle of chains and bridles could be heard by the near silent crowd of tourists that had gathered behind metal barriers at either side of Horse Guards Parade. In amongst the obligatory American and Japanese families was a tall, slim and attractive Rwandan girl, who used to go by the name of Mimi, but had recently been using her given name of Isaro Kaza Gera. She was wearing a brand new blue floral pattern dress that she had bought with a discount card she was given when she started to work for a fashion shop in Covent Garden. The placement had been specially arranged by the Immigration Services whilst her claim was being processed. She wore a long black wig in the *Beyoncé* style and her facial scar had been discreetly hidden by makeup. Upon looking at her, one would say she was an African beauty. Since starting her new job, a week ago, she had the routine of walking from her flat in Southwark to the shop in Covent Garden for her late shift, but today she had received a text first thing.

"HORSE GUARDS PARADE 10.45 AM. AMBER."

Although it was not PC Mill's number, she trusted her enough, and owed her enough, to go along with it.

Mimi was vaguely aware of the Changing of the Life Guard and that it took place at the back of Whitehall, on a large, beige, gravelled parade square. From her vantage point on the left-hand side of the square, looking up towards the imposing Horse Guards building, she could see two lines of mounted soldiers facing each other. The ones closest to her were wearing red jackets. The ones opposite were wearing green jackets. Around them was a circle of armed police officers in their black-checked peaked caps, with black bulletproof vests worn over gleaming white shirts. She scanned the faces of the mounted soldiers in green jackets opposite her. The green jackets had red trim and were crossed by a leather belt. All the men were holding short rifles propped up on their white trousered thighs, which were partially obscured by large polished black boots. In what she called her *previous life*, she had become intimately acquainted with some members of this regiment. However, she could not recognise the faces of the men she saw today, sitting as they were on large black horses, with faces shadowed under black furry hats. That was until she saw the last man at the end of the green line.

Mimi would never forget this face, even if it was disguised by a ceremonial uniform. His orange hair and ruddy, freckled face were still visible under his black hat. It was Ginger from the barracks. She had bent to his sordid wishes too many times to ever forget his face. The smell of his stinking breath and sweaty body was entrenched in her nostrils like a rude relative who had outstayed their welcome. She watched him with a hate only a thousand scars to a human soul can cause. She figured he was why she had been summoned here and was eager to see what would happen.

Between the two lines of soldiers on horseback, two ornately decorated mounted soldiers, who Mimi assumed were the officers, suddenly braced up and exchanged salutes. It appeared that the next stage of proceedings was about to commence, but what did happen, no one could have predicted. The armed police officers near the parade suddenly started to react to three black saloon cars moving at speed from the direction of the Guards Memorial on Horse Guards Road at the bottom end of the parade square. The armed officers on that side of the cordon swung around to face the vehicles, lifting their assault rifles and pointing them at the fast-approaching cars. A girl did not grow up in war-torn Rwanda without learning a thing or two about firearms and Mimi knew an assault rifle when she saw one.

Fearing a terrorist attack, the police officers started to shout, "STOP, STOP! ARMED POLICE!" Their raised, clear voices rang out across the parade ground.

The approaching vehicles started to fan out to reveal a yellow and blue marked police car in the centre of the convoy, that stopped around ten metres from the parade. The two black saloon cars took up positions either side of the white one. Mimi could make out the words *British Transport Police* around the multi-bladed police badge on the side of the blue and yellow police vehicle. The passenger doors of the black cars sprung open and she could see armed police officers wearing fluorescent yellow hats. These cops wore black jumpsuits and took up positions kneeling behind the car doors, wooden rifles raised.

This was now an armed standoff. To Mimi it seemed that the crowd took a sharp intake of breath as one. In front of Mimi, and slightly to the right, she became aware of a commotion as four men jumped the metal barrier in front of her. The men were wearing jeans and heavy jackets, but now she could see that they had put on fluorescent yellow police baseball caps. Mimi smiled to herself as the team of four men ran up and surrounded

Ginger on his startled horse. They raised their revolver handguns and pointed them straight at him.

"ARMED POLICE! PASS DOWN THE WEAPON! THEN PLACE YOUR HANDS ABOVE YOUR HEAD!"

Ginger visibly slumped in his saddle. He passed the weapon down to one of the plainclothes armed policeman. It was the fear on Ginger's face that Mimi savoured the most. She then turned to see a middle-aged female, dressed in a smart blue business suit, with a leather Police ID badge slung around her neck, alight from the marked police car and stride confidently across the parade square. Clearly a senior detective, she was flanked by two uniformed male officers.

"Officers, please lower your weapons," Mimi heard the detective say calmly, as she walked past the Met's armed police. The female detective stopped in front of where Ginger Bailey was being helped from his horse by a plainclothes BTP armed officer. Mimi could see the detective had locked eyes with Ginger like a tractor beam. Mimi listened intently.

"Thomas Bailey, I am Detective Sergeant Shelia Dean from the British Transport Police's Robbery Squad. I am arresting you on suspicion of Attempted Robbery and Grievous Bodily Harm in Liverpool Street Tube Station on the fifteenth of June 1996. You do not have to say anything, but anything you do say may be given as evidence."

Turning to one of the uniformed officers, she added, "Cuff him, please."

"And oh," DS Dean said, turning back to Ginger, "I've had a Section 18 5 PACE police search warrant authorised by my Inspector. The search teams will be commencing a thorough search of your accommodation and that sordid hell hole of a bar on the *Top Floor* of Sloane Square barracks right about…"

She stopped to look at her watch, then engaged her tractor beam. "Now."

Mimi saw that Ginger Bailey stood shocked, speechless. He took off his ceremonial hat and dropped it on the gravel. He then placed his head in his hands. His hands then went into cuffs.

By now, the army officers had got down from their horses and were remonstrating with anyone in police uniform they could find. DS Dean calmly approached them, patting her hands down in appeasement as she did so.

"Gentlemen, gentlemen. Please let me explain…" Mimi heard the detective say.

Mimi turned and hitched her brown leather handbag onto her shoulder. A huge smile on her beautiful face. As she set off to walk to work, she could see the countless flashes of tourist cameras going off. The lights caught her eye, just above her fading scar.

****

Sitting in the back seat of the Vauxhall Corsa opposite the cul-de-sac that led to The Rutting Stag, Conner felt one of his phones vibrate. He took out his personal phone to read the message displayed on the screen. It was from DS Shelia Dean.

"FIRST BLOW STRUCK. ONE IN THE BIN. SEARCHES ONGOING. WILL UPDATE YOU IF ANYTHING FOUND. I STILL OWE YOU BIG TIME! AMANDA SAYS HI SHE STARTS UNI IN SEPTEMBER!"

Conner smiled to himself at the thought of Shelia's daughter going to university. It could have all been so hugely different.

His dealer phone then started to buzz. It was Peter.

"WHITE BOY UP AND ABOUT. 10 MINS SAME PLACE. WHERE THE FUCK RU"

He looked up just in time to see Peter and two other junkies walking around the corner of the cul-de-sac from the direction of the pub, heading toward the Brewer's Street car park.

Conner grabbed the radio.

"All units, ten minutes, Brewer's Street car park. Take up your positions, please."

The units started to acknowledge over the air,

"Bravo X Ray 41 received. Bravo X Ray 42 received…"

He gave the radio to the officer in the front passenger seat. Conner was now full of excited, nervous tension as he put on his lucky sky-blue baseball cap and pulled it down over his face.

"Good luck, buddy," the driver said to Conner. He nodded back to him and exited the car to catch Peter up. It was time to be *Mark* the druggie again.

****

As Peter walked along at warp speed, trying to keep up with the other junkies, he became acutely aware that he felt fucked off, big style. It would have been too early for him if it wasn't for the fact he'd be working all night and had yet to go to bed. He'd found himself with the dregs of a whiskey in The Rutting Stag when Mark had texted him at 9 am this morning. Peter thought it typical; he had not

247

heard from Mark for ages and then suddenly he wanted to score and he was back. To be fair he was *clucking* badly as well so he had made the call to White Boy. Peter's last hit had been well over twelve hours ago in a shitty shop doorway behind Piccadilly and he had to share that with some crack whore who had gone halves. The worst thing was, when high, she kept pestering him for a fuck for a tenner. She didn't seem to get that he was in no way interested. Then he'd had an almighty argument with Ken. They loved each other still of course. But even Ken was seeing his decline. Ken had told him he looked thinner, his teeth were blackened by crack smoke, his skin was flaking and blistered. He had not taken the criticism well.

But it was not just that, as true as it might be.

Peter was all too aware that the game was getting increasingly risky with the punters. HIV was back on the scene and a lot of the *Johns* these days wanted to fight you, then fuck you. He wanted to pack it all in. Live with Ken in the suburbs. Get the whole West End scene out of his veins along with the drugs. One day, maybe.

Just then Mark ran up next to him and jolted him back to reality.

"Where the fucking hell have you been?" Peter asked him, with more spite than he intended.

Mark kept up the pace and said breathlessly, "Got banged up for a robbery. Pigs kept me in on remand, but the Judge let me go first hearing. Fucking mug."

Peter wasn't really listening.

The gaggle of junkies went through the pedestrian access door of the car park and scrambled up the piss-stinking steps to the second floor. There they waited for White Boy's blue BMW to arrive. Both men smoked in the corner of an alcove.

Peter liked Mark. He had saved him from an almighty kicking, maybe from being killed, after all. But something didn't seem to fit. He looked rough, sure. But today he seemed more stressed out. More on edge than usual. This would be the last time he would help Mark out, he thought to himself. He'd tell him after this deal. His thoughts were disturbed by the racing of tyres as the blue BMW swung up the ramp and into the car park, coming to a stop just in front of the addicts.

The window came down and the regular driver with the slicked-back hair and wrap-around shades was sitting staring straight ahead as normal. Peter had called him, so he pushed his way to the front, reminding everyone of that fact and that they should wait their fucking turn.

He went to the driver's window and saw that there were two other males in the rear passenger seats. The male behind the driver's seat was tall and muscular, with a serious face underneath a tight blonde haircut.

"One and one, bruv," Peter said, offering forty pounds.

Without saying a word, White Boy dipped into the central console and produced a small white wrap and a small brown wrap, then handed them to Peter. Nearly snapping his hand off, Peter took the precious packages and moved back to the gaggle to wait for Mark, who was now being served up, his hat pulled down over his face, keeping low. Mark was second in a group of six. He was in and out quick. Peter then saw him take his baseball cap off to wipe his brow before placing it back on his head with the peak now facing backwards as he walked away from the car.

Peter could not have realised that this was a signal to unleash a cold blue fury.

Whilst another scruffy white male was being dealt to, a large white transit van came hurtling down the vehicle ramp, stopping around twenty metres away. The van had blocked off the only vehicle exit. Suddenly the side door slid open and out poured five men in police caps and black stab-proof vests over t-shirts. Extendable batons were being drawn and racked, as shouts of, "POLICE, POLICE! STAY WHERE YOU ARE!" echoed around the car park.

From the bottom ramp, a red Vauxhall Corsa and a grey Ford Galaxy sped into the car park, unloading four more similarly dressed police officers. Two of the officers placed out long chains with tyre spikes across the front of the BMW, effectively sealing the vehicle in. The driver's door of the BMW burst open and White Boy jumped out and started to make a run for the car park wall, clearly intending to jump over. Two officers got to him first. One rugby tackled him to the floor, before the other took his arms and started to cuff him.

Peter had gone to run, but one officer, an Afro-Caribbean male with a hair comb sticking out of his hair, seemed to head straight for him, passing other junkies on the way. The cop grabbed his arms and handcuffed him where he stood.

Peter let out a sigh, which could have been relief.

Two large males got out from the back of the BMW, but they didn't panic. They came out of the car still wearing shades. One, the tallest and largest male, was wearing a red Kappa jacket, the other a black fleece. Each one carried a green two-foot-long pickaxe handle with a metal collar at the end. The remaining officers split up to take on these fearsome-looking characters between them. A split second passed, then the males from the BMW came out, swinging their wooden weapons. Red Kappa Jacket connected his pickaxe handle with a police officer at head height sending him reeling to the floor. Another officer tried to get the male in a bear hug but got the pickaxe handle in the gut. A third caught the return thrust underneath the jaw.

Then Peter saw the strangest thing he had ever seen in his life. Mark, who had been standing with the other junkies near the stairs, seem to physically change. He got taller. Filled out. He threw his hat off and walked calmly over to where Kappa Jacket was standing over the three sprawled-out officers. There was a moment of realisation between the two men, then the muscular male swung the pickaxe handle behind his head shouting with anger.

"You! You fucking crow!"

Peter saw the large man take a huge swing for Mark with his makeshift club, who ducked and then came up into the face of the man, headbutting him in the nose. The large man staggered back and gave a half an effort to swing the handle back, but Mark caught the inside of his arm before raising a knee into the inside of the man's thigh. Mark's left fist then flew out connecting with the other man's solar plexus. This caused his attacker to drop onto one knee. Mark then appeared to jump in the air, kick out his right leg behind him and summon a powerful punch with his right hand that caught the larger man in the side of his head, sending broken sunglasses into the air and the male to the floor. Two of the three injured police officers then jumped on the now prone assailant and wrestled him into cuffs before holding him down. The officer who had been hit in the head with the pickaxe handle slowly got up and stood over the now contained monster in the red Kappa jacket pinned to the floor.

Staunching a bloody wound from the side of his head, the officer said, "You're nicked for dealing controlled drugs and GBH. You *fucking* prick."

Over near the white van, the male in the black fleece had his hands over his eyes and was squealing like a madman. He was also struggling to breathe, since a whole canister of CS spray had been emptied into his face. No one helped him, and then he was nicked. Two officers took Mark down to the floor without a fight and placed him in cuffs before taking him over to the red Vauxhall Corsa and placing him in the back.

Peter sank to his knees. Maybe this was meant to happen. He dropped the wraps that had been in his hands and was promptly arrested for Possession of a Class A drug.

The plain-clothed police officer who was standing with him helped him back up to his feet and cautioned him, adding, "I suspect that the place you were immediately before coming here was The Rutting Stag pub on Duck Lane, am I right?"

Peter nodded. The officer then talked into a throat mike: "Bravo X-Ray Five-Five. Go, Go, Go. The Rutting Stag will not be showing the football today."

The officer turned to Peter. "Stick with me, mate. Don't worry, you've an angel on your shoulder. I'll make sure you see a drugs counsellor whilst you're with us. Okay?"

Peter nodded. Then he thought to himself, an angel?

Just then the red Corsa drove past him. Mark was sitting in the back. He looked very serious, as one would expect. In fact, he looked like a man being taken to the electric chair. Yet there was something else. Peter wasn't sure, it could have been reflected sunlight, or the stress, or the drugs, but he could have sworn that he had seen a halo around Mark's head.

Chapter 21

Colville Place, Fitzrovia, Central London, 1646 hours, Saturday 22nd June 1996.

After dropping Conner off at the top of Tottenham Street, the red Vauxhall Corsa and its two Brixton Crime Squad occupants sped off back to Paddington Green Police Station to carry on processing the four prisoners from the morning's *buy and bust*. Further interviews were needed, following the recovery of five hundred wraps of heroin and crack cocaine from the blue BMW and an unregistered firearm from The Rutting Stag Pub. The search of Ginger Bailey's personal flat in Sloane Square barracks had retrieved a blank-firing handgun. The Firearms Discharge Residue from the pistol matched that found on the wristband recovered in the laundry van and on Conner's clothing. The Top Floor flat in the accommodation block of the barracks had been searched, but had been mysteriously stripped bare before the police got there.

Conner was in the nick writing up his Incident Report Booklet from the morning's activities when he received a phone call from Emma at Op. Garden City. She told him that Sylvester De Lacey's constituency office had eventually got back to her. They had informed her that Mr. De Lacey was at his London home, enjoying time with his family and supporting the England Team. However, as it was police business, an address in Colville Place, Fitzrovia, had been released. Mr. De Lacey would prefer it if he wasn't disturbed today. Too bad, Conner had thought to himself.

He sorted a lift to the address straight away. Whilst in the car, he kitted himself out with his personal radio and protective equipment, covering it all up with a blue Fila tracksuit top he had found in the property store. The car AM radio had told him that the England football team had somehow made it into extra time in the quarter-final with Spain, despite the away team having the ball in the net twice, only for the goals to be ruled offside. The Spaniards had then had a solid penalty claim turned down. To say England were riding their luck was an understatement. But as he had been working on pure adrenaline since 5 am this morning, he had not thought about the football at all until that point. When he wasn't thinking of Gee, he was thinking of Amber, dying in a hospital bed.

After walking down the deserted street, past empty shops and cafes, he could see a large group of people standing on the corner of Colville Place outside The Hope and Anchor pub. The bubbling sound of chatter drifted over to him, amongst the clinking of glasses and laughter. It always amazed him how the general public carried on in blissful ignorance of the world he lived in. A thin veil between light and dark that most people didn't lift. He took up a position opposite the pub, scooped up a discarded pint glass and placed it at his feet before slumping down against the wall onto his backside. To the casual observer he would just look like a drunk taking a break from the pub. He lifted his head, lazily lit an Embassy cigarette and looked down into Colville Place past the crowd of people. It was an exclusive and leafy cul-de-sac. The three and four-storey town houses had jolly colours painted on the frontages and garage doors. Large leafy plants, in expensive terracotta pots, were scattered along the cobbled road. Despite the shadow of the looming British Telecom Tower, it was a small piece of the Cotswolds transferred to the inner cities.

He could see that the house in question was four houses down with pale blue paint covering the front and garage doors. There was a large bay kitchen window next to the front door. He took a drag on his Embassy and exhaled into the air. He had taken the heavy decision not to tell De Lacey, or more importantly the family, about the threat that was posed to them. This was his one chance to catch Gee and it was worth managing the risk. Gee was clever. He had become more and more adept at targeting his prey. De Lacey's lifestyle was busy, unpredictable, but both he and Gee knew that a *man of the people,* as De Lacey liked to portray himself, would be at home watching the football, just like any other *normal* bloke. Gee could have been inside already of course, but Conner suspected he would have heard about it by now if anything grisly had happened. He looked above the houses which were surrounded by tall office blocks bristling with CCTV cameras. There was only one way in and out. All he had to do was watch and wait. He tried to put out of his mind that the woman he loved could die on an operating table at any moment.

The realisation hit him like a truck. He loved Amber. He knew it now. The sickly-sweet feeling had always been there, from the moment he first saw her. But it had laid dormant, until fate had bought them back together, when she had stood over him in the AMIT briefing room. Her china doll face. Her curly amber hair tied back, business-like. Her athletic figure with full-rounded breasts pushing against her white blouse. The scent of her perfume, the lightest suggestion of her own sweat, showing she was a real flesh and blood woman. That had kindled a flame that had grown inside him. Her kindness, understanding and compassion were new experiences to him. His heart and soul now yearned for her to live. Yearned to be naked next to her again. The frantic sex they had experienced so far would be replaced with lovemaking. Slow, tender, all encompassing. Giving themselves to each other completely.

But she had to live. She had to.

****

"Come on now, boys, settle down. It's extra time. There's another thirty minutes," said Lady Cathy De Lacey to Clive and Henry, her two seven-year-old boys. Cathy brushed back her short black hair. She was dressed sensibly in a white turtleneck and a long red skirt.

"Oh no, really? Another thirty minutes of this nonsense?" Sylvester De Lacey muttered, looking up from the pile of papers on his lap. Other papers were spilling out from his ministerial case, which was perched precariously on the edge of a large overstuffed floral sofa.

He personally viewed Euro Ninety-Six as a colossal waste of time. He was here for the boys, who had been caught up in the whole thing. Plus, they were at school with the children of the editor of the Evening Standard and so it was worth ensuring that his sacrifice would get talked about on Monday morning. He'd even changed into jeans and a white Ralph Lauren sports shirt to help get into the spirit of the event.

"Well, if you were watching the game, you would have known," Cathy spat out, as she sat the boys down in front of the TV on a large cushion.

Both boys were resplendent in new white and turquoise blue England shirts bought from Harrods especially. She stooped down again to pick up two pop bottles and an empty packet of crisps before heading into the open-plan kitchen.

De Lacey mumbled to himself as he sipped whiskey from a cut crystal glass and went back to his papers. He'd let it be known to his constituency office that, if asked, as a *Mondeo man of the nineties,* he'd be at home watching the football. Getting behind the England team. All that patriotic bullshit. But to him it was hell on earth. A load of oiks kicking a ball about, screamed on by a load more oiks. There wasn't even a looker amongst them. Other than perhaps the tall curly-haired Liverpudlian… McManaman was it?

The match restarted, while Cathy clattered about in the kitchen. His plans for restructuring several front-line British Army regiments had received wide parliamentary support. The fall of the Berlin Wall, the collapse of Communism, even the hush-hush initiatives in Northern Ireland, had all affected the decision. There was no need to cling to the old structures. Modernisation was his rallying call. But what he was particularly looking forward to was the complete destruction of the Royal Mounted Rifles. They had nearly ruined his life. He had been blamed for the Roslaw Farm bomb. Yes, he'd been tricked. Yes, soldiers had died. But it was an organisational failing and he had taken the fall. His family name, worshipped after Waterloo, had been dragged through the dirt. Well, he would punish those at the top of the RMR with their archaic rituals and uniforms, Mess meetings and sad reunions. Even the Green Mafia, who had helped him with his *pastimes* back in the day, while he was serving at Sloane Square, would go. Along with any discrediting information they might hold on him. He would wipe the whole damned lot from the pages of history with one stroke of his *Mount Blanc* pen.

De Lacey watched Cathy come back to the living room with a large gin and tonic and sit in a distant armchair, despite there being plenty of room on the large floral sofa next to him. She looked and smiled at the boys before staring blankly at the TV screen. He had already decided that after the game he'd make an excuse and go to his club in Kensington. Seek out the company of some real men. He took another drink. The match played on.

****

Everyone in The Hope and Anchor pub was staring at a small TV screen, high up in the corner of the bar. As one, they willed on an England Goal. England had kicked off the first half of Extra Time, but it seemed clear that both teams would be happy with the lottery of penalties. The crowd noise in Wembley could be heard from the TV speakers, though the commentator was all but drowned out by the cheering and encouragement in the pub.

There was one set of eyes that was not looking at the TV. They belonged to a tall man dressed in green cargo pants and a beige safari shirt. He had a freshly shaved head and two days growth of facial hair. The glasses he wore were thick black-rimmed, but were purely aesthetic due to the transparent plastic lenses. The man was Simon Gee and he sat in the pub as comfortably as he could in his disguise. His ten years of anger, hatred and disgust had been relegated to deep inside him. They were still there of course, boiling, smouldering like the lava in a volcano. But he knew he needed to be the cold killer he had become to achieve his task. His revenge. For the first time, he readily admitted to himself what it was. There was no escaping the simplicity of it now.

This was cold, calculated revenge. Call it by its name, Boris Pasternak had once written.

And the thought thrilled him.

Although his eyes stared straight ahead, giving the appearance that he could be stoned, his ears were on high alert, waiting for a specific sound. The sound of the crazed excitement of an England goal. This would be the signal for him to carry out his plan. He had waited over a decade for this moment. He could wait for thirty minutes of extra time to play out. He was feeling noticeably confident of completing his job to kill his first abuser, Sylvester De Lacey MP, or *Mr. Fox* as he had codenamed him. Although only the penultimate name on the list, Gee was sure it was going to be his final victim. And once Mr. Fox and his family were dead, his killing spree could stop.

He felt the small vial of aftershave in his right-hand cargo trouser pocket. This would be his final confirmation. He had found out his target's address with a genuine-looking email inviting the MP to a charity pheasant shoot in a country house retreat. All that was required was a postal address for the formal invite. De Lacey's secretary had kindly provided him with the home address. She knew he would not want to miss out and it would be a lovely surprise for him. At this moment, De Lacey was in his house, no more than twenty-five metres away, with his family.

Gee was confident that they would all be dead within the hour.

The football game played out at a serene pace with the only excitement being a Paul Gascoigne shot forcing a save from the Spanish goalkeeper. Gee heard the final whistle and for the first time in two hours he looked up at the screen. It was penalties. England would go first with the ever-dependable striker Alan Shearer striding up confidently to take the first penalty. Gee stood up and walked casually out of the pub door. It was now or never.

****

From his position opposite The Hope and Anchor pub Conner had managed to get a sense of the game. It was nearly 5.30 pm and with no explosions of noise from the drinkers it was clear to him it had gone into penalties. So, it had come down to this moment. His own chance of a winning penalty. No more murders. Gee in custody. Amber alive.

Or a huge miss. A family, he himself and his girl dead.

Where is Gee? he thought to himself. Just then, his question was answered.

The side door of the pub opened.

A tall man, casually dressed, stepped out.

Conner could see that the man was too casually dressed. The new cargo pants still had shop creases. The glasses were out of place. Then he recognised the man's lanky gait.

It was Simon Gee.

Conner crouched on his haunches and started to move his radio to his mouth. He watched as Gee turned right towards the house. Conner held his nerve, waiting for the tipping point that would light the fuse to his actions. Gee walked down to one of the large plant pots, carefully lifted out a plant by the trunk and then set it down. He then lifted out a large black holdall from the plant pot, threw it over his shoulder and headed towards his target. Conner clicked the press to speak button on his radio.

"Charlie X-Ray, this is 347 Echo Kilo," he whispered softly.

"Go ahead," replied an electronic voice.

He watched in horror as Gee pulled out a large black-handled knife from the holdall and stuck it into his belt, then took out a short metal crowbar and walked over to the front door of the house, entering it within seconds.

Conner sprang to his feet and started to run to the house, blurting out over the radio, "I require urgent assistance and Firearms Units to Colville Place! Urgent assistance! Colville Place!"

"Received," the control room snapped in reply. "Units please. Armed Response Vehicles to make their way to …!"

He did not hear anymore as he sprinted to the De Lacey house. His feet, heart and mind pounding to different rhythms. It took around five seconds for him to make it to the front door. It had been jimmied open at the latch and then slammed shut, causing the wood splinters to wedge against the door frame. He could hear the sound of a female screaming inside. Conner took a step back, then charged the door with his shoulder. The door flew backwards on its hinges and he fell into the open-plan kitchen. A table had been up-turned and high stools from the breakfast bar were strewn across the stone-tiled floor, creating an obstacle course. He stepped over the stools and pulled the table to one side. He then saw a scene of chaos. In the open-plan living room, he could see the back of Gee, who was looking down at Sylvester De Lacey as he lay on his side, supporting himself on his right elbow.

De Lacey had a ragged blood-red wound in the middle of his forehead and the remains of a small glass bottle lay smashed on the floor in front of him. De Lacey looked up with absolute terror at the tall man towering over him. A female, whom Conner assumed was Mrs. De Lacey, was sitting on the floor with her back to the TV, which was still blaring out the football. She was holding two young boys tightly to her and staring at this tall man who had turned her world upside down in seconds. She was bleeding from her nose but, in contrast to her frightened husband, she had the look of defiance that only a mother could give when someone was threatening her children. Conner could see that the mother and children were wet. An oily, shiny wet.

Then he smelt the petrol.

Clearly noticing that Cathy De Lacey was looking at something behind him, Gee spun around. In his right hand the large blade pointed up to the low mock Tudor ceiling. In his left hand, and now directly over the mother and children, a lit *Zippo* lighter. Its flame danced around on top of its shiny metal box. Gee looked at Conner, immediately recognising him as the police officer who had spotted him on Maddox Place.

"Well, Well. So, this is how it's going to be, is it?" Gee said, looking at Conner with cold disdain.

Gee looked down at De Lacey. "Get up," he said, the hate evident in his tone.

De Lacey, conscious of the lighter, did what he was told. As he did so, Gee stepped behind him and put his right arm around his neck. The point of the blade next to De Lacey's Adam's apple. Gee's left outstretched arm still held the lighter. The petrol accelerant was all over the stone-tiled floor. It was clear to everyone in that room that the whole house would go up in flames in seconds if the lighter were dropped. Conner took a deep breath and assessed the situation.

"Listen, Simon, this can play out a number of ways, can't it?"

Gee looked startled at hearing his name. But he composed himself and said, with venom,

"He must die. The family as well. Don't you see?"

"No, I don't Simon, tell me. Tell me, please," Conner replied.

"I'm going to enjoy killing this pig," Gee said, pushing the blade a millimetre further into De Lacey's throat. "But it will give me no pleasure to kill a mother and her children. It really won't. But they have to die."

"No, they don't. You're in charge, Simon. We can all walk out of this. You have that gift."

Despite his calm words, sweat dripped down Conner's face. His back already soaked. The atmosphere in the room tangible. Gee adjusted his stance. Steading himself. Giving himself a more stable platform. A fighting stance, Conner observed.

Gee went on. "This piece of filth and everyone and everything connected to him must go. Only then can I tell my story. On the steps of the Old Bailey. My story. How the De Lacey's of this world abuse people. Then spit them out."

Gee pushed the blade closer to De Lacey's throat as the captive man winced in pain.

"Simon, tell me. Tell me what has led you here."

Conner was buying time, hearing chatter on his personal radio as units arrived on the scene. SO19 and Armed Response Units were taking up positions around the premises. The black, white, red and green sides of the house were all accounted for and were now within a marksman's arc.

"How can you possibly know what I've been through?" Gee asked through clenched teeth.

He tightened his grip on De Lacey's neck and pushed the blade yet another millimetre into his captive's skin. De Lacey was in a state of complete shock and remained frozen.

"I'm Ryan Conner. A cop, yes. But I wasn't always."

Conner started to edge closer to Gee. His hands up in full view.

"I know about your time in the Army. The company *tyking*. The Rutting Stag."

Gee was listening. Conner continued.

"I was at Sloane Square. I was a *crow*. Young, abused, terrified at all hours. Just like you. Where were the officers, the adults in the room? Why did they do nothing about it?"

Conner held the man's stare. "I also know it never leaves you. But this is not the answer, Simon. Too many people have died already."

"Then you know why he must be killed. Have you read the inscription above the Old Bailey, *Punish the wrongdoer*? This is my job and I will have my day in front of the world's media to tell my story."

Gee pushed the blade into De Lacey's straining neck. A speck of blood appeared. The politician's eyes were wide, expecting death.

"No! Stop!" Conner shouted.

****

At the junction with Colville Place and Tottenham Road, a collection of police vehicles had gathered. Police tape had sealed off the road whilst simultaneously keeping everyone inside the pub. Nobody really noticed. The police sealing off a street was an everyday occurrence in London. The Mobile Tactical Firearms Commander, referred to as *Foxtrot One*, and three firearms officers dressed in black body armour and *Kevlar* helmets, were holding a *bonnet briefing* on a marked up five series BMW. It had been parked out of line of sight from Colville Place. The group were joined by the Duty Uniformed Inspector, and they all studied a map of the area. A radio, perched on the bonnet of the car, burst into life.

"Foxtrot One receiving? Its Sierra five."

Sierra Five was one of the five sniper callsigns sent by the Met's Elite *SO19* from New Scotland Yard.

"Foxtrot One, go ahead," the Tactical Firearms Commander replied.

"Guv, we have visual on three white males. Conner has his back to us. A male, likely to be Gee, has hold of De Lacey. Wait… Gee has a knife to De Lacey's neck. Received so far?"

Foxtrot One grimaced. "Yes, go ahead,"

A few seconds of dead air were followed by, "Gee has a lighted Zippo in his left hand. The family are also in the room. It looks like Gee's intending to blow the whole house up…over."

"Received," Foxtrot one replied. "Maintain a view of the suspect through the scope. If he goes out of sight let me know."

Foxtrot One then turned to the other officers stood around him. "Fuck."

They all knew what it meant. As long as Gee had the lighter and the family were in the building, they could not shoot Gee and risk him setting fire to the whole place.

"We're going to need a negotiator, an ambulance and the London Fire Brigade. Also make sure no one gets out of that pub," Foxtrot One said to the uniformed Inspector.

The Inspector nodded and walked off, talking to control on his radio.

Foxtrot One looked at the remaining Firearms Officers. "I'll call the on-call Silver Commander. He won't like me ruining his Saturday afternoon with this."

****

Simon Gee, his knife still drawing blood from De Lacey's neck, looked at Conner.
Conner tried again.

"There *is* another way. Listen. I can see the wife and kids. Haven't you wondered why I haven't asked you to let them go?"

Gee glanced at Cathy De Lacey hugging her children, who were crying in her arms. Then he looked back at Conner.

"Because they are the only thing keeping you alive," Conner said, pointing at them. "Look, the police are out there. They are working on the basis that us three are expendable. I'm sorry, Mr. De Lacey, but they are. Simon, there are police snipers' rifles trained on you at this very moment. But they won't shoot you while you have the lighter and there's a risk of setting the family alight. The Met don't want that in the papers tomorrow. I want you to make it out of this, Simon. I want you to have your day at the Old Bailey. Tell the world what happened. Bring down the whole fucking lot of them!"

Conner adjusted his feet. Edging a few centimetres closer to both men.

"De Lacey can spend the rest of his life where he belongs, in some stinking hole, with his reputation in complete tatters. Unable to come back from the shame this time. Did you know he was the officer in charge when the Roslaw farm bomb went off?"

Gee had heard of the bombing of course. The loss of life was marked by the Royal Mounted Rifles every year on its anniversary.

"I was there in that building, Simon. I have lived with the effects of the explosion for four years. The deaths of my brothers-in-arms. Because of that pathetic little shit. I have every reason to want him dead. But this not the way to get revenge. One more death of anybody in this room is one too many."

Conner could see De Lacey was looking at him with a new intensity. The man's eyes seem to acknowledge his own failures. A failed soldier, a failed husband and father, a failed man. De Lacey wept uncontrollably. His past had finally caught up with him.

"I understand why you needed to find him. But you've found him now. Take him to court, tell the world what happened," Conner added.

Gee took a deep breath. "I'm sorry about the girl. I thought it was you running into the shop. But what could I do? I had yet to finish my job."

Conner said nothing.

"I didn't really hate the other men I have killed. It just seemed like... like the right thing to do. They were all part of the abuse system. They all deserved to die, but I didn't *hate* them. It was just a... just a blood lust that would come over me. The years of anger and disgust of them. Of myself," the killer said, in a resigned tone.

Gee took another deep breath and closed his eyes for a split second. Conner edged closer.

"I'm tired," Gee said, now staring directly at Conner. "I have been in this pursuit for so long. And here I am. The police are here. The press will be here. The story will come out. You, Ryan, you can tell the story."

"No, Simon. No, it must come from you. It was all before my time."

Conner sensed the situation was shifting in a bad direction.

Gee quickly turned to look at Cathy and the children. Then turned back to face Conner.

Gee's body was tense, his face stern and focused. Conner could see a clarity of purpose come over the Tall Man, as he became action personified.

"Rot in hell, *crow,*" Gee said, as he stuck the blade into De Lacey's throat, straight into the carotid artery.

Thick, dark red spurts of blood arced out of the politician's neck and he slumped to the ground, desperately clawing at the open wound. Cathy and the children screamed and hugged each other closer. Conner's radio burst into life with sudden chatter. Simon Gee put both his arms out wide. He turned the knife downwards, but did not drop it. Blood trickled off the blade onto the stone-tiled floor and mixed with the petrol. His left arm still outstretched, the lighter still burning in his left hand. Conner realised he was too far away; he could not get to Gee before he dropped the lighter. He accepted his fate. He thought of Amber. Maybe she was already on the other side waiting for him.

Gee stood in this twisted crucifixion form. Then he focused on Conner and spoke in a calm voice.

"Stand easy, brother."

Conner could see in Gee's eyes, just for a split second, the proud young man who had gone to Sloane Square barracks full of excitement and hope. Only to be turned into a vengeful killer at the hands of the Green Mafia and a sick abuser.

"The job's done," Gee said.

Conner saw Gee slowly and deliberately flick the lid of the lighter closed, extinguishing the flame. In an instant, the front bay window was pierced, and a sniper's bullet entered Gee's head, dropping his lifeless body immediately to the floor. The knife and the closed lighter flew off into the corners of the room, far out of harm's way. Within seconds, the front door burst open and four firearms officers ran in, their assault rifles raised to eye level as they scanned for further threats. Two officers went straight for Sylvester De Lacey and started to work on his neck wound. It was in vain. De Lacey had joined his ancestors. The other two officers quickly assessed that there was nothing to be done for Gee, fragments of his skull and brain matter spread out over a wall and the floor. One officer continued to the family and started to pour bottles of water over them to dilute the accelerant, stripping them of their clothes and dressing them in white paper suits.

Nobody said anything to Conner. Nobody checked to see if he was all right. He was a cop, so he had no other option but to be all right. He stared dead ahead at the TV that was still playing. David Seaman, the England goalkeeper, had saved the final penalty. He was bouncing up and down, waiting for his team mates to join him in celebration. The crowd cheered wildly at their new hero.

England were into the European Championship Semi –
Finals for the first time. Tomorrow the papers would be full
of it. That game had a clear winner. Conner's less so. He
turned and walked out of the house.

Chapter 22

Giuseppe's Ice Cream parlour, Leicester Square, London, 1004 hours, Thursday 27th June 1996.

The light summer rain pattered against the large front window of the Haagen Dazs ice cream parlour. Ryan Conner sat alone, looking out onto Leicester Square towards the Odeon cinema and the Moon Under the Water pub. Street cleaners in luminous orange suits were out in force, scooping away the detritus of the previous night's riot. England had gone out of the European Championships following a penalty defeat to Germany. The England faithful had not taken it well and had occupied Trafalgar Square for several hours before it turned to violence against the police and rival fans. It had spilled out into the surrounding streets shortly after. Conner had slept through it, having turned the game off at the end of the ninety minutes, somehow knowing how it was going to end. There had been lots of endings. Euro '96, *Cool Britannia*, the strategic defence review, Gee's reign of terror. All of them had come to a sudden stop in that week.

He had tried not to think about Simon Gee since Saturday. He'd spent his days being interviewed as a significant witness to De Lacey's murder. The more he talked it through, the more he wondered who was bringing justice to the world. Who was punishing the wrongdoer? The police or Gee? Probably both, in their own way. The police shooting took precedence over everything else. The papers were full of salacious headlines about *the MP and the Sex Killer*. It was all over page six, the football still taking up pages one to five. But there was no large outpouring of grief for a posh politician. Not even from his family, it seemed. London's gay community had thanked the Met Police for its actions in finding Gee and putting a stop to the murderous rampage that was terrorising their community, but insisted more must be done to prevent it happening again. And they were probably right.

Gee would be recognised as a serial killer, having killed more than the magic number of five people. Conner was sure that this was not Gee's intention. A missing person on the City of London Police's missing database, by the name of Bernard West, had been identified as the likely first of Gee's victims. Murdered at the Albert Embankment and pushed into the Thames. A search of Gee's flat had revealed a list with all his victims' names on it. All except one, which had been mysteriously blacked out by the time it was booked into property. This worried Conner. He felt that there were bigger actors in this play. Viv Mason, who had avoided any connection with any of the crimes, was one. Fairfax the other. But there were others above them, he was sure. Gee's wild allegations about a high-profile sadomasochistic sex ring had made little more than a paragraph in the tabloids. The scandal of Sloane Square barracks' links to organised crime did get more press attention. There was outrage from some military chiefs keen to distance themselves. A Parliamentary enquiry had been promised. It would take years. Heads would roll, perhaps, eventually. Conner doubted much would be done.

Turning from the rain-speckled window he looked at the empty chair opposite him where Amber should be.

Just then the chair slid back on its legs. There was a clatter, as walking sticks were dropped against the back wall and a large chocolate and hazelnut ice cream in a round paper tub was dropped on the table. Amber Mills collapsed into the chair and stared with intent at her extravagant dessert.

Conner looked at her and laughed. "Are you all right there?"

"What?" she said, through a mouth full of double chocolate. "I've been waiting weeks for this."

Amber had lost some weight and her face was still grey in places. She also struggled to walk unaided. But her hair was long and bright and red. As she sat there, alive, stuffing her still gorgeous face with ice cream, he thought that he had never seen such a beautiful sight. She had been released from hospital that morning and he had offered to drive her to her parents for a recovery period. When she had come round, she had insisted on giving a statement accepting full responsibility for the situation that led to her assault. This had made the investigation into him quickly evaporate. It had also allowed him to get back into a policing role. He had been made a Detective Constable. Although not with AMIT, who dropped him like he was hot, but by *Chief* Detective Inspector York from Operation Atlantic, who had glided up a rank on the back of the Test Purchase operation's success. This was in no small part, York accepted, thanks to Conner's initiative. He would start in the Minor Beat Crimes Unit at Charing Cross on Monday. He would also remain a Test Purchase Operative, though not in Central London. His time here was done.

For now, however, he was looking forward to spending some time with Amber.

He looked at her, then asked. "When you were lying on the floor in the newsagents, I said some things, that, well, you know. I mean, could... could you hear me?"

He felt his cheeks going red. "It's just … well, I sort of meant what I said… but.. if you don't feel the same, that's sort of fine…"

Amber swallowed her ice cream and then leaned over and kissed him gently on the mouth.

"The very thought of being *your girl* kept me alive. I love you," she smiled, her eyes staring intently into his. "Now, shut up and eat your ice cream."

Conner picked up his spoon and saw she was nodding at the tub, urging him to get stuck in. He scooped up a large dollop of strawberry gelato and made a big show of putting it into his mouth. She laughed. They ate peacefully together, not needing to say another word.

****

Pines Villa, Saffron Waldon, Essex. 1123 hours, Thursday 27th June 1996.

The sound of the front doorbell rang out around the large country house.

"I'll get it, darling," Provost Marshall, Brigadier Sir Hugh Fairfax shouted upstairs to his wife.

Opening the front door, he saw a motorcycle courier in a black tinted helmet holding a brown paper parcel. The parcel was handed to him, and the motorcyclist left.

Shutting the door, his wife shouted down to him, "Who was it?"

"No one, Dear, just a parcel delivery. I'll handle it."

He went into his study.

Turning quickly, he locked the door and placed the package on his desk as he sat down in a brown leather swivel chair. Opening it up, he found that inside was a brand new Motorola mobile phone. He switched it on and as soon as it picked up a signal, it rang. He answered it.

"It's the Supreme Worshipful Master," a voice said on the other end of the line. It was a commanding voice. One of impeccable breeding.

"Good morning, Worshipful Master," Fairfax said, trying to sound as relaxed as possible.

"Now, this business with Sloane Square and our *assets,* how bad is it?"

"Well, yes, it was an embarrassment, but operationally for the Supreme Lodge it's absolutely fine. It was unfortunate that it ended with the closure of Sloane Square barracks, the disbandment of the Royal Mounted Rifles Mounted Regiment and with it, of course, our Green Mafia London detachment. But the Mechanised Infantry Regiment will remain and our Green Mafia assets will be suitably placed within the surviving regiment. Fortunately, Master Mason made it out unscathed. Those lost to the Criminal Justice system will be taken care of when they come out. I have it on good authority that there will be lots of work for private security firms in the Middle East in the not-too-distant future. Those individuals currently in prison will be perfect for this venture."

Hearing positive mumbles from the other end of the phone, Fairfax went on.

"And of course, the original plan was an enormous success. We had Gee take care of all the loose ends on the list we sent him. The small bottle of De Lacey's aftershave had the desired effect."

Fairfax purposefully omitted that the last name on the list had been the Supreme Worshipful Master himself. The voice on the end of the phone. This had been on the insistence of the American Supreme Lodge to prevent some future, unmentioned *difficulties*. However, that part of the plan had clearly failed and was unlikely to be resurrected anytime soon. It was worth remaining cordial with him, Fairfax had realised. He continued.

"The *CivPol* took care of Gee as we had hoped and his allegations have been minimised thanks to our friends in the media. If Gee hadn't killed De Lacey at his house, it would have been in the street or in a smutty club. De Lacey had brought nothing but disgrace to the Royal Mounted Rifles since he joined. And of course, his plans to downsize the Army have disappeared with him. No, the Supreme Lodge Council are extremely happy with the outcome."

"And your... *specialist* services? Will they continue?"

"Why, of course, Supreme Worshipful Master, nothing gets in the way of business... or, in this case, pleasure."

There was silence on the line until the voice said, "Very good, my Lord Provost. Thank you for your insight. Excellent work overall. I will let you enjoy the rest of your weekend."

"Thank you. Thank you, Your *Royal* Highness."

The phone went dead.

The End

Printed in Great Britain
by Amazon